HARMONY CABINS

REGINA HART

Dafina
Books

Kensington Publishing Corp.

http://www.kensingtonbooks.com

DAFINA BOOKS are published by

Kensington Publishing Corp.
119 West 40th Street
New York, NY 10018

All Kensington Titles, Imprints, and Distributed Lines are
available at special quantity discounts for bulk purchases for
sales promotions, premiums, fund-raising, and educational
or institutional use. Special book excerpts or customized
printings can also be created to fit specific needs. For details,
write or phone the office of the Kensington special sales manager: Kensington Publishing Corp., 119 West 40th Street,
New York, NY 10018, attn: Special Sales Department, Phone:
1-800-221-2647.

Dafina and the Dafina logo Reg. U.S. Pat. & TM Off.

ISBN-13: 978-0-7582-8654-3
ISBN-10: 0-7582-8654-6
First Kensington Mass Market Edition: February 2014

eISBN-13: 978-0-7582-8655-0
eISBN-10: 0-7582-8655-4
First Kensington Electronic Edition: February 2014

10 9 8 7 6 5 4 3 2 1

Printed in the United States of America

To my dream team:

- *My sister Bernadette, for giving me the dream*
- *My husband Michael, for supporting the dream*
- *My brother Richard, for believing in the dream*
- *My brother Gideon, for encouraging the dream*
- *My friend and critique partner, Marcia James, for sharing the dream*

And to Mom and Dad, always with love

CHAPTER 1

Audra Lane strode with manufactured confidence to the vacation rental cabins' main desk and faced the man she thought was the registration clerk. She curled her bare toes against the warm polished wood flooring and took a deep breath.

"You're probably wondering why I'm wearing this trash bag."

"Yes."

That was it. That single syllable delivered without inflection or emotion in a soft, bluesy baritone.

Audra's swagger stalled. She tugged her right earlobe.

Maybe that was his way. His manner wasn't unwelcoming. It was just spare. He'd been the same when she'd checked into the rental cabins in Where-the-Heck-Am-I, Ohio, less than an hour earlier.

In fact, the entire registration area was just as spartan as the clerk. Despite the large picture windows, the room seemed dark and cheerless in the middle of this bright summer morning. There weren't chairs inviting guests to relax or corner tables with engaging information about the nearby town. It didn't even offer a coffee station. Nothing about the room said, *Welcome! We're glad you're here.* There were only bare oak walls, bare oak floors, and a tight-lipped clerk.

What kind of vacation spot is this?

Audra pushed her questions about the room's lack of ambience to the back of her mind and addressed her primary concern.

She wiped her sweaty palms on her black plastic makeshift minidress. "I'd left some of my toiletries in my rental car. I thought I could just step into the attached garage to get them, but the door shut behind me. Luckily, I found a box of trash bags on a shelf."

She stopped. Her face flamed. If he hadn't suspected before, he now knew beyond a doubt that she was butt naked under this bag.

Oh. My. God.

She'd ripped a large hole on the bottom and smaller ones on either side of the bag for a crude little black dress, which on her five-seven frame was *very* little.

Audra gave him a hard look, but his almond-shaped onyx eyes remained steady on hers. He didn't offer even a flicker of reaction. His eyes were really quite striking, and the only part of his face she could make out. When he'd checked her into the rental, she'd been too tired after her flight from California to notice his deep sienna features were half hidden by a thick, unkempt beard. His dark brown hair was twisted into tattered, uneven braids. They hung above broad shoulders clothed in a short-sleeved, dark blue T-shirt. But his eyes . . . they were so dark, so direct, and so wounded. A poet's eyes.

How could the cabins' owner allow his staff to come to work looking so disheveled, especially an employee who worked the front desk? Did the clerk think he looked intimidating? Well, she'd been born and raised in Los Angeles. He'd have to try harder.

Without a word, the clerk turned and unlocked the cabinet on the wall behind him. He chose a key from a multitude of options and pulled a document from the credenza.

"Sign this." He handed the paper to her.

The form stated she acknowledged receipt of her cabin's spare key and would return it promptly. Audra signed it with relief. "Thank you."

"You're welcome." He gave her the key.

A smile spread across her mouth and chased away her discomfort. Audra closed her hand around the key and raised her gaze to his. "I don't know your name."

"Jack."

"Hi, Jack. I'm Au . . . Penny. Penny Lane." When he didn't respond, she continued. "Thanks again for the spare key. I'll bring it right back."

"No rush."

"Thank you." Audra turned on her bare heels and hurried from the main cabin. That had been easy—relatively speaking. At times, she'd even forgotten she was wearing a garbage bag and nothing else. It helped that Jack hadn't looked at her with mockery or scorn. He'd been very professional. Bless him!

Jackson Sansbury waited until his guest disappeared behind the closed front door. Only then did he release the grin he'd been struggling against. It had taken every ounce of control not to burst into laughter as she'd marched toward him, the trash-bag dress rustling with her every step.

He shook his head. She'd been wearing a garbage bag! Oh, to have seen the look on her face when the breezeway door had shut behind her— while she'd been naked in the garage. Jack gripped the registration desk and surrendered to a few rusty chuckles. They felt good. It had been a long time since he'd found anything funny.

He wiped his eyes with his fingers, then lifted the replacement key form. A few extra chuckles escaped. She'd signed this document, as well as the registration, *Penny Lane.* Jack shook his head again. Did she really expect him to believe her parents had named her after a Beatles song?

Jack lifted his gaze to the front door. She'd given a Los Angeles address when she'd registered. Who was she? And why would someone from Los Angeles spend a month at a cabin in Trinity Falls, Ohio, by herself under a fake name?

"Benita, when you told me you'd made a reservation for me at a vacation rental cabin, I thought you meant one with other *people*," Audra grumbled into her cellular phone to her business manager, Benita Hawkins.

Although still tired from the red-eye flight from California to Ohio, she felt much more human after she'd showered and dressed.

"There aren't any people there?" Benita sounded vaguely intrigued.

"The only things here are trees, a lake, and a taciturn registration clerk." Audra's lips tightened. Her manager wasn't taking her irritation seriously.

"Hmmm. Even better."

Audra glared at her phone before returning it to her ear. She could picture the other woman seated behind her cluttered desk, reviewing e-mails and mail while humoring her. "What do you mean, 'even better'?"

"I told you that you needed a change to get over your writer's block. You're having trouble coming up with new songs because you're in a rut. You see the same people. Go to the same places. There's nothing new or exciting in your life."

That was harsh.

Audra stared out the window at the tree line. She'd noticed right away that none of the windows had curtains. The lack of privacy increased the cabin's creepiness factor.

A modest lawn lay like an amnesty zone between her and a lush spread of evergreen and poplar trees, which circled the cabin like a military strike force. In the distance, she could see sunlight bouncing on the lake like shards of glass on the water. The area was isolated. Audra didn't do isolated. She'd texted her parents after she'd checked into the cabin to let them know she'd arrived safely. Maybe she should have waited.

"This place is like Mayberry's version of the Bates Motel." She turned from the window. "How is this supposed to cure my insomnia?"

"Writing will cure your insomnia."

"Have you been to these cabins?"

"No. When I was growing up in Trinity Falls, Harmony Cabins went into bankruptcy and was abandoned. They've only recently been renovated."

"I'm coming home." But first she'd take a nap. The red-eye flight was catching up with her. She wasn't safe to drive back to the airport.

The cabin itself was lovely. The great room's walls, floors, and ceiling were made of gleaming honey wood. The granite stone fireplace dominated the room. But a large flat-screen, cable-ready television reassured her she'd have something to do at night. The comfortable furnishings that were missing from the main cabin were scattered around this room, an overstuffed sofa and fat fabric chairs. The dark décor was decidedly masculine. That would explain the lack of curtains at the windows. Men probably didn't think about details like that.

"You promised me you'd give it thirty days, Audra." The clicking of Benita's computer keyboard sounded just under her words. "I sent the rental a nonrefundable check for the full amount of your stay in advance."

Audra frowned. Benita's check had allowed her to register as Penny Lane. "It was your check, but my money. If I want to cancel this anti-vacation vacation, I will."

They both recognized the empty threat. The cost

of a monthlong stay at a rental cabin was too much to waste.

Benita's exasperated sigh traveled twenty-four hundred miles and three time zones through the cell phone. "You owe the record producer three hit songs in four weeks. How are they coming?"

Audra ground her teeth. Her deadline was August 4, twenty-five days from today. Benita knew very well she hadn't made any progress on the project. "How can you believe this place is the solution? You've never even been here."

"Do you really think I'd send you someplace that wasn't safe? I have family in Trinity Falls. If there were serial killers there, I'd know."

Audra tugged her right earlobe. She was angry because she was scared, and scared because she was outside her comfort zone. "I don't want to be here. It's not what I'm used to."

"That's why you *need* to be there. And this is the best time. Trinity Falls is celebrating its sesquicentennial. The town's hosting its Founders Day Celebration on August ninth. I'll be there."

"One hundred fifty years. That's impressive."

Benita chuckled. "I'll see you in a month."

Audra stared at her cell phone. Her manager had ended their call. "I guess that means I'm staying." She shoved her cell phone into the front pocket of her tan jeans shorts and turned back to the window. "In that case, I'll need curtains."

The chimes above the main cabin's front door sang. With three keystrokes, Jack locked his laptop and pushed away from his desk. The cabins had had more activity today than they'd ever had before.

Jack hesitated behind the registration desk. It wasn't a surprise to see the chair of the Trinity Falls Sesquicentennial Steering Committee had returned. Doreen Fever was a determined woman.

"Afternoon, Doreen." He knew why she was there. She wanted every citizen to be involved in the festivities surrounding the town's 150th birthday. The problem was, Jack wasn't a joiner.

"I'm still amazed by how much you've accomplished with the rentals in so little time." Doreen gazed around the reception area.

"Thank you."

Doreen was the sole candidate for mayor of Trinity Falls. She also was the artist behind the bakery operation of Books & Bakery, and the mother of Jackson's former schoolmate, though she looked too young to have an only child who was just two years younger than he was. Her cocoa skin was smooth and radiant. Her short, curly hair was dark brown. And her warm brown eyes were full of sympathy. Jack didn't want anyone's sympathy. Not even someone as genuine and caring as Doreen.

"I hear you have a lodger." Doreen folded her hands on the counter between them.

How did the residents of Trinity Falls learn everyone else's business so fast? His guest hadn't even been here a full day. "Not by choice."

Confusion flickered across Doreen's features before she masked it with a polite nod. "A young woman."

"I noticed."

"I'm glad to see the cabins' renovations are going well and that you're taking in customers."

"Thank you."

Doreen gave him a knowing smile. "The elementary school was grateful for your generous donation. I take it that was the check from your guest? Are you sure you don't need that money to reinvest in the repairs?"

"The school needs the money more. I appreciate your stopping by, Doreen." He turned to leave.

"Jack, you know why I'm here." Doreen sounded exasperated.

Good. He could handle exasperation. Pity pissed him off.

He faced her again. "You know my answer."

"The town will be one-hundred-and-fifty-years old on August ninth. That will be a momentous occasion, and everyone wants you to be a part of it."

Jack shook his head. "You don't need me."

"Yes, we do." Doreen's tone was filled with dogged determination. "This sesquicentennial is a chance for Trinity Falls to raise its profile in the county and across the state. You, of all people, must have a role in the Founders Day Celebration."

"That's not necessary."

"Yes, it is." Doreen leaned into the desk. "This event, if done well, will bring in extra revenue."

"I know about the town's budget concerns. I have an online subscription to *The Trinity Falls Monitor*." Reading the paper online saved Jack from having to go into town or deal with a newspaper delivery person.

Doreen continued as though Jack hadn't spoken. "If we host a large celebration with high-profile guests, we'll attract more people. These tourists will stay in our hotels, eat in our restaurants, and buy our souvenirs."

"Great. Good luck with that." He checked his watch for emphasis. It was almost two o'clock in the afternoon. "Anything else?"

She softened her voice. "I know that you're still grieving Zoey's death."

"Don't." The air drained from the room.

"I can't imagine how devastated you must feel at the loss of your daughter."

"Doreen." He choked out her name.

"We understand you need time to grieve. But, Jack, it's been almost two years. It's not healthy to close yourself off from human contact. People care about you. We can help you."

"Can you bring her back?" The words were harsh, rough, and raw.

Doreen looked stricken. "I can no more bring back your daughter than I can resurrect my late husband."

Paul Fever had died from cancer more than a year ago. He'd been sixty-seven. In contrast, leukemia had cut his daughter's life tragically short.

Jack struggled to reel in his emotions. "People grieve in different ways."

Pity reappeared in Doreen's warm brown eyes. "I went through the same feelings. But, Jack, at some point, you have to rejoin society."

"Not today." Some days, he feared he'd never be ready.

Caring about people hurt. He'd loved his ex-wife and his daughter. He never again wanted to experience the pain losing them had caused. If anything, the experience had taught him that it was better not to let people get too close.

The persistent ringing shattered Audra's dream. She blinked her eyes open. Had she fallen asleep?

Her gaze dropped to the song stanzas scribbled across the notebook on her lap. Was it the red-eye flight or her lyrics that had lulled her to sleep?

She stretched forward to grab her cell phone. "Hello?"

"Did we wake you?" Her mother asked after a pause.

Audra heard the surprise in the question. "It was a long trip." She refused to believe her writing had put her to sleep. "Is everything OK?"

Ellen Prince Lane sighed. "That's what we're calling to find out. We thought you were going to call us when you arrived at the resort."

"I sent you a text when I landed." Audra scrubbed a hand across her eyes, wiping away the last remnants of fatigue.

"A text is not a phone call." Ellen spoke with exaggerated patience. "How do we know that someone didn't kidnap you and send that text to delay our reporting you missing?"

Audra rolled her eyes. Her mother read too many true-crime novels. Her father wouldn't have suspected foul play was behind a text from her.

"I'm sorry, Mom. I didn't mean to worry you."

"This whole idea worries me." Her mother made fretting noises. "Why couldn't you have stayed in Redondo Beach to write your songs? Why did you have to go to some resort in Ohio?"

Audra wanted to laugh. No one would mistake Harmony Cabins for a resort. But this probably wasn't a good time to tell her mother that.

"We discussed this, Mom. Benita thought a change of scenery would cure my writer's block." And even though she had her doubts, Audra didn't want to add to her parents' worries.

Ellen tsked. "How long will you be gone?"

They'd discussed that, too. "About a month."

"You've never been away from home that long."

"I know, Mom."

"You don't even know anything about that resort."

"Benita's friend owns the cabins. I'm sure I'll be comfortable here."

"How will you eat?"

"There's a town nearby. I'll pick up some groceries in the morning."

"What do they eat there?"

Audra closed her eyes and prayed for patience. "I'm in Ohio, Mom. It's not a foreign country. I'm sure I'll find something familiar in the town's grocery store."

Ellen sniffed. "There's no need to take that tone."

"I'm sorry."

"Your father's very worried about you, Audra."

Yet her mother was the one on the phone. "Tell Dad I'll be fine. The cabin is clean and safe. There are locks on all the doors and windows. I'll be home before you know it." She hoped.

Audra looked toward the windows beside the front door. She needed curtains. She didn't like the idea of the windows being uncovered, especially at night. She'd feel too exposed. She checked her wristwatch. It wasn't quite three in the afternoon. It wouldn't be dark until closer to nine at night. She had a few hours to figure something out, like hanging sheets over the windows for tonight.

Her mother's abrupt sigh interrupted her planning. "Your father wants to talk with you. Maybe he can get you to see reason."

Audra rubbed her eyes with her thumb and two fingers. This experiment was hard enough without her mother's overprotectiveness.

"My Grammy-winning daughter!" Randall Lane boomed his greeting into the telephone. He'd been calling her that since she'd been presented with the Song of the Year Grammy Award in February. Before that, she'd been his Grammy-*nominated* daughter.

Audra settled back on the overstuffed plaid sofa. "Hi, Daddy."

"Will you be home in time for my birthday?"

She frowned. Her father's birthday was in October. It was only July. "Of course."

"That's all that matters."

"Randall!" Ellen's screech crossed state lines. "Give me back that phone!"

"Your mother wants to speak with you again. Have a nice time in Ohio, baby."

Her mother was as breathless as though she'd chased her father across the room. "Aren't there coyotes and bears in Ohio? And mountain lions?"

Audra's heart stopped with her mother's questions. She was a West Coast city woman in the wilds of the Midwest. Talk about being a fish out of water.

She swallowed to loosen the wad of fear lodged in her throat. "They don't come near the cabins."

"How do you know?"

"I just do," she lied. "I'll be fine."

"I think you should come home, Audra. What does Benita know about writer's block? She's your business manager, not a writer. I'm your mother. I know what you need. You need rest."

Her mother had a point. Audra hadn't had a full night's sleep ever since she'd taken the Grammy home.

She stood and paced past the front windows. "Benita may be right. Maybe I need to get completely out of my comfort zone to jump-start my writing."

Ellen sniffed again. "Well, I disagree. And so does Wendell."

Audra stilled at the mention of her treacherous ex-boyfriend. They'd broken up three months ago. Her mother knew that. "What does he have to do with anything?"

"He's been trying to get in touch with you. He wants your forgiveness."

That made up her mind. She was definitely staying at Harmony Cabins for at least a month. "Please don't tell Wendell where I am. Even if I forgive him, we're never getting back together."

"What has he done? You never told me why you broke up."

Shame was a bitter taste in her throat. "Wendell used me. I'm not giving him or anyone else the chance to do that again."

~⊱ CHAPTER 2 ⊰~

Early Saturday morning, Audra locked her cabin door, then stretched her arms high above her head. Her bright orange running jersey slid up her torso. She leaned left, then right, stretching the muscles of her back and sides. Audra jogged in place as she set the stopwatch feature on her digital wristwatch. It was only six-thirty, eastern standard time, three-thirty back home. She'd do an easy thirty-minute run out, then retrace her way back.

Her footsteps crunched along the gravel path, then abruptly silenced when the surface changed to dirt. A warm mid-July breeze followed her, carrying the scents of morning dew, grass, and pine from her isolated cabin toward the nearby lake.

"Aren't there coyotes and bears in Ohio? And mountain lions?" Her mother's question stalked her.

Audra stumbled on the smooth path. Why had Ellen planted that fear in her mind? Maybe jogging in the woods wasn't a good idea. She didn't know this area. She couldn't assume it would be as safe as the path four miles from her Redondo Beach townhome.

She was almost to the clearing surrounding the lake when she saw a figure sprint from the wood on the other side.

Jack!

He was a blur of gray T-shirt and black shorts. His feet barely touched the ground. Audra gasped, jumping back. She crouched beside some bushes. Her heart thundered in her ears. Her body screamed with tension. What the hell was chasing him?

She shot a look back toward the tree line behind him. Even after several breathless seconds, the path remained empty. Her attention returned to Jack. He'd slowed to a walk.

Oh, for Pete's sake! Was that the way he completed his morning run, with a sprint to the end of the path as though the hounds of hell were hunting him? She wished she'd known that before. Audra bent over, trying to catch her breath. But she kept a wary eye on Jack.

Without warning, he stripped his sweat-soaked T-shirt over his head. Her breath lodged in her throat. Again. She could barely see him on the other side of the lake. Still, her fingers shook with the need to trace his taut sienna back. She could almost feel the heat and dampness of his skin. There was something carnal about him that stirred a longing deep inside her that she didn't recognize.

Audra's gaze followed Jack as he crossed the whimsical blond-wood bridge back to the rental cabins' side of the lake. He continued on the path to the main cabin. Only after he was out of sight did Audra exhale.

She found an easy pace that carried her over the same bridge and into the woods across the lake. Her pulse quickened. Her stomach muscles quivered with nerves. Audra shook her head. She had to step out of her comfort zone and confront her fears. Jack had gone running on this trail and had returned in one piece. It must be safe. Right? She replaced her mental images of lions, tigers, and bears with one of Jack, bare-chested and sweaty. The trick vanquished her fears. Now her breathing was shallow for other reasons.

Two hours later, Audra had showered and dressed after her workout. She skipped down her weathered front steps and started toward the main cabin. It was almost half past eight o'clock. She bent her head back and gazed through the leaf-laden tree branches. The sun shone on the green leaves framed against the bright blue sky. Beautiful.

Audra arrived at the main rental cabin's front door; this time, she was fully dressed and wearing shoes. She entered and closed the door before turning toward the registration desk—and Jack.

"Good morning."

"Ms. Lane." His smooth, deep voice made the greeting more formal.

His braids were even more disheveled this morning than they'd been yesterday. And his beard . . . was he channeling his inner ZZ Top? Audra's thoughts flashed to the 1980s music video of the pop band's hit song "Sharp-Dressed Man." Jack could use some help with that.

"You can call me, um, Penny."

Jack didn't respond. His onyx eyes were steady on hers. What was he thinking? Was it too much to hope he'd forgotten the garbage bag she'd worn the last time she'd come to the cabin? Probably.

Audra smoothed the neckline of her lime green cotton blouse. "Do you have a map of the town? I'd like to get a few things, like groceries and curtains."

"Curtains?"

"There are a lot of windows in the cabin, but none of them have curtains. I feel exposed."

Jack stared at her in an unnerving silence for seconds before turning to the gray metal file cabinet behind him. He plucked a trifold brochure from a folder and returned to the desk. He spread the map across its surface, then picked up a pen.

"Groceries and curtains." He circled a section on the map.

Audra leaned closer to study the area he'd marked. She caught his scent, soap and sandalwood. Audra glanced up, startled to find him once again staring at her. She stepped back.

"Thank you. Could you recommend a place where I could get breakfast?"

Jack paused before scanning the map again. He drew another circle in a location that appeared in the heart of town. "Books and Bakery."

Her smile returned. "You aren't much of a talker, are you, Jack?"

"No, Ms. Lane."

"Please call me Penny. Or does your management have a policy against employees addressing guests by their first names?"

"No, ma'am." Finally a flicker of reaction flashed into those serious eyes. Just as quickly, it was gone.

Audra gathered the map. "Thank you for your help."

Jack's nod was curt.

She turned to leave. Was everyone in Trinity Falls as antisocial as the desk clerk? If so, she'd demand Benita return her money.

Audra was having one new experience after another. Last night, she'd slept in an isolated cabin in the woods, using spare sheets and towels as makeshift curtains. This morning, she'd gone jogging in the forest. Now she was going to experience small-town life. If new experiences were the measurement of success, at this rate, she'd finish writing the contracted songs by the end of the week.

I hope you're happy, Benita.

It was a short drive into Trinity Falls. Audra was instantly charmed by the redbrick roads, quaint streetlamps, manicured front yards, and rows of 150 YEARS STRONG banners, proclaiming the town's upcoming sesquicentennial. She followed the map's directions to the Trinity Falls Town Center and parked her rental car in front of Books & Bakery. The town and its shopping center looked like something out of a fairy tale. Audra expected a crowd of little people to swarm her, shouting, "Follow the Yellow Brick Road!"

She stepped from her silver Toyota Camry and stood observing the town center. The little slice of commerce in this modern-day Mayberry was comprised of six stores grouped in a semicircle around the parking lot: Are You Nuts?, Fine Accessories, Books & Bakery, Ean Fever—Attorney-at-Law, Skin Deep Beauty Salon, and Gifts and Greetings.

Were the residents of the enchanted town under the spell of the Good Witch or the Wicked Witch? She approached Books & Bakery with caution. But when she opened the door, a sense of warmth and cheer greeted her like an old friend. She forgot she was in an unfamiliar place, surrounded by strangers.

Audra took in the dark hardwood flooring and bright, inviting wall displays. The scent of lemon wood polish lingered in the air. Sesquicentennial banners similar to the ones that lined the town roads hung from the bookstore's ceilings and draped the walls.

Special-interest tabletop displays and overstuffed red armchairs drew Audra farther into the store. The bookcases were made of the same dark wood that shone beneath her feet. New releases were shelved beside perennial best sellers. The rows upon rows of books mesmerized her. Only hunger kept her focused on her destination—the bakery.

Audra followed the aisles, making mental notes of the sections to linger over after breakfast. The inventory included local artist crafts, like framed artwork, greeting cards, and jewelry.

She glimpsed glossy magazine covers as she wound her way toward the smells of fresh pastries and coffee, and the sounds of banter and laughter. She skimmed the titles on the mystery and romance shelves and glanced toward the science-fiction and fantasy section.

"You must be the new guest at Harmony Cabins." A woman's voice hailed her.

Audra tensed at the greeting. How did the attractive, older woman behind the counter know who she was? Her warm brown eyes twinkled and she smiled as though she were happy to see Audra. Short, curly brown hair framed her round, cocoa face.

Audra stopped in front of the bakery counter. "Yes, I am."

The stranger offered her right hand. "Welcome to Trinity Falls. I'm Doreen Fever, the café manager."

Audra accepted Doreen's hand. "I'm Au . . . Penny Lane." Her face heated with her slip.

Doreen released her hold and offered Audra a menu. "Well, Penny, what would you prefer, a late breakfast or an early lunch?"

"I'm hungry enough for both." She requested eggs, wheat toast, and coffee before settling onto a bar stool, leaving an empty seat between her and the other patron at the counter.

Doreen brought her a mug from a supply behind the counter and filled it with coffee. "Your breakfast will be right up."

"Where are you from?" The question came from the patron beside her. She was a beautiful woman, with long ebony hair and café au lait skin.

"Redondo Beach, near Los Angeles."

"Really?" The woman's movie star features brightened. She migrated to the empty bar stool between them, bringing her mug of coffee with her. "I'm Ramona McCloud, mayor of Trinity Falls, although my term is over in six months. Do you live near the beach?"

Audra absorbed all of that. "A few miles away."

"Wow." Ramona spoke the word on a sigh. "Why aren't you there now?"

Audra tugged her right earlobe. "Where?"

"At the beach."

"I needed a break." Or so Benita claimed, repeatedly.

Ramona laughed. "That's like saying you need a break from paradise. Beaches and beautiful weather—if I lived in Los Angeles, I'd never leave."

"Now you want to live in Los Angeles?" The deep voice startled Audra.

The newcomer was about six feet tall and built like a running back for a professional football team. He walked past Audra and placed a quick kiss on Ramona's full lips. His rugged, dark good looks held Audra's attention.

"That depends." Ramona gave the man a flirtatious glance. "Are you going to Los Angeles?"

"No, temptress, I'm going to Philadelphia."

"Then so am I." The love shining in Ramona's ebony eyes made her even more beautiful.

"Knock it off. I'm about to eat breakfast." A querulous voice interrupted the lovers' exchange.

Audra turned to find another tall man on the bar stool beside her. His long, lean figure sprawled elegantly on the seat. The humor in his midnight eyes belied the scowl on his model good looks. Whereas the first man looked like a professional football running back, this one reminded her of a wide receiver.

Audra glanced around at the tables, filling up

behind her. She hadn't imagined the café at Books & Bakery would attract so many people. She waited for her discomfort of crowds to return. It didn't.

Ramona gestured toward the handsome man beside her. "Penny Lane, this is Dr. Quincy Spates. He's the new professor of history at the University of Pennsylvania."

Quincy shook her hand. "Welcome to Trinity Falls."

Ramona continued. "And the degenerate behind you is Darius Knight. He's lucky to be gainfully employed as a reporter with *The Trinity Falls Monitor.*"

"Penny Lane, huh?" Darius's eyes were curious as he offered Audra his hand. "I was surprised to hear Harmony Cabins had a guest. What brings you to Trinity Falls?"

Audra shook the reporter's hand. "I'm here on vacation."

Darius cocked his head and released her hand. "I hadn't realized anyone outside of Trinity Falls knew the cabins existed."

A tall, slender woman in a royal blue skirt suit entered the café. Her confident strides carried her behind the counter. "I didn't know Jack had any cabins that were fully renovated." She offered Audra her right hand. "Welcome to Trinity Falls. I'm Megan McCloud."

Audra returned her greeting, trying to remember everyone's name. Apparently, Jack was the only antisocial person in town, the taciturn hermit in the enchanted forest.

On Audra's right, Ramona sipped her coffee. "Megan owns Books and Bakery."

Audra's eyes widened. "It's a wonderful bookstore. I can understand why it's so popular."

Megan grinned. "Thank you. What do you do?"

Audra tensed. "I'm a musician."

Darius leaned forward. "What instrument do you play?"

Ramona lowered her coffee mug. "You should talk with Vaughn Brooks. He's Trinity Falls University's band director."

Doreen reappeared with Audra's breakfast. "I doubt Penny wants to talk shop on her vacation."

Audra sighed with relief—for both the food and the interruption. She hated lying to these nice people.

Megan crossed her arms. "The books Jack ordered came in. Would you mind taking them to him when you return to the rental cabins?"

"No, not at all." Audra sipped her coffee.

Megan nodded. "Thank you."

Doreen topped off Audra's coffee. "How long will you be with us?"

"About a month." Audra bit into the wheat toast. The bread tasted homemade. "Delicious."

Doreen flushed with pleasure.

"A month?" Ramona's eyebrows rose. "That's some vacation."

"Ramona, are you prying into someone else's personal life?" Another tall, dark, and handsome stranger materialized.

Ramona gasped. "Hardly. That's Darius's job."

The new arrival walked to the counter and leaned forward. Megan met him halfway. They exchanged a quick kiss over the salt-and-pepper shakers, sugar packets, and napkin holders.

He then stepped behind the counter to kiss Doreen's cheek. "Hi, Mom."

Doreen cupped his jaw. "Would you like some breakfast?"

He shook his head. "Just coffee, please. I've already eaten."

Was she watching a Saturday-morning tradition? The camaraderie among these friends was so natural. They were more like an extended family. In contrast, the people in Los Angeles she considered friends were more like well-acquainted strangers. Was this what small-town living was like? If so, she envied them.

Megan took Ean's hand as he started past her and nodded toward Audra. "Ean Fever, this is Penny Lane."

Ean shook her hand. "Welcome to Trinity Falls. I'm glad Jack's finally renting out his cabins."

Audra frowned. "Jack? Do you mean the desk clerk?"

Doreen laughed. "And handyman, janitor, and whatever else. Jack owns Harmony Cabins."

Audra's jaw dropped. "I thought he was an employee."

Quincy shook his head. "We shouldn't be surprised that Jack didn't introduce himself."

"He probably didn't see a reason to." Megan poured herself a mug of coffee.

"That's no excuse." Ramona turned to Audra. "He didn't tell you who he is?"

Audra frowned. "He just said his name was Jack."

Quincy put his hand on Ramona's shoulder. "Ramona, Jack probably didn't want to make a big deal about it."

Ean sat on the other side of Quincy. "It's not like Jack to call attention to himself."

"In what way?" Audra's curiosity had ballooned.

"You have to tell her now." Darius shook his head. "You've made it worse by bringing it up."

Ramona grinned like the cat that swallowed the canary. "Jack is Jackson Elijah Sansbury." She paused, drawing out the suspense. "He's the great-great-grandson and sole descendent of Trinity Falls' founding family."

Audra nearly choked on her coffee. The man she'd thought of as the rental cabins' front-desk clerk was actually a member of the town's founding family?

"Wow."

❧ CHAPTER 3 ❧

Who was knocking on his private cabin's front door? Jack pushed himself from his armchair. He tossed the book he'd been reading onto the coffee table and padded barefoot across his great room.

He eased his frustration by yanking open his front door. Then he froze. His cabin guest stood on his porch. She wore the same green top and orange capris from this morning. He missed the trash bag.

Her presence on his property was putting him through a range of emotions he hadn't allowed himself to feel in almost two years. Amusement when she'd strutted to his registration counter, wearing nothing but a garbage bag; surprise at finding her standing on his porch; and, judging by the stirring in his shorts, desire at the sight of her.

"Yes?" The copper doorknob bore into Jack's palm.

She offered him a Books & Bakery plastic bag. "Megan McCloud asked me to give these to you. They're the books you ordered."

"Thanks." Jack took the heavy package from her. He didn't mean to look at her shapely calves, rounded hips, trim waist, and full breasts. It just happened. He swallowed. "Anything else?"

"Am I the only guest here?" She folded her arms under her chest, drawing his attention back to her cleavage.

Jack's palm slipped on the doorknob. "Yes."

He shouldn't have agreed to let Benita's friend stay here. She had to leave. Something about her was having an effect on everything in him.

Audra's gaze drifted from him to the lawn beyond his porch. "I hadn't realized the cabins would be so isolated."

He clung to the doorknob. "They are."

She returned her attention to him. "You really aren't much of a talker."

Why did she keep saying that? What did she want from him? Jack's attention was drawn to her ebony hair and its explosion of curls. He'd bet the cabins they'd feel like warm silk between his fingers. His grip tightened on the doorknob.

Audra continued. "Have you ever gone fishing?"

Jack gave himself a mental shake. What had she asked him? Something about fishing? "Yes."

Her expression brightened. "I've never been. Could you teach me?"

"No." The word shot from his lips with the desperation of a man trying to keep himself afloat on turbulent waters.

The light in her champagne eyes dimmed. "I'd really like to learn. I don't spend much time outside the city. Actually, I don't spend any time outside the city. I'd like to take advantage of this opportunity.

You know, to go fishing, hiking, sailing. But I need someone to show me how."

"No." He couldn't spend that much time alone with her. She was a danger to his way of living. He'd cut himself off from people and caring. Caring hurt.

"Why not?" The disappointment in her catlike eyes almost persuaded him to change his mind.

Jack was stoic. "Is there anything else?"

Audra searched his eyes. She seemed about to say something. Jack braced himself against her appeal.

"No, thank you." She turned and walked away.

He closed the door, working his numbed hand from its knob. *Why can't people leave me alone?*

In his younger years—before his wife and daughter—he wouldn't miss an opportunity to get to know a beautiful woman. But his circumstances had changed. Now he didn't want to get close to anyone ever again. He'd been hurt before. Badly. He didn't want to go through that again. But his cabin guest was drawing him like the proverbial moth to a very seductive flame. How close could he get before he caught fire?

"What name did you pick?" The clicking of Benita's computer keyboard accompanied her voice down the airwaves to Audra's cell phone. It was Saturday evening and Benita was still working.

"Penny Lane." Audra leaned forward to rest her guitar on the oak coffee table in front of her.

Silence descended. Even the constant click of

Benita's keyboard hung suspended. Had she lost the call?

"'Penny Lane'?" Benita's voice was thick with disdain. "Was that the best you could do?"

"What's wrong with it?"

"The residents of Trinity Falls aren't stupid." Benita exhaled a heavy breath.

Audra imagined her manager ripping her fingers through her short, straight hair. "I never said they were." She rose from the sofa, offended. "If you think you could have come up with a better name, you should have."

"Do I have to do everything?" The clicking sound returned, louder. "I found the resort. I made the reservations. I paid for the cabin in advance—"

"With my money."

"Do I also have to come up with the cover story?"

Audra gripped the cell phone with her left hand and planted her right fist on her hip. "Why do I even need a cover story?"

Benita sighed again. "Because when they learn you're a celebrity, everyone in Trinity Falls—population fifteen hundred—will follow you around town."

"No one knows the songwriters, Benita. They're all about the singers." Audra wandered from the dark plaid sofa to the front window. "Besides, even if Jack knew my real name, I doubt he'd care."

"Just make sure you don't fall in love with him."

"With Jack?" Audra called an image of the grumpy cabin owner to mind.

"He was one of the handsomest guys in high school." A printer whirred to life in Benita's office.

"That's really saying something. In my day, Heritage High was full of cute guys."

Audra frowned, trying to imagine what Jack looked like under his layers of fur. "He must have fallen on hard times."

Benita's hum was noncommittal. "You're not out there to rescue anyone, either."

"What are you talking about?" Audra turned away from the window.

"You know you're always trying to help people." Papers shuffled. A stapler snapped. "That's how Wendell was able to get over on you."

"I don't want to talk about Wendell." Or his five months of treachery. Audra paced past her sofa—and bitter memories of the way Wendell had used her.

"Then just concentrate on those three songs so you can come home."

"Good-bye, Benita." Audra disconnected the call and tossed her cell phone on the sofa.

Just concentrate on those three songs. Her manager made it sound so easy. But Audra had never had such a hard time with her songwriting. She shoved her hands into the front pockets of her shorts and wondered about someone else who was having a hard time.

What happened to Jack to transform him from a high-school heartthrob to Sasquatch?

"I have three top priorities that I want to address during my first term as mayor—strengthening education, repairing infrastructure, and improving emergency services." Doreen Fever trembled with excitement as she shared her plans with her boyfriend, Leonard George.

They sat at her dining room table after preparing dinner together in her cozy kitchen. She'd made the spaghetti and meat sauce. He'd made the salad.

Leonard drizzled more Italian dressing onto the half-eaten bowl of vegetables. "Don't you think you should wait until you're elected before you start making plans on what you're going to do?"

Doreen gave Leonard a sharp look. The lack of enthusiasm in his voice puzzled her. What could be wrong? "I'm running unopposed."

"But you aren't in office yet." Leonard continued eating his salad.

"I can't wait until I'm in office to figure out which issues I want to tackle first." Doreen forked up some lettuce. "I have to hit the ground running."

"I'm glad you know what you want to do when you're in office. But do we have to talk about that tonight?"

Doreen paused with her fork halfway to her mouth. "Not if you don't want to."

"All you ever talk about now is what you're going to do or planning to do as mayor of Trinity Falls." Leonard's voice was laden with exasperation. "I know you're excited, but can't we talk about something else for just this one night?"

She was speechless. Had she been talking too much about her plans? "I hadn't realized I was monopolizing our conversations."

"You are." Leonard stabbed several vegetables

with his salad fork. "There are other things in our relationship that we could talk about."

"Like what?"

"Anything else."

Doreen swallowed a sigh. He wasn't making this easy. "Name something and we'll talk about it."

Leonard chewed and swallowed a mouthful of vegetables. "You could ask me about my day."

Doreen dropped her fork. "I did while we were cooking. I thought I'd cheer you up with a more positive topic."

"I may not have anything good to say about the math class I'm teaching this summer, but I don't want to talk politics, either." Leonard finished his salad and moved on to his spaghetti.

How is he able to argue and eat at the same time? Doreen toyed with her salad for a long, tense silence before shoving it aside. "You know what you *don't* want to talk about, but you can't tell me what you *do* want to discuss."

"That's right."

"Can you hear how annoying that is?"

"No." He looked puzzled.

Doreen played with her spaghetti. "When you figure out what you want to talk about, let me know." She shoved a forkful of pasta into her mouth and chewed. The food settled like barbells in her stomach.

"I don't understand why you're upset." Leonard continued after a tense silence. He'd already cleaned half of his plate. "How would you feel if I talked about my work all the time?"

"You do." Doreen lowered her fork. *Is he kidding?*

"No, I don't."

Arguing the point wouldn't get her anywhere. "Are you still opposed to my being mayor?"

"It's your decision." He avoided her eyes.

Doreen sighed. "In other words, yes."

"You know how I feel about you, Dorie." He lowered his knife and fork, and his voice. "I want to marry you. I don't want to talk about education, infrastructure, or emergency services. I don't even want to talk about teaching math or coaching football. I want to talk about building a life with you. What are we going to do this weekend? Where are we going on vacation over Christmas break?"

Emotion lodged in her throat. Doreen swallowed it. "I care about you, Leo."

"But you care more for the memory of your dead husband. It's been almost a year and a half, Dorie."

"When I lost Paul, my whole world changed."

He reached his right arm across the table. His fingers were just short of touching her hand. "I'm not looking to replace him. I'd just like a bigger role in your life."

She cared for Leonard. But did she love him? She wasn't sure. She did know she didn't want to lose him. But neither did she want to lose herself—which she feared would be possible with Leonard.

"You have all that I can give for now. Is it enough?" Doreen held her breath.

Leonard sat back on his chair, allowing his arm to draw back to the edge of the table. "For now."

His tongue may have spoken the words she wanted to hear, but his eyes carried an ultimatum that chilled her heart.

* * *

It was 12:27 A.M. Audra was tired, but she wasn't at all sleepy. *Damn it!*

She sat on the top step of her cabin's oak porch. Because of her morning jog, she didn't fear an encounter with wildlife any longer. Her body was still on California time, believing it was only 9:27 P.M. But then it should also think she'd been up since four in the morning. She tugged on her hair and squeezed her eyes shut. *Sleep already!*

All of the light from the cabin's great room poured through the open door behind her, relieving some of the night's oppressive blackness. She glared at the notebook in her fists. An entire page of crossed-out lyrics scowled back at her.

She'd been in Trinity Falls two solid days. She still had writer's block. She still had insomnia. This was stupid. She should drive to the airport right now—without taking the time to change out of her nightgown and robe—and wait for a flight to Los Angeles International Airport. Only desperation to meet her three-song contract by August 4 kept her from giving up on Benita's stupid plan to go into self-exile.

Damn it. Audra exhaled. She had to relax if she was to get any sleep tonight. She lifted her gaze to the sky. *Good grief!* The heavens were blanketed with stars. She'd no idea there were so many of them. Beautiful. She inhaled a long, calming breath and drew in the smell of pines, earth, and fresh air so different from the city. The crickets were rather chatty. Would she be able to sleep with all that noi—

Her eyes widened. Her spine stiffened. Was that rustling? Was it coming from the bushes? What was causing it? The wind? A bear? A coyote? What was that other animal her mother had listed? *Oh, my God!*

Her heartbeat outpaced her thoughts. In her mind, she saw herself racing into the cabin and bolting the door behind her. In reality, her body wouldn't move. She was fossilized with fear. *Oh, my God!* Audra strained again to listen. If it was a bear, would it chase her if she ran? How fast did bears move? Should she lie on the stairs and pretend to be dead?

"Hello, Ms. Lane." Jack stepped from the bushes and entered the pool of light spilling from her cabin.

"Oh, my God." Audra pressed her hand to her chest. Her voice shook with residual terror. She was as breathless as though she'd run a forty-yard dash in less than three minutes. "You scared the *crap* out of me."

"Sorry." He slipped his hands into the front pockets of his baggy brown shorts. His muscles rippled under his short-sleeved forest green T-shirt.

"I thought you were a bear." Audra struggled to catch her breath.

"I'm not."

With anyone else, Audra would have thought he was trying to be funny. But Jack didn't appear to have a sense of humor. He didn't appear to be very talkative, either. His conversation was so sparse it bordered on nonexistent.

She gave him a suspicious look just in case. "Are there bears or other wild animals nearby?"

"Not usually."

That is hardly reassuring.

Audra grasped the neckline of her robe. Her gaze darted to the shadowed outline of the trees behind him before narrowing on his face—or what she could see of it hidden between his unkempt hair and overgrown beard. "Why were you skulking in the bushes?"

"I wasn't."

She gave him a sharp look. Did she hear humor in his voice? Was he laughing at her? Impossible. "What were you doing then?"

"Walking, Ms. Lane." Jack shrugged.

The movement reminded Audra of the way he'd looked, ripping his T-shirt off over his head, and the sight even from a distance of his hard, sculpted, sweaty torso.

Audra gave herself a mental shake. "You don't have to call me 'Ms. Lane.' I'd rather you used my first name."

Jack cocked his head to the side. "What is it?"

"I . . . I gave it to you." The lie didn't sit well.

Jack shook his head. "'Penny Lane' isn't your name. It's a Beatles song."

Audra was speechless. Jack had known she was lying all along. His dark, direct gaze remained steady on hers. He didn't seem angry. He seemed curious—and slightly amused.

She found her voice. "Some people are named after songs."

"You weren't."

Audra couldn't continue the lie. He'd seen right

through it. She wasn't comfortable with misleading him, anyway. But suppose he recognized her real name? Benita had warned her against telling people who she was. Well, it was a chance she'd have to take. Besides, Jack didn't strike her as a groupie.

"My name is Audra Lane."

Jack narrowed his gaze. "Really?"

Audra smiled at his suspicion. "Yes, that's really my name."

Jack studied Audra Lane's mass of dark curls, searched her makeup-free features, then considered her worn and faded yellow cotton robe. Her bare toes peeked from beneath its hem.

It was hard to reconcile this fresh-faced young woman with the sleek and sophisticated star whose photo had been all over the Internet after she'd earned the Grammy Award for Song of the Year. He probably shouldn't tell her that, though. For one thing, she might get offended. For another, she obviously didn't want to be recognized. Why else would she take a fake name, even one as ridiculous as "Penny Lane"?

"Hello, Audra Lane."

"Hello, Jackson Elijah Sansbury." She smiled at his surprised expression. "The people at Books and Bakery told me you were the great-great-grandson of the town's founder."

"Did they?" Jack's jaw tightened. What else had they told her?

"Don't try to deny it." Her smile blossomed into a grin that seemed to bathe him in warmth right down to his bones. "Five independent sources confirmed Ramona McCloud's information. I think it's pretty cool."

"Do you?" He needed to leave. Every kind word, hint of humor, and soft smile chipped away at his protective walls. He was starting to feel human again. He wasn't ready for that.

"What are you doing out so late?"

"Insomnia." The reminder of his inability to sleep brought back his irritation like a comfortable old coat.

She gave him a knowing nod as she rose to her feet. "Then you and I have that in common."

She was a little over average height, but she seemed shorter than she'd appeared in the photos he'd found on the Internet. And her robe covered the killer legs her garbage bag minidress had exposed. Shame.

He finally processed her comment. "You have insomnia?"

"Yes." She tightened the belt to her robe. "Is your insomnia the reason you've wandered to my cabin?"

He felt another unfamiliar trace of humor. "Walking relaxes me."

Her gaze swept their surroundings—the tall, old trees and the gravel path that bisected the well-manicured lawn. "I can understand why. I'm surprised more people haven't discovered this place. It's a hidden treasure."

Warmth of pride and pleasure battled the coldness within him. "I don't advertise."

"Why not?"

"Don't want guests."

Audra's winged eyebrows flew up beneath her

bangs. "Why own the cabins if you don't intend to rent them?"

Jack folded his arms over his chest. "It's a hobby."

"Some hobby." Audra chuckled. "I guess I should consider myself lucky to have connections. How do you know Benita Hawkins?"

"It's a small town."

She wrapped her arms around her slender figure. "Yes, it is. I'm not used to this much quiet or the lack of streetlights."

"Then why are you here?"

Audra chuckled. "I keep asking myself the same thing." She turned to reenter her cabin. "Good night, Jackson Elijah Sansbury. I hope we both sleep well."

"Good night." Jack stayed long enough to watch her close the door behind herself. Then he turned to head back to his cabin.

He hadn't felt this alive in a long time, a very long time. His senses were heightened. The stars that blanketed the sky shone brighter. The scent of the evergreens bordering the path was stronger. The leaves rustling in the midnight breeze sounded like music. But since he felt more energized than he had felt in months—possibly years—would he be able to sleep at all tonight?

CHAPTER 4

Muffled hammering shattered the still morning. Audra followed it down the graveled trail bisecting a nearby clearing. As she'd suspected, Jack was wielding a hammer on the porch steps of a neighboring cabin identical to hers. Her footsteps crunching on the path must have alerted him. He stood as she approached.

His left bicep bunched as he wiped sweat from his forehead. His onyx gaze fixed on her. His eyes were so compelling—secretive, dark, and vulnerable—for such a gruff, tough man.

Audra's gaze drifted from his impressive arm and chest muscles to his hair. It was past time for him to redo his braids, if that was the style he wanted. They were so unruly—Audra couldn't determine his intent. Was he trying to invent a new look? His beard could use some tidying as well. Were small woodland animals nesting in there?

"Good morning." Audra savored this new opportunity to get the stingy cabin owner to string together a more generous sentence, something longer than five words.

"Morning."

She was just warming up. "What are you doing?"

"Repairs."

Hmmm, this is harder than it seems. Audra racked her brain for a question that would require more than a one- or two-word answer. "What do you have left to do on this cabin?"

"A lot."

Wow, he's a tough subject. She gave him a hard look. Was he doing this on purpose? His sharp sienna features, visible above his beard, gave away nothing.

Audra shoved her hands into the front pockets of her linen shorts and let her attention drift over the cabin behind him. "You don't have a website, and Benita didn't have much information on your cabins. I was nervous about coming at first."

"Why?"

Audra gave him a wide-eyed stare. He'd sounded curious. That must be a good sign. "I think everyone fears the unknown. Don't you?"

He shrugged his broad shoulders. "Maybe."

Audra stared at his teal green T-shirt. The simple cut, rounded neckline, and small pocket above his left pectoral seemed familiar. Was this the same shirt he'd worn yesterday?

She gestured toward his torso. "How many shirts do you have like that?"

Jack glanced at his chest. "Seven."

"One for each day?"

"Yes."

She'd been teasing. Was he serious? "That's . . .

very frugal. What do you do when you run out of T-shirts?"

"Laundry."

He was good at this game. Audra had been so sure he wouldn't have a one-word answer for that question.

She tried again. "What happens if you forget to do the laundry?"

Jack gave her a puzzled look. "I don't."

Audra gave up. "I've kept you from your work long enough. Sorry."

"No problem." Jack struggled not to laugh, which was getting harder to do around Audra.

She was so obviously disappointed that she hadn't gotten him to talk more. He'd enjoyed the mental challenge of thwarting her. Maybe a part of him was glad Audra Lane had arrived on his rental cabins' property.

She stepped back. "Still, I didn't mean to interrupt you."

"Why did you?"

She shrugged. "I was restless. You know, I wouldn't bother you if you had other guests I could talk with."

"Maybe." Why was he glad there weren't other renters on the property? Did he want her interrupting him?

Audra narrowed her eyes. "Are you doing this on purpose?"

His lips twitched, despite his best efforts. "What?"

Her eyes widened. "You're deliberately giving curt answers to my questions."

Jack's grin broke free. "Am I?"

"Oh!" Audra spun on her heels and marched away, kicking up gravel behind her.

Jack's shoulders shook with humor. He felt lighter than he'd felt in years. It was as though in the three days that Audra had been on the property, her presence was healing him, removing the scars of fear, grief, and bitterness that his daughter's death and his ex-wife's betrayal had left behind. She'd ripped open the lid of his coffin and was breathing life back into him.

Jack returned to his hammering. Maybe he shouldn't have been such a jerk to Audra. He'd had fun, though. But if he'd answered her questions, perhaps she'd have answered his.

What was she doing here?

What was she working on?

Why had she chosen to travel under such an obvious pseudonym? She'd have called less attention to herself by using her real name.

Audra wasn't on her porch that afternoon. Jack didn't pretend not to be disappointed. Then he heard the music. He slowed his footsteps on the graveled path that led to her front steps.

A soft, tentative voice drew him up the stairs. He stood beside the front window and listened to the voice tell him about broken promises, lost time, and the crushing weight of other people's expectations.

The music stopped. "Shoot! Shoot! Shoot!" Pure frustration powered the exclamations.

After a brief silence, Audra picked up the song

from the beginning. The uncertain chords of an acoustic guitar accompanied the lyrics. Indistinct humming filled the open spaces when she ran out of words.

Jack cocked his head. It wasn't her best work. After he'd seen the article on her Grammy wins, he'd found her work on the Internet and played a few of the music videos. The songs were strong, memorable, and entertaining. It wasn't just the vocal talent of the popular artists who showcased the songs; it was Audra's abilities as a songwriter.

Her voice was soft and uncertain right now, but he heard its underlying appeal. Had she recorded any of her own work? Would she ever consider it?

His knuckles rapped on Audra's front door. Jack froze. Why had he done that? He hadn't intended to let her know he was there. The cabin became still. The silence penetrated the thick wooden door. Jack stepped back, debating the wisdom of leaving.

"Who is it?" Audra's tone was gruff bravado.

He couldn't resist a smile. "Jack."

Another brief silence. Jack sensed rather than heard her footsteps carrying her toward him.

The door opened just a crack, as though Audra wanted to verify his identity.

Jack held her cautious gaze. "Bears don't knock."

Audra gave him a sarcastic look before joining him on the porch. "Considering the similarities in your appearance, I'm surprised you do." She softened the gibe with a cheeky grin.

"I was housebroken years ago." Jack deadpanned his response.

"That's a relief." Audra pulled the front door closed.

She was still teasing him. How long had it been since someone had done that? How long had it been since he'd wanted to tease someone back? About as long as it had been since someone had made him laugh, long before Zoey's death.

Audra strolled past him to the porch's railing and looked up at the cloudless blue sky. "It's so beautiful here."

"Yes, it is." His gaze traveled up from her bare feet and long shapely legs to her gold linen shorts and hot pink T-shirt. She looked as bright and warm as the day.

"And quiet. Except for the crickets that come out at night." Audra glanced over her left shoulder. "Were you creeping around in the woods again?"

He ignored her question. "I heard your music. It was good."

Audra sighed. "No, it wasn't."

"I wouldn't say it was good if I didn't think it was."

"I know. You're not the kind of person who tells social lies. You speak your mind—when you speak at all."

Jack heard the humor in her voice. "I'm speaking now."

Audra feigned concern. "Does it hurt very much?"

"You're full of smart remarks today, aren't you?"

Audra tugged her right earlobe. "I'm sorry. I'm not usually this sarcastic."

"Are you a singer?" Jack watched her closely. Would she tell him the truth?

She arched a brow. "Why? Do you know someone who could make me a star?"

"I'm serious. You have a good voice. You could have a future in the music industry."

Audra shook her head. "I know at least a dozen people who are much, much better singers. But they'll never make it in the industry. They have the vocal talent, but they're not entertainers."

"That's important?"

"It's half the battle."

"Why couldn't you be an entertainer?"

"That's way out of my comfort zone." She shrugged one slender shoulder. "This whole vacation is out of my comfort zone. But Benita thought it would be good for me."

"She was always a know-it-all, even as a kid."

Audra's smile made the day even brighter. "I think she's right in this case. That's the reason I asked you to be my guide."

Jack stiffened. "Why?"

"To give me a tour of the town—"

"Trinity Falls isn't that big."

"Take me hiking—"

"Follow that path." Jack inclined his head toward the distance.

"And fishing."

He gave her a hard look. With her hypnotic smile and seductive warmth, Audra Lane was a threat to his numb, solitary lifestyle. And now she was proposing they spend even more time together. That wouldn't be wise.

"No." Jack crossed to the stairs.

"You won't tell me why not?" Her voice followed him down the porch steps.

"No."

"Ah! You've returned to your chatty self. Welcome back." Her voice was full of laughter that was even more enthralling than her music.

Jack's lips twitched with reluctant humor. No, it wasn't a good idea to spend hours alone with Audra Lane. Right now, she was giving him all he could handle. She was making him feel again, and that scared him far more than those bears she was certain waited in the woods.

That night, Jack tried to stay away, but he wasn't strong enough. Or perhaps Audra's lure was stronger. She wasn't on her porch, but he heard music again. This time, it was a full band, not just a guitarist. And the singer was familiar.

Jack followed the sound to the back of Audra's cabin. The area was well lit. The back door was open, allowing the cabin's lights to shine over the gray-and-white stone patio. A laptop stood open on the wooden bench. It was plugged into the exterior wall. Music played from the computer. Mary J. Blige belted out one of her self-esteem anthems, "Just Fine." The music was compelling. The words were empowering. But it was the woman on the patio who held him captive as she moved with abandon to the beat of the music.

Audra still wore the gold shorts and formfitting hot pink T-shirt she'd worn that afternoon. She swung her hips with the beat of the music, letting her body flow with the song. Muscles in his torso knotted with a half-forgotten sense of yearning. Audra raised her arms high above her head and pumped her hips. Jack's palms itched with the desire to trace his hands along the curves of her body. He clenched his fists and took a step back. At the same time, Audra spun on her bare toes to face him.

Her scream stripped the silence. She stumbled back, falling awkwardly onto the bench behind her. She pressed a fist to her chest. "Oh, my goodness! You scared the crap out of me! Again!"

Jack felt as guilty as a seven-year-old child caught searching his parents' bedroom for his Christmas present. That actually had happened to him. "I'm sorry."

"Why are you always creeping around in the woods?"

"I wasn't creeping." Jack stepped into the light.

"Then what were you doing?" Audra's voice no longer shook.

"What were *you* doing?" It was a childish response but the only one he was prepared to give at the moment.

"Dancing."

"Why?"

She dragged a hand through her hair. "I thought the exercise would help me sleep."

"Still having trouble sleeping?"

"So are you. Why else would you keep creeping around in the woods?" She pressed a couple of keys on her laptop. Mary J. Blige became silent. The screen glowed blue, then became dark.

"I wasn't creeping around."

"Then what were you doing?"

Cornered. In the sudden silence, he heard the crickets in concert. "I came to see you."

"Why?"

"To tell you . . . I'd take you fishing."

What? Where had that come from?

Her champagne eyes sparkled. "Really?"

No. But the slow smile brightening her pixie features turned his mind to mush. "Sure. I'll take you fishing in the morning."

He hadn't meant to offer to teach her. What would make him say that he would?

"You could have waited until the morning to tell me."

A reprieve? "No, I couldn't. We need to leave no later than five."

Her eyes stretched. "In the morning?"

"Yes." Jack breathed more easily.

Audra wouldn't want to wake up that early. Five o'clock in the morning here was two o'clock in the morning on the West Coast. There was no way she'd adjusted to eastern standard time yet. She'd only been here three days.

"OK." Audra popped off the bench and collected her laptop. "I'd better say good night."

Jack gaped. "That's OK with you?"

"I'm excited." Audra flashed him a bright grin over her shoulder before bending to unplug her computer from the patio outlet.

Jack dragged his eyes from the firm curves of her derriere. "Five o'clock isn't too early for you? We're three hours ahead of the West Coast."

Audra straightened. "I can do the math. I've been getting up early to jog, but I can always exercise later in the day."

"You've been jogging in the mornings?"

She held her laptop close to her chest. "I've seen you coming back from your run."

Why hadn't he seen her? It bothered him that someone had watched while he'd exercised his demons.

"What time will we be done fishing?" Audra's question redirected his train of thought.

"We can stay as long as you like." He felt a curious combination of fear and anticipation.

It had been years since he'd gone fishing with someone. He didn't mind his own company, but could he handle Audra's? She was changing him. The fact he was here proved that. He'd avoided human contact for the past sixteen months, but Audra had the power to pull him from his self-imposed exile after his daughter's death. Should he fight it? Could he? Did he want to?

Audra almost vibrated with excitement. "Should I bring anything? What should I wear?"

Jack fought to resist her and his longings. "I'll pack our lunch." He nodded toward her. "What you're wearing now is fine."

More than fine. Maybe he should ask her to wear sweats.

"Great." She glanced at the serviceable black watch on her wrist. "Good night."

"Night."

What had he gotten himself into? Jack watched his guest enter the cabin, then close and lock the patio door between them. A light green curtain he'd never seen before swung in its large, rectangular window. She was even changing his cabins.

Jack walked back to his cabin. His heart was pounding. Was it anxiety or excitement? Audra Lane's presence was having an almost magical effect on him. How much longer could he resist her? Did he even want to?

CHAPTER 5

Jack had been serious when he said he'd come for her at five o'clock, Monday morning. Audra opened her door to find him on her porch. He wore black cargo shorts and black hiking boots. Today's T-shirt was gunmetal gray.

"Is this T-shirt number four or five in your collection?" Audra let him in, nodding at his sculpted torso.

"It's Monday. This is T-shirt number one." He stopped close enough for her to feel a hint of his body's warmth. In his left hand, he held two fishing rods.

Audra gestured toward the cooler in his right. "Is that our lunch?"

"Peanut butter and jelly sandwiches." He set the cooler on the floor near his feet.

"Grape jelly?" She noticed the navy blue pack strapped to his back.

"Is there any other kind?"

"You have hidden depths, Mr. Sansbury." Audra

strained to see the man beyond his unkempt hair and overgrown beard. Most of his features were hidden, but his onyx eyes twinkled at her. Her heart tripped at this all-too-rare glimpse of emotion.

Audra settled onto the dark plaid fabric sofa. She shoved her feet into ankle-high coffee-colored hiking boots.

Jack offered her a fishing rod. "Do you know how to use this?"

"I've never even seen one in real life."

"You're kidding." Jack lowered the rod.

A thought occurred to Audra. She gave Jack a sharp look. "Am I going to have to put a worm on this?"

"I have artificial lures."

Relieved, Audra took the rod to examine it. It was longer than she'd imagined, about five feet, and supple. She shook it a few times. "I had no idea fishing rods were so flexible."

"You've really never been fishing?"

"Never." The cork grip was comfortable in her hand. What kind of metal was the handle made of? Graphite?

"You've led a sheltered life."

"Perhaps." Audra examined the aluminum reel and nylon line. "Don't people go fishing to relax? How hard could it be?"

"Right." He collected the cooler, walked to the door, and held it open for her. "Are you ready?"

"I think so." She led him outside. The fishing rod felt light in her fist.

Jack watched her check the locks on her front door. "Afraid the bears will steal your guitar?"

"If they're like you, they'll just lurk around in the

bushes waiting to scare me half to death." She walked past him and down the porch steps.

Moonlight eased the velvet darkness. Their footsteps, crunching over the graveled path, battled back the thick silence. Trinity Falls was foreign from her life in Los Angeles. L.A. was full of traffic noises, crowds, and artificial lights. But after four days, Audra was used to the quiet here. Perhaps Benita was right, as much as she hated to admit it. This alien environment may be what she needed— and not just to bring back her creative muse. She felt reinvigorated by the silence that blanketed her at night, crickets that sang her to sleep, and the fresh forest scents that filled her lungs.

"Where are we going?" *Why am I whispering?*

"To the lake."

Audra jumped when Jack responded in a normal voice. "Why did we have to come out so early?"

"Why didn't you ask me that last night?" There was humor in his voice.

"I was afraid if I asked too many questions, you'd change your mind."

"I still might."

Audra allowed the silence to resettle. Any further comments might be considered questions. She couldn't risk Jack canceling their outing. Each step that brought her closer to the lake ratcheted her excitement.

Finally the lake came into view. Jack stopped a distance from the whimsical bridge and shrugged off his backpack. He opened it to withdraw a wide, faded blanket, which he spread near a large maple tree that must have guarded the lake since the dawn of time.

He waved her closer to him. "I'll show you how to set your lure."

More than fifteen minutes later, the sun had stretched into the sky. Birds had gathered for their morning meeting. The temperatures had risen. But Audra still hadn't baited her fishing rod or cast her line. She glared first at the uncooperative worm substitute, then Jack.

He shrugged. "'Don't people go fishing to relax? How hard could it be?'"

Audra's brows lifted to her hairline. He was giving her words back to her. "I miss the grumpy desk clerk."

"He's right here."

Audra didn't think so. The humor in Jack's eyes so captivated her that she forgot more than half of his face was covered by hair.

She tugged away her gaze to check her watch. It was after five in the morning. "Why do people fish for relaxation? This isn't relaxing."

Several minutes later, she'd finally baited her line. Frustration roiled anew when it came to casting it.

"Come on. You're almost there." Jack's warm, strong hands covered hers, guiding her through the motion.

Audra was ready to return to bed by the time their lines were cast. She settled beside Jack on the blanket, mimicking his pose: legs crossed, both hands on the pole. "If I had to fish to survive, I'd starve to death."

Jack threw his head back and laughed. Audra gaped. He used his right index finger to lift her chin and close her mouth. "You'll collect flies."

"I'm sorry." Audra's skin was still warm from that single touch even after his hand had dropped away. "There was a time I didn't think you ever laughed."

In a blink, his smile disappeared as though it had never been there. "I haven't had a reason to."

"Maybe you should go fishing more often."

"Maybe." Jack looked away.

Audra did the same. A companionable silence settled over them. Audra gained confidence as they recast their lines periodically—until she felt a tug on the rod.

"I've got something." She struggled to hold on to her fishing rod while she rose to her feet.

Why was she nervous? Was it because she was afraid? Of what? *Failing.* The realization went through her like an electric charge. Was that the reason for her writer's block? After her Grammy win, did other people's expectations seem too high?

She felt Jack behind her. His hard arms pressed against her waist as he once again covered her hands with his to guide her. He was warm, strong, and steady at her back. His presence gave her confidence. Together, they reeled in her fish and put it in the bucket.

"Oh, my gosh! Did you see it? Isn't this amazing?" Audra's heart raced with excitement.

Jack smiled. "Yes, it is. That's a white bass. Perfect size for eating."

She didn't care if he was humoring her. Suddenly she was having the time of her life. Audra managed to bait and cast her line by herself, then settled back onto the blanket—but not for long. Jack's line came alive with his catch. She didn't know whether her hovering around him was a help or a hindrance to his reeling in the fish. She just wanted to be a part of the action.

After they put Jack's fish in the bucket, Audra returned to the blanket. Her gaze traced the deep green tree line nearby, the white trellis bridge arching over the lake, the silver blue water dancing in front of them. "It's so beautiful here."

"It is." His voice was calm, confident. At peace.

"It's more than beautiful. It's enchanted."

"Like a fairy tale?"

Was he laughing at her again?

Audra gave this more relaxed Jack a considering look. She liked what she saw—or rather what she could see between his beard and his braids. Thick black eyebrows slashed across his high forehead. Deep-set, almond-shaped onyx eyes communicated a sharp mind with a hint of pain. Sensuous lips were half masked by his black beard and moustache.

She arched a brow, challenging him. "Are you an expert on fairy tales?"

A jolt slammed through Jack as his mind jerked back to his past. He'd read Disney versions, Hans Christian Andersen, and *Grimm's Fairy Tales* to Zoey every night before bed. His eight-year-old daughter had had an insatiable appetite for the stories.

"I've read my share." Jack swallowed to ease the dryness in his throat.

"If this really were a fairy tale, which one would it be?" Audra shifted toward him. The movement distracted Jack from his thoughts. Thank goodness.

Jack stored away the bittersweet memories of his little girl and considered Audra's question. He surveyed the proud old trees and playful lake. "*Alice in Wonderland*?"

"No way." Audra gave in to laughter.

It amazed him how she could make him smile. "Which fairy tale would you choose?"

"With your gruff attitude and these isolated cabins, it would definitely be *Beauty and the Beast.*"

His gaze moved over her pixie features. "Would you be Beauty?"

Audra shook her head. "I never said that."

He would. "I guess we each have our own fairy tales."

Audra's dark curls danced in the gentle breeze. Her champagne eyes searched his face. "You know, if you'd like, I can redo your braids."

Jack fought the urge to smooth a hand over his hair. Audra's expression held neither criticism nor disdain. Still, his cheeks burned with embarrassment. He hadn't thought much about his appearance in months. Years? Not since Zoey had gotten sick. Without his daughter to prompt him, he'd thought about it even less after she died.

"No, thanks."

A pretty pink blush rose in Audra's cheeks. "I'm sorry. I didn't mean to offend you. You're doing me a favor by teaching me how to fish. I wanted to repay you."

Jack's gaze dropped to her mouth. Her lips drew him like a thirsty man to water. They were moist, slightly parted, and pink as candy. Suddenly he wanted a taste more than he wanted his next breath. Before he could change his mind again, Jack swooped in and claimed her lips.

He felt Audra's gasp against his lips before he sealed her mouth with his. Her touch, her scent, transported him to another place and time, down the rabbit hole. Jack pressed a little deeper for a better taste. His heart stuttered, then beat hard and fast after having felt nothing for so long. The darkness that had borne down on him for years eased. Her warmth was healing him. And for a moment, Audra had responded. He was sure she had. He'd brushed his tongue across the seam of her lips. They'd softened beneath his touch before she pushed away.

Jack blinked to focus on her face. Concern and remorse chilled him when he saw where his beard had chafed her chin and cheeks. He wanted to soothe the areas, but feared she wouldn't want him to touch her again.

What was happening to him? Had hiding in these cabins so deteriorated his civility and self-control that he now resembled an untamed beast?

Audra frowned. "That's not the way I repay my debts."

"You don't owe me anything."

"Then what was that?"

A hungry man seeking sustenance? A blind man reaching out to see? "I don't know."

Audra's expression said, *I don't believe you.* "I don't do flings."

"I'm sorry." Jack scrubbed his left hand over his beard. "It sounds stupid, but I don't know what came over me."

Audra rose. "Thank you for the fishing lesson."

She was leaving? Of course. He'd crossed the line and made her uncomfortable.

Jack stood with the bucket. "Would you like the fish?"

"I at least want the one I caught." Audra's half smile gave him hope that he could redeem himself.

"Fair enough." Jack helped Audra collect their belongings before escorting her to her cabin.

He was beginning to believe he needed redemption. He'd been alone in the dark for so long. Could Audra, with her warmth and light, draw him from the cold darkness his life had become since Zoey's death? Did he deserve saving?

"Good morning, Simon. What can I get for you?" Doreen masked her surprise at finding Simon Knight at Books & Bakery's food counter at eight o'clock, Tuesday morning. The retired pharmacist had never appeared this early before.

Simon waved her off. "Nothing, thanks, Doreen. I've already eaten."

The mystery deepened. "Then what can I do for you?"

"I want to tell you first, and in private, before I make a public announcement." He bounced on the toes of his black loafers. "I'm running for mayor."

Doreen stared at the older man for seconds that felt like minutes. "You're running for mayor? It's mid-July. The campaign filing deadline was December."

"I'm starting a petition to join the race. I just need about five hundred signatures to get my name on the ballot."

Was this some kind of joke? But Simon wasn't known for his sense of humor. Rather, he was a thorn in the side of anyone who ever tried to get anything done for the benefit of the town's nearly fifteen hundred residents.

Doreen crossed her arms. "Simon, you've lived in Trinity Falls all of your life. You've never been a member of any civic organization. You've never participated in any improvement campaigns. You've never even attended a town meeting. Why have you decided to run for mayor?"

Simon stood straighter, looking down his broad nose at Doreen. "The residents of Trinity Falls deserve to have a choice of mayoral candidates. We haven't had a two-candidate competition for three election cycles."

"Is that going to be your campaign platform, giving the town a choice for mayor?" Did she sound as incredulous as she felt?

Ramona McCloud, the current mayor, was not running for reelection. Instead, she'd made the life-changing decision to leave Trinity Falls next month with her boyfriend, Doctor Quincy Spates. That meant Doreen was the only registered candidate for the election. She'd been prepared to challenge Ramona for the office, though. She'd understood how their visions for Trinity Falls were different and why. In contrast, campaigning against Simon would be like kickboxing smoke.

Simon gave her a smug look. "My platform will be the sesquicentennial celebration."

Doreen frowned. "I'm chairing the Trinity Falls Sesquicentennial Steering Committee. You're not even a member."

Yet another example of Simon's lack of civic participation. Why did he want to be mayor?

Simon wagged his right index finger. "The

sesquicentennial—in particular, the Founders Day Celebration next month—is our best chance to raise the town's profile and boost tourism . . . if it's done correctly."

Doreen narrowed her eyes. "Meaning?"

"I'm going to position the outcome of the mayoral election as a judgment on the sesquicentennial events. Will the steering committee you're leading raise the town's profile? Will it increase tourism or draw regional, if not national, attention?"

Doreen's laugh was short and shocked. "So I do all the work, while you just sit back and judge the outcome? How convenient for you."

"That's not what I said."

Doreen continued as though she hadn't heard him. "The only flaw in your campaign strategy is that the celebration—in particular, Founders Day—is going to be a success."

"How?" Simon bounced on his toes again. "You can't even convince Jack Sansbury, the last member of our founding family, to attend the celebration."

Doreen unclenched her teeth. "The sesquicentennial is going to be a success. But what about your lack of government experience?"

"I'm willing to learn. I'm up for the challenge."

"Are you talking about on-the-job training?" Was he serious? "I already have experience working with town agencies through my volunteer positions on civic committees."

A movement in Doreen's peripheral vision drew her attention past Simon and corked her growing head of steam. Her regular morning customers were arriving. Her son, Ean, joined Quincy, Ramona, and Simon's son, Darius.

Doreen glared at Simon. "We'll continue this later."

"Now, hold on, Doreen." Simon glanced over his shoulder. "Now that I've given you the courtesy of advance warning, I'm ready to announce my candidacy."

"You mean your petition." Doreen fumed. Her soon-to-be challenger preened at his pending spotlight.

Simon didn't appear to hear her. "Good morning." His voice boomed as though he was already on the campaign trail. "How's everybody this morning?"

Darius gave his father a suspicious look. "What brings you here so early?"

"I have some news I'd like to share with you good people." Simon rubbed his hands together. "I'm running for mayor."

"You missed the filing deadline." It was the first thing that popped into Darius's brain and out of his mouth.

Simon waved his hand dismissively. "I'm circulating a petition, which I expect all you good people to sign."

The older man's guffaws grated on Darius's ears. Apparently, after thirty-three years, he still wasn't immune to being embarrassed by his parents. "That's not funny. It's unethical to coerce people into signing your petition."

Simon's grin didn't waver. "We're all friends here."

Darius put a firm hand on his father's shoulder and spoke to his friends. "Go ahead and order your breakfast. I'll be right back."

He steered Simon to the farthest table in the bakery.

Simon shrugged off Darius's arm. "What are you doing?"

"I'll ask you the same thing. Why are you talking about running for mayor?"

Simon sent his son a resentful glare as he straightened his dark green jersey. "The residents of Trinity Falls deserve a choice of mayoral candidates. We haven't—"

"Cut the crap." Darius's head ached from his father's bullshit. He pulled out a chair and sank onto it. "Save the pompous speeches for strangers. Tell *me* the truth."

Simon settled onto the seat across from Darius. "I want to be the next mayor of Trinity Falls."

"Why?"

"It's my civic duty."

"Bullshit. You've never been civic-minded."

Simon's brown cheeks flooded an angry red. "Who are you to approve or disapprove of the reason I'm running for office? I can run for mayor if I damn well choose."

Darius ignored Simon's temper and scrutinized the angular features that were discomfortingly similar to his: high forehead, dark eyes, broad nose, and full lips. "Does Mom know what you're doing?"

"I told her."

"And?"

"I don't have to ask your mother's permission to do anything. I'm a grown man. The only person I need to please is me."

Translation: Ethel Knight was pissed. Great. Another reason for his parents to be at odds.

"You don't know anything about being mayor. You don't know the first thing about running a town."

"How hard could it be?" Simon sneered. "If Ramona McCloud can run Trinity Falls, so can I."

"No, you can't." Darius's voice was flat. "Get a hobby if you're worried about retirement."

"I'm not worried about my retirement," his father grumbled.

"This race is too important for you to use it as a way to draw attention to yourself."

Simon's brow beetled with fury. "What does that mean?"

"You know exactly what I'm saying. You love being the center of attention. That's why you want to run for mayor."

"That's not true." Simon seemed actually to believe his words.

Darius ignored his father's interruption. "Trinity Falls isn't your toy. The mayor's office isn't a game."

Simon stood, pushing the chair under the table. "This isn't a game to me."

Darius held his father's gaze. "Public servants aren't allowed to have secrets."

Simon spread his arms. "I have nothing to hide."

"Are you sure?"

"Positive." His father turned and walked away.

Simon Knight wanted the town to believe he was an honest, responsible family man. Darius knew the truth. His father's life was a lie. Simon's reckless decision to run for mayor would have devastating consequences for his entire family when those lies were exposed.

Anger and fear stewed in Darius's gut. He had to convince his father that for once in his selfish life, Simon needed to make a decision that wasn't all about Simon.

CHAPTER 6

When was the last time he'd come to Trinity Falls? Jack couldn't remember. It was at least a year and a half ago. Zoey had been alive. But Tuesday evening, Jack pulled his silver Toyota truck into the Trinity Falls Town Center and parked in front of Books & Bakery. He ignored his sudden craving for Doreen's Trinity Falls Fudge Walnut Brownies. That wasn't the reason he was here.

The streets on the way into town had been lined with sesquicentennial banners. He had conflicting emotions over their proclamation, 150 YEARS STRONG. He was proud his family had founded something that continued to endure, but he regretted that the legacy would end with him.

Jack climbed from his truck and followed the sidewalk that ribboned the center's stores. He paused in front of a shingle that read, EAN FEVER, ESQ. It was shortly after six o'clock. Ean must have left for the day. His old friend had visited him three or four times since Ean had resigned his partnership with a

New York City law firm and returned to Trinity Falls. Each time, Jack had sped Ean on his way. He wasn't ready to reconnect with old friends or rejoin the community. It was too soon to start caring about people again.

He continued past Gifts and Greetings, Tilda Maddox's gifts and card store. Customers meandered in and out of Are You Nuts?—the shop where Vernon Fox sold peanuts and candy. Business looked brisk in Fine Accessories, Grady Weatherington's shoes, purse, and accessories store. Few people recognized Jack. Some hailed him, making his name a question. Was it the beard?

Then there were the ones who just stared with pity, dismay, or fear. He hated that. It was one of the reasons he never ventured into town anymore. Jack did his best to ignore them as he progressed toward his destination, Belinda Curby's Skin Deep Beauty Salon.

The bell above the salon's front door played a jaunty tune, drawing unwelcome attention to his arrival. What was he doing here?

"Hey, Jack." Belinda greeted him as though it had been days rather than a year since she'd last seen him. She stood at her station, halfway across the room, tending to her patron. The young woman with pink-and-purple-tinted hair gaped at him.

"Belinda." He forced himself farther into the salon.

The large, rectangular interior was bright and even more colorful than Belinda's client's hair. Green tile climbed away from the silver flooring and halfway up the walls. The top half of the wall was a medley of reds, oranges, and white. Silver stylist chairs ringed the perimeter. Customized black porcelain sinks huddled in the center of the room.

Three other stylists—two women and a man— were in various stages of caring for their customers while trying to appear as though they weren't staring at him.

"It's been a minute since I've seen you." Belinda spoke over her shoulder.

"Just about." It would have been even longer if he'd been able to forget the beard burns he'd left on Audra's skin. Was coming here the right thing to do?

"What brings you in today?" Belinda's gentle question confused him even more.

Jack hesitated, silenced by his growing unease.

"Isn't it obvious, Belinda?" Novella Dishy, the older stylist, asked the rhetorical question. Jack recognized her from his days of picking up his ex-wife after her salon appointments. "He's here for a damn haircut. And that beard has *got* to go. Jack, who told you that that was a good look for you?"

The thin young stylist whose station was behind Novella's giggled. Jack didn't recognize her but the male stylist was Glenn Narcus.

"Novella." Belinda shot her employee a quelling look.

Jack fingered his beard. He preferred Novella's candor to Belinda's protectiveness. But why would Novella think his beard was a fashion statement?

"I wasn't going for a look."

Novella made a disapproving face before adding more creamy white stuff to Nessa Linden's hair.

Nessa had been a Trinity Falls Town Council member for years.

"What made you start to care again, Jack?"

The sugary sweetness of Nessa's question set Jack's nerves on edge.

"Not sure I do."

The bell above the front door chimed a welcome interruption. Jack turned as Darius entered the salon.

The newspaper reporter grinned at him. "Thought I recognized your truck in the parking lot. Come to get your nails done?"

Irritation knitted Jack's brows. "Is that why you're here?"

"I'm here for the view." Darius shared his cover model smile with the room. "Evening, ladies and Glenn."

A chorus of replies and giggles poured past Jack. *Why am I here?* Jack started toward the exit.

Darius caught his arm. "No manicure? My mistake." He folded himself onto a bright orange plastic chair in the waiting area and drew Jack down beside him. There was laughter in his dark eyes.

Jack scowled as he sat. "There's a reason you're still single."

"Hey, Darius."

Darius leaned forward to see into the styling area. "Well, hey, yourself, Michelle. How could I have missed you sitting over there?"

The young woman with the rainbow hair giggled with pleasure. "Ms. Belinda's going to make my hair all one color."

"I bet you'll look just as pretty then, too." Darius winked. "Evening, Ms. Novella."

Novella waved her thin comb at him. "Save your attentions for the empty-headed young girls who want them."

"All I did was say hello, Ms. Novella. Any hidden meanings are purely a figment of your vivid imagination." Darius settled back on his chair.

Novella blushed as the salon filled with laughter.

Jack chuckled. "Still have all the town's single women fighting over you?"

"If that's your intel, you need to check your sources."

"What are you two talking about over there?" Novella yelled to be heard over the dryers.

Darius raised his voice in return. "Ms. Novella, you know it's not polite to eavesdrop on other people's conversations."

The older woman gasped. "I'm not eavesdropping! I just want to make sure you talk some sense into Jack. That man is *not* leaving here looking like that. It could ruin the salon's reputation."

Darius' silent chuckles shook his shoulders. "Jack can make his own decisions, ma'am. And Belinda doesn't seem concerned."

Jack lowered his voice. "Novella Dishy is just as mean as she's ever been."

"What are you saying, Jack?" Novella shouted.

Jack closed his eyes briefly. "Just catching up with Darius, ma'am."

Darius watched him intently. "Man, I wish I could say you looked good, but . . ."

Not him, too. Jack scowled. "Don't lose sleep over it."

"The only reason it bothers me is that I know it would bother Zoey."

Jack gave Darius a sharp look. "What the hell are you talking about?"

"Don't you know how scared she was to leave you alone? With her and Kerry gone—"

"Don't bring Kerry into this."

"This isn't about her." Darius shifted toward him. "It's not about you, either. It's about Zoey. She was worried you wouldn't have anyone to take care of you."

Jack looked away. It was killing him to hear how scared his daughter had been as she was dying. But she hadn't been afraid for herself. She'd been worried for him. Hearing that made him feel worse. But Darius's words kept coming.

"How do you think she would feel if she saw you now? You don't look anything like her beloved dad."

"Stop it." Jack's pulse raced.

"What would she think if she saw what you allowed to happen?"

"Stop." Jack couldn't catch his breath.

"How do you think she would feel, knowing her worst fear has come true? You look more like the Beast from her favorite fairy tale than her father."

Jack jerked toward his tormentor. This was the second time someone had compared his appearance to the beast in "Beauty and the Beast." "I know what you're doing."

"No one said you were stupid."

Jack breathed heavily. "And you're smarter than you look."

"Don't let that get around."

"Don't worry." Jack stood. "Belinda, do you have time for me?"

Silence settled over the salon.

A huge grin stretched the salon owner's painted lips. "Jack, honey, I'll make time for you."

A round of applause and shouts of encouragement broke the peace.

Jack turned in time to see Darius walk out of the salon. He'd thought his friend would want to watch the fruits of his manipulation. They'd see each other again, though. For now, Jack was more interested in Audra's reaction to his soon-to-be neater appearance.

"Mom, why do you need the cabin's address?" Audra adjusted her hold on her cell phone. She wandered the great room Wednesday afternoon, hoping the movement would help her understand her mother's train of thought.

Ellen exhaled an impatient breath. "Suppose I need to get in touch with you?"

"You have my cell phone number. You don't need the cabin's address." Audra paused beside the front window and tipped its curtain aside. The sun was bright and warm on the front lawn. A gentle breeze ruffled the leaves along the tree line.

"I can take care of myself, Mom. I wish you'd stop smothering me and making me afraid to try new things."

The past six days in the small town of Trinity Falls, she'd grown more than she had in her thirty-one years in Los Angeles.

Her mother sniffed. "I didn't realize I was doing that."

"You were." It was with Jack's company and encouragement that she felt comfortable enough to explore.

She hadn't seen him since Monday. She missed the grumpy rental owner. She'd been going to Books & Bakery, but her new friends' company wasn't the same. However, Audra had gone jogging later this morning deliberately to avoid Jack and memories of their brief but powerful kiss. Obviously, the strategy wasn't working, since her mind seemed consumed with both. Audra let the pale green curtain swing back into place.

Ellen continued making her case. "I need the resort's address, Audra. Suppose something happens to you and I can't reach you on your phone? Are the address and phone number secret? You can't even tell your own mother?"

Audra smothered a sigh. "OK, Mom. I'll give you the information. You don't have to lay on the guilt trip."

She crossed the great room on her way to her bedroom. She'd left the rental's brochure in her nightstand. She read its main address and phone number to her mother, waiting while Ellen repeated the information to her.

"Good." Ellen's voice was full of satisfaction. "Now your father and I can rest easier, knowing exactly where you are."

"How's Dad?" Audra returned the brochure to her nightstand and closed the drawer.

"He's fine. He's worried about you, though. He hasn't said anything, but I can tell."

Audra rolled her eyes in amusement. "Please tell Dad there's no need for either of you to worry about me. I'm fine."

"There's no reasoning with your father about this. He won't relax until you're home." Ellen paused. "When are you coming home?"

Audra held on to her patience. She loved her mother, but sometimes . . . "My deadline is August fourth."

Ellen hesitated. "Have you spoken with Wendell?"

"No, Mom. Wendell and I broke up months ago. You know that." Audra sank onto the edge of the bed.

"I know the two of you had a disagreement, but you can work through it. He wants to talk with you."

"He used me, Mom."

"He cares about you, Audra. He worries that you work too hard. So do I. He understands that there's more to life than work. That's something you need to know, too."

"I've been having some fun here." Audra lay back on the bed. The mattress was heavenly, not too hard and not too soft. Just perfect.

"What have you been doing?"

"I went fishing Monday."

Why had she mentioned that? It just reminded her of Jack—and a kiss that had been so wonderful, even if it had been so wrong. He'd smelled of fresh air and pinecones. His lips had been soft and warm. His taste had been . . . Audra sprang upright.

Ellen exhaled. "I'm glad you're finding time to have fun, although fishing doesn't sound like much fun to me."

Audra's laughter was forced. "You should try it. I didn't think I'd enjoy it at first, either."

Yet, how much of her enjoyment had been from fishing and how much had been due to Jack? She didn't want to examine that question too closely.

Ellen gave her a noncommittal hum. "What else have you been doing?"

"I met some very nice people."

"Other tourists?"

Audra stood and left the bedroom. "No, townspeople. Trinity Falls is celebrating its sesquicentennial."

"Oh, one hundred and fifty years. That's nice."

Audra walked to the great room. She stopped beside the dark fabric sofa and stared at her guitar resting on its cushions. "The town's hosting its Founders Day Celebration August ninth."

"Oh, that's too bad. They're going to have it right after you leave."

"I was thinking of staying for it."

"But, Audra, you said your deadline is August fourth. You're already going to be gone so long."

"It's just a few more days, Mom." Audra settled onto the sofa. "I'd better get back to work."

"Oh, all right. But give Wendell a call."

"Mom . . ."

"He's sorry, Audra."

"I don't care. 'Fool me once, shame on you.' He won't have a chance to fool me a second time."

"Don't be so hard. Call him." With that, Ellen disconnected the call.

Call him? Perhaps when hell froze over. She needed someone who was real. Someone she could trust. But where do you find someone like that?

* * *

The knock on her door Wednesday afternoon came just as Audra was getting ready to wash her lunch dishes. There was only one person who would visit her, Jack.

Her heart leaped and executed a series of spins like a champion figure skater. She hadn't realized quite how much she'd missed seeing him yesterday.

Audra took a moment to catch her breath before crossing the cabin. She pulled the door open—and stared at a stranger with an ice box.

"May I help you?" Disappointment sat like a brick in her gut.

He was a handsome stranger. His smooth sienna skin was taut over a broad forehead, high cheekbones, long nose, and stubborn jaw. His lips were sensuously full and curved in a teasing smile.

"Have you forgotten me after just one day?" a familiar, bluesy baritone asked.

Audra's jaw dropped. *"Jack?"*

Jack smoothed his right hand over his cheek. His beautiful onyx eyes twinkled at her. "Do I look that different?"

Audra raised both brows. "I had no clue what you looked like under all that hair."

His beard had hidden a lot. She had no idea he had such a sexy neck. If it weren't for his memorable eyes and unforgettable voice, she wouldn't have recognized him at all. How was it possible this *GQ* cover model was the same Grizzly Adams wannabe she'd met just six days ago?

"May I come in?" Jack's question woke Audra from her trance.

"Of course." She stepped back, pulling the door open wider.

"Thank you." Jack crossed her threshold.

Audra's gaze tracked his loose-limbed gait. She could look at him forever. His army green cargo shorts showed off his long, muscled calves. His collared brown shirt complemented his skin.

"Did you go shopping yesterday?" Audra locked her front door.

"No." Jack faced her from the center of the room.

Audra shook her head with a smile. "So you do have more than seven T-shirts. I can't believe I fell for that."

Jack's unrepentant grin took her breath away. "I never said I only had seven shirts. I said I had seven like the one I was wearing."

Audra couldn't stop staring at him. "What inspired this makeover?"

"It was time."

Something in his voice alerted her that his transformation wasn't a whim. Did it have anything to do with the shadows in his eyes?

She gestured toward him. "What do you have in the cooler?"

He looked at the carrier as though he'd forgotten it was in his hand. "An afternoon snack. You said you wanted me to be your guide."

"Where are we going?"

"Hiking."

Audra's brows leaped with pleased surprise. "Am I dressed properly?"

Her skin warmed as Jack's eyes skimmed her peach T-shirt and ice blue shorts.

His attention settled on her feet. His voice was rough. "You just need some shoes."

He met her gaze and there was something beyond simple appreciation in his eyes.

Audra's blush deepened. She'd forgotten about the hot pink polish on her toenails. The manufacturer named it Wet Kiss. It had seemed innocent until she'd met the heat in Jack's gaze.

"Are sneakers OK?" Her voice cracked.

"Yes."

Audra escaped to her room, primarily for her socks and sneakers, but also to give herself a stern talking-to.

You've seen handsome men before, Audra. Los Angeles is full of them. So why are you acting like a head case just because the Wolfman had exfoliated and turned into the Sexiest Man Alive?

She pulled on her socks, slipped into her sneakers, then tied her laces. *So the Beast now looks like every woman's idea of Prince Charming. Get over it.*

Audra took a deep breath, then rejoined Jack in the great room. He didn't tease her this time when she stopped to check that her cabin was secure before wandering into the woods with him. The mid-July afternoon sun wasn't too harsh. And the path Jack took was heavily shaded. The air was rich with the scents of moist earth and lush foliage.

Audra listened to the birds singing in the trees, chipmunks scrambling in the underbrush, and the wind rustling leaves overhead. They must have been walking for about ten minutes before she realized Jack hadn't spoken a word. She slid him a sideways look. His newly clean-shaven features looked relaxed—content—as he strolled beside her.

They continued still farther down the path. Unease trickled through her.

Why isn't he talking?

And how well did she know this man who was leading her deeper into the forest?

HARMONY CABINS 51

They remained still farther down the path

they'd edged through th...

the rented cabin...

And how well did she know this man who was

leading her deeper into the fore...

~CHAPTER 7~

"What's on your mind?" Jack met her gaze.

Audra swallowed a lump of sudden panic. "I was wondering why you aren't talking." *And where you're leading me?*

"I'm imagining how you'll react when you see where I'm taking you."

"Where are we going?" She leaned into the path as it grew steeper.

"You'll see."

Audra stopped abruptly, forcing Jack to wait with her. "How do I know you're not some sort of psycho killer?"

Jack's expression was somber. "If I were, would I wait six days to kill you? You've met other people who know you're here."

That made sense in a creepy way. "I guess not."

"Trust me. I won't hurt you. And you'll like where we're going." He tossed her a smile that made her heart jump and shout.

"When we first met, you wouldn't give me five

words. Now you've taught me how to fish. You're taking me hiking, and you've smiled at me twice today. That's three miracles. Call the pope."

Jack wrapped his right hand around her bare upper arm to get her moving again. His skin was warm and just a little rough. "And the Oscar for Best Dramatic Performance goes to Audra Lane."

"You see? That's what I'm talking about." She allowed him to draw her forward. "What's behind these changes in you?"

"Not what, *who*." Jack stopped again, holding her with his gaze. "I've been changing since you walked into my cabin, wearing your fancy little dress."

Audra's heart skipped. Why would he say that? What had she done to change him? Although, after Wendell, she didn't trust herself to examine his words too closely. "You mean the trash bag? So you *were* laughing at me."

"On the inside. I'm only human." He released her arm, letting his fingers trail along her sensitive skin.

Audra shivered at his touch. "I appreciate that you didn't laugh on the outside. I was embarrassed enough."

Jack used his hand on the small of her back to nudge her forward again. "That's me, Mr. Sensitivity."

"More jokes. Amazing." Audra tilted her head. "How have I changed you?"

Jack started to walk again. "I'd been alone for a long time. Then you arrived. You make me want to be around people again. Part of me is relieved. I like this change. Although another part of me isn't ready."

"What made you close yourself away in the first place?"

Jack didn't respond for a long time. "Maybe I'll tell you one day."

They continued in silence. Audra was shaken by Jack's claim that she'd had such a strong effect on him. What had she done that had been so special? Convinced him to teach her how to fish?

An unfamiliar rushing noise sounded in the distance. Audra looked around. "What's that?"

"You'll see."

She slid him a look. "A man of mystery, as well as sensitivity."

Jack just smiled.

They hiked a little farther up the path until it leveled off and they stepped into a clearing. Audra gasped.

Jack swept his left arm to encompass their surroundings. "This is Trinity Falls."

The horseshoe-shaped clearing was twice the size of a football field. She and Jack stood at its base. Before her was a carpet of deep green grass framed by stately poplar and white ash trees.

At the center of the clearing was the source of the rushing wind she'd heard: a waterfall. Audra walked closer to its edge, which was framed by a sturdy metal safety fence. She felt its power as the water poured into the stream below, pushing gusts of wind and mists of water up and over her.

Jack smiled at Audra's reaction. Her eyes were wide. Her lips parted. She looked transfixed. *She looks like she belongs, a woodland fairy queen exploring her kingdom.* He'd been right to bring her here. He hadn't enjoyed this scenery with anyone since Zoey

had become ill, nearly four years ago at the age
of six. Before then, she'd made the trip with him
frequently. He'd never come to the clearing with
Kerry. She wasn't fond of nature.

Jack set the cooler beside a nearby tree and approached Audra. She stepped back from the edge
and stretched her arms wide. She spun to him. Her
face, arms, and T-shirt were damp from the waterfall's mist. Her cloud of curly dark hair played in
the breeze. Her warm caramel features glowed
with pleasure. Her bright grin lifted her lips and
his heart. "This place is remarkable. It's just like a
fairy tale."

"I'm glad you approve." Jack's laughter came
more easily now. Those muscles had warmed since
Audra's arrival.

The waterfall fed a skipping stream that was born
at its feet. The water danced over rocks and continued far into the distance. Jack fell into step beside
Audra as she explored the clearing's perimeter,
following its tree line. She exclaimed at the red-
shouldered hawks and merlins, soaring above the
water and dancing on the wind. She laughed at the
squirrels racing each other up and over tree trunks.
Watching her pleasure in this special place made
Jack see it in a new way, too. It did seem enchanted,
almost magical.

She turned to lead them back the way they'd
come. "I feel like Snow White and the Seven Dwarfs'
next-door neighbor."

"Or Cinderella. Her pets helped with the chores."

Audra's winged eyebrows leaped toward her hairline. "You *do* know your fairy tales." Her champagne

eyes sparkled with pleasure. "Are these woods part of the rental cabins' property?"

"No, it's part of the county's park system. But not many people come here."

Her eyes widened. "Are you serious? I'd come here every day."

He believed her. The mental image of the two of them spending long, lazy hours together in the clearing melted another chunk of ice from his heart.

Jack led Audra back to the cooler. Together they spread the blue-and-white plaid picnic blanket under the tree. It was the same blanket he'd taken when they'd gone fishing. They removed their shoes, then sat cross-legged on the blanket to share the lemonade and fresh fruit he'd packed for their afternoon snack.

Audra popped a seedless black grape into her mouth as she looked over their surroundings. "You must be so proud of your ancestors for establishing this town."

"I am." Jack bit into an apple.

"Now Trinity Falls is one hundred and fifty years old." She gave him a curious look. "How have you managed to remain humble? I'd run up and down the streets every morning, screaming, 'I'm king of the world!'"

He smiled at her imitation of Leonardo DiCaprio's famous line from *Titanic*.

"My parents made sure I was well-grounded." He sipped from his thermos of lemonade. "I had chores and a part-time job. But most importantly, my parents taught me to give back to the community."

"Your parents sound incredible."

"They were incredible." They were his heroes. He'd assumed he and Kerry would have a family just like the one he'd known. But everything had gone wrong.

"I bet you were the most popular boy in high school." Audra's voice pulled him from the past. "You're from a prominent family. I bet you were a star athlete. All the girls in your school probably chased after you."

Jack set down his thermos. "What about you? Did all the guys ask for your phone number?"

She gave him a self-deprecating smile. "I was a nerd. Prom night, I was home re-reading *Harry Potter and the Goblet of Fire.*"

Jack winced. "Really?"

"Really. What about you?"

"I had a date."

"Of course you did."

They were tucked into the trees, all alone. The sounds of the waterfall underscored their isolation. Jack felt himself pulled in Audra's direction.

"What was wrong with the boys in your high school?" His voice was huskier than he'd intended. "Were they blind or just stupid?"

Audra gave him a skeptical look. "Don't worry. I'm not a self-conscious adolescent anymore."

"You don't look like one either." Jack leaned in slowly, claiming her mouth with his own.

The taste of her sweetness today was as intoxicating as the first time he'd kissed her. Her lips were soft and supple beneath his, making him forget everything except her scent, her feel, her warmth. He slid his tongue across her lips and she opened for him, welcoming him closer to her. Jack followed her without hesitation.

Audra's head was spinning. She uncrossed her legs and fell back onto the blanket, clutching onto Jack for dear life. He swept his tongue into her mouth and Audra moaned at the intimacy. Fireworks went off behind her lowered eyelids. And this was just a kiss, warm and wet and deep, but still just a kiss. She'd been kissed before. It had never felt like this, though. She pressed her fingertips into his muscled shoulders as her world spun away from her.

Audra trembled as Jack's hands moved over her body. His palm caressed her left breast through the thin cotton of her T-shirt. He molded her fullness and stroked her tip until her nipple tightened with need. Audra arched her back, pressing her breast tighter into his hand. The feel of his fingers tracing her, learning her, drew her deeper under his spell. She forgot where she was. She forgot what she'd been doing. All she knew was here and now, and a hunger that moved her body restlessly beneath his. Heat built inside her. She scored her fingertips down his tapered back, pulling him closer to her. Kissing him harder. Drawing his tongue deeper into her mouth.

She sighed as Jack freed her lips to taste her neck. His hand slid to her waist. There was a tug at the waistband of her shorts, then his hand slipped inside to smooth over her hips. She pressed her head back, gasping for air. Jack licked her collarbone and palmed her derriere. The cornucopia of sensations kept her off balance. An ache was growing between her thighs. Her bare legs shifted beside his.

She needed to touch him, needed him to feel what she was feeling. She slipped her hands under Jack's shirt. The heat from his skin scorched her palms. She traced the taut, smooth muscles of his back and drew him closer, wanting more of his touch. Wanting to ease her ache.

Jack kissed her again. Audra opened her mouth, deepening their bond, drinking him hungrily. Jack's hand caressed its way to her lower abdomen. He slid his fingers between her thighs, separating her folds and pressing one finger against her. Audra's body shivered. In shock or in need? Both.

Audra tore her mouth free. She grabbed hold of Jack's wrist, stopping his movements. Embarrassed, she bit her lip, squeezing her eyes shut. Her hips wanted to rock against the pad of his finger. Her thighs shook with the strain to resist him, to resist herself. Her body wanted him there so badly, and in so many ways. But . . .

"I can't." Audra met Jack's heated gaze.

Jack's chest heaved in a deep sigh. He released her, rolling away to sit with his back to her.

Heaven knew he'd stoked a fire in her body that only his touch could feed. But neither her heart nor her mind was ready for this.

Audra laid her forearm across her eyes. "We've only known each other six days. I'm leaving in three weeks."

"It's a bad idea for both of us." Jack's voice was tight.

"I'm sorry."

"Don't be."

Her body hummed and her knees shook. Would she be able to stand? "As much as I'm tempted, I've never had a casual relationship."

"I understand."

Audra didn't remember helping Jack repack the cooler. She didn't recall leaving the waterfall or walking down the hill through the woods. Her mind didn't clear until they arrived at her cabin. The gravel path crunched beneath her sneakers. She didn't remember putting those on again, either.

Jack climbed her porch beside her. "Did you eat the fish you caught Monday?"

She could still feel his hand between her thighs and he wanted to talk about fish? "Yes. It was delicious."

"I was thinking of cooking mine for dinner tonight. Will you join me?" His quiet question caused the muscles at the tops of her thighs to pulse again.

Should she? "I don't know if it's a good idea for us to spend more time together."

"I'm not suggesting we take our clothes off." Jack's onyx eyes probed hers. "But I was serious when I said you're changing me, and for the better. I haven't laughed or even smiled much since . . . in a very long time. I'd like to get to know you."

Either he was telling the truth or that was the best pickup line she'd heard in her thirty-one years of life.

She was playing with fire. Twice he'd shown her that with a look, a touch, or a taste, he could make her forget her best intentions.

But the fact was she wanted to get to know him better, too. "All right."

Jack's smile was her reward. "I'll see you at seven." He turned to leave.

"Should I bring anything?" Her question stopped him.

"No, I've got it covered." And he winked at her. He actually winked.

Audra dug her keys from her front pocket, then let herself into her cabin. This was the way she would have felt if she'd had a date to her high-school prom.

Jack had showered, shaved, ironed his clothes, and changed, then changed again in his private rooms in the main cabin. He was pulling together the ingredients he'd need for dinner with Audra when the bell sounded above the front door of the rental cabins' office.

She was early!

On the heels of that panicked thought, Jack realized something was wrong. Audra wouldn't enter through the rental cabins' office. Jack strode through his kitchen and great room to the main cabin's registration desk.

He didn't bother to mask his impatience when he found Simon Knight waiting for him. "What can I do for you, Simon?"

Simon looked around, spreading his arms wide to encompass the entire room. "Very nice."

"Thanks."

"You see, Jack. That's the kind of man you are."

The other man leaned into the desk, bringing him closer to Jack. Too close.

Jack stared him down without responding.

Simon straightened. "You're the kind of man who picks himself up and keeps moving forward despite the roadblocks and inconveniences that get in his way."

Jack shoved his fists into the front pockets of his black Dockers. "Which one was it?"

Simon looked confused. "Was what?"

"My daughter's death. Was it a 'roadblock' or an 'inconvenience'?"

The softly voiced question seemed to catch Simon off guard. "That isn't what I meant. Of course your daughter's death was a terrible tragedy."

"Tell me what you want, then leave."

Simon straightened his shoulders. "Trinity Falls is celebrating its sesquicentennial."

"And?" Jack's patience was nearing its end.

"We're planning a Founders Day Celebration as part of the festivities."

When Jack didn't respond, Simon continued. "As the sole surviving member of our town's founding family, you should be the keynote speaker for the Founders Day events." Simon made the pronouncement as though he were presenting Jack with the keys to the town his family had settled.

"No." Jack had taken two steps toward his office before Simon's shocked words stopped him.

"Wait. What?"

Jack faced him. "I told Doreen I won't make any speeches."

Simon gaped. "You have to represent your family and the town during this celebration."

Jack considered his unwanted visitor. What wasn't Simon telling him? "Why are you here?"

"To convince you to participate in the sesquicentennial celebrations. You owe it to the town."

"If you think the event needs more speeches, make one yourself."

"People expect a member of the founding family to be represented on Founders Day."

Jack returned to the registration desk. "What is this really about?"

"What do you mean?" Simon's gaze slid away.

Jack's suspicions increased. "You're not on any of the town's planning committees. You've never come to the cabins before. In fact, this is the first time I've seen you in almost four years. So why the sudden interest in what I'm doing and whether I'm involved in the sesquicentennial?"

"The celebrations are important to the town."

"Then why aren't you on any of the committees?"

Simon's expression became stubborn. "I've been busy. Until June, I had a very demanding full-time job."

Jack crossed his arms over his chest. "Doreen has a full-time job. She's also running for mayor and chairing the celebration committee."

Simon's brown eyes crackled with anger. "What kind of mayor can't convince a member of the town's founding family to say a few words during its Founders Day Celebration?"

A lightbulb came on. "Is that what this is about?"

"Trinity Falls deserves to have a real mayoral election. For too many years, our candidates have been running unopposed. That's not a democracy."

Jack arched an eyebrow. "So you're going to run against Doreen."

"You don't think I'm a viable candidate?"

"No."

Simon's eyes grew wider. "Why not?"

The answer should have been obvious. "Doreen has been a force in this community for as long as I can remember. She's in the newspaper all the time, raising money for emergency services and the elementary school, campaigning for lights in Freedom Park. What have you done for the town?"

Simon's face flushed. "I have ideas for the town, including ways that we could bring in more tourists for the sesquicentennial."

"Doreen wants to do the same thing."

Simon's manner cooled. "But Doreen's going to fail, and I'll use that failure against her to win the election."

"You'll do it without me." He left before he said something he'd regret. Jack had learned his lesson sixteen months ago. No one would use him ever again.

CHAPTER 8

Jack was as nervous as if this were a real date. Audra arrived at seven o'clock Wednesday night. With just a smile, she lifted the suffocating pressure from his chest. The bright light within her drove the dark shadows surrounding him back into the corners of his cabin.

"Are you going to let me in?" Laughter bounced in her voice.

"Sorry." Jack moved out of her way. He watched her cross his threshold. Her light blue top draped her high breasts. Her matching capris hugged her slim hips. He could stare at her all night. Forever.

What was it about her that pulled him after he'd spent so many months pushing people away? What did he need from her? And what would happen to him when she and her bright light returned to L.A.?

Audra stood in the middle of the great room, taking in her surroundings. What did his home look like through her eyes? The honey-wood walls, stone fireplace, and large flat-screen T.V. were identical to the ones in Audra's cabin. So were the dark plaid sofa and matching armchair. But there were no curtains at his windows and the area rug tossed onto his floor was a darker shade of brown. The room was clean but spartan. It looked more like a rental cabin than Audra's. His shoulders slumped.

She turned to him. "Something smells wonderful."

"Dinner's almost ready." Jack led her to the dining room.

With just the small maple table and matching chairs, the dining room was even more depressing than the great room. Why hadn't he added a bookcase or artwork or even a table centerpiece? Something that made it seem more like a dining room than a mess hall.

He brought the bowls of mixed salad before serving the baked fish with asparagus and crusty bread.

"Would you like butter for your bread?" Jack was so out of practice. His conversation was putting him to sleep. Was it having the same effect on Audra?

"No, thank you. This is fine." Her smile seemed stiff. Was it his imagination?

Their dinner conversation was stilted. The moments of silence were awkward. How could he make it better? "More iced tea?"

"Not yet, thank you. I haven't finished this one."

"All right." Perhaps it was just nerves, at least on his part.

"This fish is delicious." Her compliment rescued his dampening thoughts. "Did you cook it yourself?"

"Do you think I ordered takeout from Trinity

Falls Cuisine to pass off as my own?" Jack's smile broadened as the blush rose in Audra's cheeks.

"I'm sorry. I didn't mean to offend you. I'm just having a hard time picturing you behind a stove."

"Why?"

"It's not the way I see you. Do you wear an apron?" Her full pink lips curved in a teasing smile that both calmed and aroused him.

He was fascinated by that smile. "How do you see me?"

"Fishing. Hiking. Cutting wood."

"You've never seen me chop wood."

Audra shrugged. "I can still picture it. But I can't see you being domestic."

"You'd be surprised."

"Believe me, I am." She gestured toward her half-eaten dinner. "And impressed."

Jack's laughter eased the lingering tension in his neck and shoulders. Now their conversation flowed more naturally. After dinner, he cleared the table, insisting Audra make herself comfortable while she waited for dessert. He returned with coffee and two plates of Boston cream pie.

Audra's champagne eyes widened. "You bake as well?"

Jack set the coffee and pie in front of Audra. "The pie's from Books and Bakery." He offered her a fork before taking his seat.

"Doreen is a wonderful baker." Audra's moan of pleasure stirred intimate muscles that had been dormant too long for Jack.

He cleared his throat. "Yes, she is."

"You cook, you fish, you're gainfully employed. Why aren't you married?"

"I don't get out much." Jack gave her a wry smile before taking another mouthful of pie.

"Why is that?"

He avoided her eyes. "I like my privacy, but there isn't much of that in Trinity Falls."

"But people here admire you. They care about you."

Jack swallowed more pie. "Are you asking a question?"

Audra considered Jack—the way he shifted on his chair, the way he avoided her eyes. Why did the idea of his neighbors speaking well of him make him uncomfortable? "I suppose I am. Why did you exile yourself to the woods?"

"It's what I prefer."

"But why? What happened two years ago that made you choose to live away from people?"

"That's personal." His knuckles paled as he gripped his coffee.

"So is sleeping together." Audra met his gaze. "It's clear we're attracted to each other, but I can't share my body and nothing else. I'm not built that way."

Jack stood from the table, pacing away from her. Audra followed him with her eyes. Would he tell her to leave or ask her to stay? Did she have the right to ask him to share his biggest secret?

His voice came low and tight. "Sixteen months ago, my daughter died."

Shock chilled Audra. Her words poured on a breath. "I'm so sorry. What was her name?"

"Zoey. She was six years old when she was diagnosed with leukemia. She died before her ninth birthday . . ." Jack's voice drifted away.

"So young." Audra's eyes stung with unshed tears.

"The chemotherapy treatment was as bad as the disease." Jack rubbed his face with his right hand. "She grew weaker right before my eyes. She was already so little. She died less than two years later."

That explained so much about Jack: his isolation, his previously unkempt appearance, the pain in his poet's eyes.

Audra dashed tears from her cheeks. "What happened to Zoey's mother?"

"She left before Zoey died." Jack faced Audra. "Don't feel sorry for me. I don't need anyone's pity."

Audra blinked at his angry words. "I'm sorry Zoey died, but I don't pity you. I admire you."

"Why?" Jack's question was thick with suspicion.

"A lot of people would have crumbled. Your daughter died. You lost your wife—"

"I didn't lose her. She left."

"But you're still standing."

"Barely." Jack massaged the back of his neck as he moved restlessly across the room.

"You've had some setbacks. That's understandable."

"'Setbacks' imply I'll return to fight another day. I don't know that I will."

Audra gestured toward him. "Have you looked in a mirror lately? You already have."

"Thanks to you." His expression shifted from stubborn resistance to surprised confusion.

Audra shook her head. "This isn't about me. It's all about you."

"Or us." When he spoke, his voice was deep, warm, and compelling.

"Can there be an 'us,' Jack?" Audra ignored the thrill of excitement that burst through her at the thought of being with this man. "I've just broken up with someone, and you're mourning your daughter."

"So?"

"Is a casual relationship between us a good idea?"

"Why not?"

Audra shook her head, pulling her fingers through her hair. "For you, sex is a physical act. For me, it's a lot more."

Jack returned to the dining table, looking into Audra's eyes. "You're a dangerous woman, Audra Lane."

She frowned. "Why?"

"Because you make me want things I shouldn't want. You make me want to feel again."

"You've been in Trinity Falls for almost a week. Have you left your cabin yet?" Audra's manager asked the question Thursday morning in lieu of the traditional cell phone greeting.

Audra scowled. "I have. Several times."

"Really?" Benita's skepticism was annoying.

"Why don't you believe me?"

"Because I know you."

The hissing sound in the background indicated her manager was making coffee. Audra checked her watch. It was just after ten o'clock in the morning, which meant it was seven o'clock in Los Angeles. Benita started her days early to accommodate her East Coast contacts. She pictured Benita standing beside the coffeemaker in her sterile office. This probably wasn't her first cup of java, though. And there was no guarantee additional caffeine would improve her mood.

Audra returned her guitar to its case and leaned back against the overstuffed sofa. "I've gone fishing, hiking and jogging. I've also explored your hometown. It's very pretty."

"Pretty boring." Benita snorted. "There's nothing to do. And most of the inmates are crazy."

Audra thought about yesterday's hike with Jack, fishing with him at Pearl Lake, talking with the townspeople at Books & Bakery. She'd enjoyed those experiences more than she'd expected. Maybe over time it would become boring, but she couldn't imagine that.

"There's plenty to do. And the people here are nice, which is probably why you think they're crazy."

"Who'd you go fishing and hiking with?" Benita's rapid-fire question dismissed Audra's response.

Audra propped her feet on the honey-wood coffee table. "Jack Sansbury, the guy you didn't tell me owns the cabins."

"No way." Benita tapped a couple of keys on her laptop. "I heard Jack became a recluse after his daughter died. How did you convince him to leave his cabin?"

"I asked him." A wave of sadness rolled over Audra as she thought of what Jack had been through.

Audra set her papers on the coffee table and pushed herself off the sofa. She crossed to the front window, poking the curtain aside. How could his ex-wife have left him and their daughter? What kind of person was she? Audra couldn't fault Jack for tucking himself away in the cabins. What would she have done in his place?

Benita hummed. "That's it?"

"Why is that so hard to believe?" Audra listened

to stainless-steel tap against a ceramic surface as Benita stirred her much-needed coffee. Her manager usually took three packets of sweetener and a third of a cup of French vanilla creamer. Audra's teeth ached at the thought of that much sugar.

"Listen, Audra. I'm glad you're getting out and trying new things. That's what I wanted for you when I booked you into the cabins."

"So you said." She turned from the window.

"Yes, I did. I was sure the change of scenery would cure your writer's block. Just be careful."

"Of what?" Audra gave her manager her full attention now.

"You're coming off of a bad relationship. Jack's had some things happen in his past, too—"

Audra interrupted the other woman. "His daughter died and his wife left him."

"So you see? You're both vulnerable right now."

Audra circled the sofa. "I know. You don't have to remind me that Wendell was a mistake."

Benita grunted. "Wendell is a jackass. Kerry's the mistake."

Audra frowned. Benita had lost her. "Who's Kerry?"

"Jack's ex. Listen, just be careful. Don't become distracted by a vacation romance."

Audra planted her right hand on her hip. "If I'm on vacation, why are you calling me?"

Benita's sigh blew through the cell towers. "How's the writing coming?"

Audra glared at the coffee table and her pages of disjointed notes. "Not well."

Her manager sighed again. "Are you still having trouble sleeping?"

"Yes." Although Audra had a feeling her stress was

less about her writing and more about the recluse down the road.

"The clock's ticking, Audra." Benita was tapping her pen against her desk.

"I can't hear it over your constant nagging."

"Believe me. You'd rather hear my nagging than a music producer's complaints."

Her manager had a point. "I'll have something to you soon."

"Do you need an extension on your deadline?"

"No." Audra reclaimed her notes from the table. "I'll keep working on the songs. I just need to clear my head."

"All right. Keep me posted." Benita disconnected the call.

Audra tossed her cell phone to the other side of the sofa. The lyrics were stuck in her brain, just out of reach. She needed to get them out. How?

"Shouldn't you be at work?" Jack led Darius into his great room Thursday afternoon.

"I'm on my lunch break." The reporter gave him a critical once-over. "You look better."

"Is that why you're here?" Jack folded himself onto his armchair and rested his right ankle on his left knee.

"Don't flatter yourself." Darius sank onto the sofa. "My father wants to be mayor of Trinity Falls."

"I know. He stopped by yesterday."

Darius' scowl darkened. "He also wants a prominent role in the Founders Day Celebration. What made you think that would be a good idea?"

"Me?" Jack frowned at the other man. "How's that my fault?"

"He said you suggested it."

Jack's memory returned. "I didn't realize he'd take me literally."

Darius' sigh was deep. "I know you don't want any part of Founders Day or the sesquicentennial in general. But Doreen doesn't need my father's interference on this, as well as the campaign."

"I know." Jack scrubbed both hands over his face. "How can I fix this?"

Darius stood to prowl the great room. "No one can reason with either of my parents, especially my father."

How could two self-centered people like Simon and Ethel Knight have a caring offspring like Darius? Their selfish genes must have canceled each other out.

"Doreen can handle him." Jack hoped.

"Probably." Darius stopped in front of the fireplace with his back to the room. "Even if my father gets his name on the ballot, I won't vote for him."

Jack empathized with his friend's conflict. He'd never vote Simon into public office, either. Not while he was sober. "You have to decide who'd be the better choice. No one can make that decision for you."

Darius turned to Jack. "Who do you think your great-great-grandfather would vote for?"

Jack frowned. "Why?"

"He founded this town. Who do you think he'd want to run it right now?"

"I don't know." Jack lowered his right leg to the floor and leaned forward on his chair. "He founded the town in 1864. Women weren't even allowed to vote. But it's obvious Doreen's more committed to Trinity Falls."

Darius nodded. "A hundred and fifty years. What do you think Ezekiel Sansbury would say about the fact that his town survived when so many others failed?"

Jack had wondered the same thing over the years. What would his great-great-grandfather say about the town's longevity? How would he feel?

"He'd probably be pretty damn proud. Wouldn't you?" Jack stood. "The town has had its struggles—the economy, civil rights. But we've weathered every storm and emerged even stronger."

Darius arched a brow. "What's preventing you from saying those words on your great-great-grandfather's behalf during the Founders Day Celebration?"

Jack shook his head, in part amusement and part irritation. "You're a master manipulator."

"Zoey's death was devastating to everyone who knew her. She was a smart, kind, and caring little girl who deserved a full life. Don't you think she'd want you to have a role in the celebration?"

"You played that card when you convinced me to get a shave and haircut."

"It worked."

Jack rubbed the back of his neck. "I'm not looking forward to being on exhibit, Darius."

"That's obvious."

Jack paced the room, trying to escape his agitation. "I don't want people watching me in pity, whispering about me and my family."

Darius shoved his hands into the front pockets

of his black pants. "Since when do you care what people say, either to your face or behind your back?"

"Easy for you to say. You've never been the subject of public scrutiny."

Darius's brows jumped up his broad forehead. "Do you think it's easy being the son of Simon and Ethel Knight?"

Jack conceded Darius's point. His friend's parents seemed to stage frequent scenes in public. "I'm not ready, Darius."

"Do you want someone else to make that speech? My father, perhaps?"

Jack gave him a sharp look. "What makes you think Simon would try to speak for my family?"

"You implied it would be a good idea for him to take your place for Founders Day."

"Shit."

"What are you going to do about it?"

Jack stared at the honey-wood flooring of his cabin. The silence stretched as he considered his options. Was he ready to emerge from his self-imposed exile and rejoin his community, the community his ancestors founded? Or would his neighbors' concern and pity serve as painful reminders of Zoey's death?

He lifted his eyes and met Darius's gaze. "If anyone speaks for my family, it will be me."

"What does that mean?"

"I'll take part in the Founders Day Celebration."

Darius inclined his head with a smile. "Good. I'll tell my father."

CHAPTER 9

Doreen couldn't have looked more surprised if she'd opened her door Thursday evening to find Santa Claus waiting on her porch in the middle of summer.

Jack smiled at her expression. "May I come in?"

"Of course." She seemed to collect herself.

It had been years since he'd been to the Fever residence. Memories of visiting Doreen's son, Ean, while they were still in high school, returned. Despite the new carpeting, furniture, and wall treatment, the home still felt familiar.

Jack shoved his hands into his dark gray walking shorts. His palms were sweating. What was he doing?

"Am I interrupting your dinner?" It was five in the evening. Jack had put off this meeting for as long as he could.

"You're not." Curiosity had nudged out shock in Doreen's eyes. "I'd heard you went to Belinda's salon. You look good. Can I get you anything?"

"Ice water would be great. Thank you." He followed his hostess into her kitchen and took the seat at her blond-wood table.

Doreen joined him, handing Jack one of the two glasses. "It's great to see you, Jack. But I can't help wondering why you're here."

Jack took a fortifying gulp of the ice-cold water. "I'll participate in the Founders Day Celebration."

Doreen's face glowed with pleasure. She pressed her hands together in a silent clap. "That's wonderful! Jack, we were so hoping you'd—"

"I'll give a speech, but don't expect it to be long."

Doreen laughed. "Promise you'll say something more than 'Thanks for coming.'"

Jack smiled. "I promise."

"This really will be an exciting day. The celebration's going to start with a parade down Main Street, featuring civic groups, the high school and junior high school marching bands and cheerleaders, and the town council members."

Jack felt obliged to respond. "Great."

"Ramona and several of the former mayors will give speeches."

That surprised him. "They're returning to Trinity Falls for the sesquicentennial?"

"Of course. Scores of former residents are coming home for the event, too."

"I'm amazed." And humbled.

Doreen continued. "The university's concert band will perform. Then, in the evening, we'll have a fireworks show and more music. So, what do you think?"

"Sounds great." Jack finished his water.

"Are there any events you'd like to add?"

"No, you're doing a great job. Thanks, Doreen."

"Thank *you*." Her round cocoa cheeks flushed. "But are you sure there isn't anything we should add? Perhaps we could present a plaque to your family."

"That's not necessary."

Doreen smiled. "You're a lot like your parents, Jack. They didn't like being in the limelight, either."

Jack stood. "I don't want to help plan the celebration. Just tell me when to show up and what to do. But don't expect me to participate in more than one event."

Doreen rose with him. "That's fair enough. I'm really glad you changed your mind about being part of Founders Day. It wouldn't have been complete without you."

Jack didn't know what to say, so he changed the subject. "Thanks for the water." He put his empty glass in the sink, then turned to leave.

Doreen accompanied him. "I heard Simon went to see you."

"Is it true he wants a role in the event?"

"I've assigned him to escort one of the floats."

Jack smiled. "Good thinking."

"It's good to see you smiling again." Doreen unlocked her front door. "I'm curious."

"About what?"

"What made you change your mind about participating?"

"Not what, who. Darius. He can be a real pain." Jack crossed the threshold without looking back.

Darius was annoying, but he'd also been right. The Sansbury family had to be represented during

Founders Day. Still, Jack couldn't shake the feeling he'd agreed to something that would change him in a way he wasn't ready for.

Jack wandered the woods of the rental cabins' property. It was after midnight, but he couldn't sleep. He'd tried reading and watching television. He'd even done laps in Pearl Lake. But his mind was too restless to sleep. So he'd left his cabin, seeking solace in the woods. It wasn't surprising that his steps led him to Audra.

Her porch was empty. He experienced a hot rush of déjà vu as music floated to him from the back of her cabin, a full band—not just a guitarist—accompanied by a familiar singer. Jack followed the sound.

Just as before, the cabin's light poured through the back door, illuminating the gray-and-white stone patio. Audra's laptop lay open on the weathered patio bench. Her compact disc drive played another Mary J. Blige song, "Real Love." Nearby, Audra interpreted the music with sensuous movements of her gently rounded figure.

She wore her summer uniform of brightly colored T-shirt and shorts. Her reactions to the music were fluid and uninhibited. Mesmerizing. His body responded to her, growing warmer. He imagined his hands cupping her slim, undulating hips, her muscles flexing beneath his palms. He envisioned his body pressed to hers. She braced her legs apart and moved her torso from side to side. Jack swallowed. Audra lifted her arms above her head and moved her body. Jack groaned, squeezing his eyes closed briefly as a sweet, sharp ache ricocheted throughout him. Audra spun on her bare heels. Her scream was short, more of a gasp, as she jumped a foot off the ground.

"You. Must. Stop. Doing that." Audra pressed both palms against her chest. The fright in her eyes ripped at his heart.

"I'm sorry."

"I accepted your apology the first time. If you were truly sincere, you wouldn't have done it again." Audra crossed to her laptop. Her voice shook with the remnants of fear.

Jack followed her. "What are you doing?"

"Turning off the music."

Panic. "Why?" Was she leaving?

"What are you doing here, Jack?" She silenced the CD, then dropped onto the bench beside it.

"I couldn't sleep."

"Neither could I."

"Dance with me." He hadn't danced in years, but he had the sudden urge to give himself over to the music. Her music.

"I don't feel like dancing anymore." She sounded like a sulky child.

Jack smiled. "One dance." He typed commands into her laptop. He selected Mary J. Blige's "Be Without You," then offered Audra his hand.

She frowned at him. "That's a ballad."

"Perhaps you can't sleep because you're dancing to the wrong music. Try slowing down."

The idea of holding Audra in his arms made the blood rush through his veins. His heart thundered in his chest. His breath hitched in his throat.

Audra hesitated. Her skeptical gaze shifted from

his hand to his eyes. Finally she moved into his embrace. In her bare feet, she fit comfortably under his chin. He wrapped his arms loosely around her slender frame and let the music guide his movements. Together they swayed to Mary J. Blige's achingly romantic song of a woman urging her husband to stay strong with her. He closed his eyes and breathed in her scent, lavender and powder.

Audra's arms slid up his shoulders to wrap around his neck. He stepped back to look down into her upturned face. Her champagne eyes had darkened. Their bodies rocked together. With one finger, Jack traced the gentle sweep of Audra's left cheek, the soft curve of her mouth. Her lips parted. Jack's body stirred.

He lowered his head until his mouth met hers. Her lips were soft and giving. Her taste was so sweet, like the remnants of a dream before waking. Jack held her tighter. He deepened their kiss, eager for her to nourish his soul. Audra opened beneath his demands, inflaming him even more. He stroked his tongue across hers. Audra pressed her body against him and opened wider.

Her sweetness, softness, heat, and strength nearly overwhelmed him. He ached for her as he'd never ached for anyone before. He needed her more than he'd imagined he'd need anyone ever again. He committed her touch and shape to memory with a long, slow caress from her firm breasts to her rounded derriere. His palms burned.

Jack cupped Audra's hips against his arousal. He tore his mouth from hers. "I need this, Audra. But is this what you want?"

Audra's answer was to pull him closer. She kissed

him hard and hungrily. Her tongue swept inside his mouth, searching him, learning him, making his body smolder and his breath catch. Jack's legs shook. He broke the kiss and lifted Audra from her feet. Cradling her in his arms, he carried her into her cabin. He kicked the door shut behind them and strode across the great room to her bedroom. Her passion was a drumbeat in his mind, echoing throughout his body. He wanted this night with this woman more than he wanted the sun to rise in the morning. His muscles tightened with an almost painful urgency. Jack released Audra to stand on her own and stepped back.

"Are you sure?" His voice was rough. The words forced from him. What if she said no? Would he have the strength to walk away? Jack gritted his teeth and waited.

"Very sure."

He exhaled. He pulled a condom from his shorts pocket and laid it on her nightstand.

Audra's eyes sparkled. "You were confident."

"Hopeful."

Their shared humor eased his urgency to join with her. Right. Now.

He shed his clothes, never looking away from Audra as she slipped off her own. He gave thanks for her summer uniform—two scraps of cotton and two bits of silk. She stood before him in glorious nudity—firm curves, toned muscles, long limbs.

Audra's tongue stuck to the roof of her mouth as Jack revealed his muscled chest, ripped abs, slim hips, and powerful thighs. Where should she start? As she played with the hair on his chest, his muscles quivered beneath her touch.

Jack took her wrists and drew her arms behind her back. Her body shivered as she pressed her breasts to his chest. Jack claimed her mouth for a mind-melting kiss and Audra fell into the sensation. She opened wider, drawing his tongue deeper. Her nipples tightened. Her sex dampened. She suckled his tongue in the rhythm she wanted him to take her. Jack's erection flexed against her. Audra moaned her approval.

The room rocked and Audra's eyes popped open. Jack was walking her backward toward her bed. He nudged her onto the mattress, then he came down on top of her, holding most of his weight off her.

Audra leaned away. "Wait. There's something I want to do first."

Jack hesitated before rolling off her.

Audra straddled him. She drew her fingers down his chest. "Mind if I play?"

His onyx eyes gleamed. "Can I play, too?"

"Soon." She kissed and licked her way down his chest to his stomach, nipping his waist before claiming his shaft. Jack growled low in his throat. The sound filled her with feminine power. Audra took him slowly into her mouth. Jack's hips tensed, rising off the mattress. She teased him, caressed him, squeezing and stroking until his chest rose and fell.

"Turn around." Jack's husky command startled her.

Did he mean to . . . ?

Jack propped himself on his elbows. The heat in his poet's eyes made his intentions clear before he repeated the words. "Turn around. Lay over me."

Audra's thighs went limp. Arousal upon arousal pooled in her core. Shaking with desire, she clumsily turned, scooting backward until she was able to reclaim him with her mouth. Her heart beat so fast, too fast. She was intensely aware of her position in relation to Jack's face. This was new territory for her. *Oh, my goodness.*

Her hand shook as she palmed him again. Audra covered his tip with her mouth, drawing him deep, loving on him. Then Jack touched her. His fingers parted her folds. Shock—hungry and electric— flashed through her. Her nipples pebbled. Her core dampened. Her body trembled. *Oh, my goodness.*

His fingers explored her, inside and out. He kissed her deeply, intimately, shifting his mouth over her most sensitive flesh. Audra's eyes widened at the way he used his tongue. It was rough against her, exploring her with broad strokes and intimate caresses. He licked and nipped. Like an erotic puppet master, he commanded her body to rock against him. Audra rolled her hips, lost to the sensation of Jack's mouth covering her spot as she tried to continue sucking his shaft. But this feeling was too much, too intense. She ached. Her body burned. She rocked faster and faster until pleasure exploded through her.

Breathing hard, Audra turned onto her back beside Jack. Her core continued to pulse with pleasure. Audra lay limp as Jack shifted away, then rolled the condom over his erection. She gasped as he pulled her beneath him and again as he surged into her with one smooth stroke.

He stretched her with his fullness. Audra's hips rose to meet him as desire built in her again. Jack lowered his head to suckle her nipple. He teased its tip with his tongue and nipped it with his teeth, demanding so much and giving even more. His urgent abandon fed her own. He moved on her with a rough, raw masculinity. Audra answered his challenge. She wrapped her legs around his hips and took him deeper. Jack's fingers played with her other breast, pinching the nipple. He ministered to it with his teeth and tongue. Audra was frantic.

She clenched her core around his erection. Jack groaned. The sound spurred her own excitement. Arching his back, he buried himself even deeper within her. He rubbed himself against her. It was too much. It wasn't enough. Her body tightened as Jack continued to thrust home, rocking against her as her muscles became unbearably taut. Then he touched her right there. *Yes! Yes!* She convulsed under him like a live wire. Wave after wave of pleasure burst in and around her again. Jack pulled her closer in his embrace. He drove into her once, twice, then again . . . until his body shook, prolonging her climax with his own.

For several long moments, they held each other. Audra sighed with deep contentment. Her muscles were sweetly drained. "I'm going to sleep well tonight."

Jack kissed her shoulder, the touch gentle with affection. "So am I."

Audra was especially hungry Friday morning. Was it the thorough lovemaking she'd enjoyed the night before or the grueling jog with Jack she hadn't liked as much this morning?

After their hour-long race—it hadn't been a jog—Audra had offered to cook their breakfast. She didn't speculate on her reason for wanting to spend her morning with the sexy rental owner or her reaction to his criminally beautiful smile. Instead, she'd crawled back to her cabin to clean up and cook.

Minutes later, Audra stepped from the shower and dried off. As she dressed in lemon yellow shorts and a lime green tank top, she realized she was humming a melody she'd never heard before. She hurried from her bedroom and found her spiral notebook where she'd left it on the coffee table. Her cellular phone chirped at her. Audra ignored it, focusing on the song in her head. She roughed the music on a fresh sheet of paper.

The chirping stopped only to begin again as she turned toward her bedroom. The caller identification read *Restricted*.

She answered it anyway. *What the heck? I'm in a good mood.* "Hello?"

"I was beginning to think you weren't going to pick up." Wendell's voice teased her.

Audra's mood took a nosedive. The troll had blocked his phone number. "I told you not to call me. Ever. Again."

His low chuckle used to be appealing. Now it set her teeth on edge. "You didn't mean it."

"Actually, I did." Audra started back to her bedroom. Her bare feet were soundless against the honey-wood flooring.

"Come on, Audra." Wendell lowered his voice to a wheedling huskiness. "You were angry then."

"I still am." She pulled a comb through her hair

with short, jerky motions of her right hand. Her dark brown curls were still damp from her shower.

"I handled things badly. I was wrong."

"So was I. I thought we were in a relationship."

"Give me a chance to make it up to you, honey."

"Don't call me that." Audra tensed with remembered heartache, shame, and anger. She marched from her bedroom. "Your baby's mother is the one you should be pleading with. She's the one wearing your ring. Call her and stop pestering me."

Wendell sighed. "Come home, honey. Let's talk about this."

A knock on the front door interrupted Audra's tirade.

Jack!

"I told you not to call me that." Audra pulled open the door. She offered Jack a forced smile.

Jack's expression dimmed to concern when he saw her. His gaze swung from her cell phone back to her eyes. "Everything OK?"

Audra nodded before returning to Wendell's call. "Good-bye."

"Audra, wait! We need to talk. Honey, I miss you."

Audra barely heard Wendell. She watched Jack wander farther into her cabin. Her gaze drank him in. He looked good in his navy T-shirt and gunmetal gray shorts. He looked even better naked. Audra's body warmed at the memory.

"Stop calling me. I mean it." Audra hung up, ignoring Wendell's entreaties.

Jack turned to her. "Problem?"

"The ex." She forced her mind away from the call and toward the gorgeous man in front of her.

Could she kiss him? She wanted to, but they hadn't discussed the rules of their relationship.

"Is your ex a problem?"

"No, we broke up more than a month ago." Audra set her cell phone on the coffee table. "But I have a more important question. Are we allowed to touch each other outside of the bedroom?"

A slow smile stretched Jack's lips and weakened Audra's knees. "Yes."

"I love a man of few words." She closed the distance between them and twined her arms around his neck.

Jack settled his large hands on her waist and drew her into his body. Audra's senses came alive. Her temperature rose; her nipples tightened; her pulse raced. All that before he even lowered his head to hers.

His lips were warm and cool, soft and firm. His taste was pure heaven. When he deepened the kiss, Audra molded her body to his. Jack held her tighter. Her head spun. She couldn't catch her breath.

Shaken by the intensity of her feelings, Audra broke the kiss and made herself step back. She dug her short nails into the palms of her hands. "I promised you breakfast."

"What's on the menu?" Unasked questions hovered in Jack's eyes.

Audra wasn't ready to address them. She escaped into the kitchen. "Bacon, waffles, and blueberries."

"Blueberries?"

Audra paused to look at him. Her voice was sharp with concern. "Are you allergic?"

"No, but—"

"Then don't knock it." Audra led the way into the kitchen.

Blueberries? Jack still had his doubts, but at least there would be bacon. "Do you need a hand?"

"Just keep me company."

He settled on the maple chair, at the matching square kitchen table, and treated himself to the pleasure of watching Audra. She was dressed in sunshine with her bright yellow shorts and green top. She moved around the kitchen with efficiency, collecting the makings of their breakfast. In moments, bacon sizzled in the frying pan, waffles browned in the toaster, and coffee brewed in its machine.

Jack let Audra steer the conversation with light topics: their morning jog, fishing, and what they each planned to do today. But as she fixed their plates, his curiosity got the better of him.

"Whose idea was the breakup?" He stood to take their breakfast plates to the table.

Thankfully, Audra didn't pretend not to understand his question. She set a mug of coffee beside his plate. "Mine."

He'd suspected as much. "Why?"

Jack took his seat and sipped his coffee. She'd remembered he took it black with only one sugar. Every time he was with her, it got harder for that stubborn block of ice to remain around his heart.

Audra settled on the chair across from him. She sketched circles of syrup all over her waffles, then passed the bottle to Jack. "It was a combination of things—his fiancée and their unborn child."

Jack's brows lifted. "I see."

"It took me a while, but so did I." Audra sliced into her waffles.

Jack picked up a blueberry and examined it suspiciously. "Did you confront him?"

Audra sipped her coffee. "Wendell—"

"'Wendell'? That's his name?"

Audra ignored his interruption. "He said they'd broken off their engagement."

"But you didn't believe him?"

Audra gave him a wry smile. "You didn't see the ring."

"Suppose there hadn't been a ring?" Jack ate the blueberry. It wasn't bad.

Audra shook her head as she chewed a forkful of waffles. She added a blueberry. "I don't deal in hypotheticals. The fact is, there's a ring. There's a fiancée and she's pregnant with Wendell's child. He told me he cared about me, but all the while, he was leading a double life."

"So the problem is you don't trust him?"

Audra frowned. "Could you?"

"No."

"We both got into a relationship with people we couldn't trust. What does that say about us?"

"It says more about the people we trusted. Do you think you could ever trust him again?"

Audra stabbed a blueberry with her fork. "Hiding a fiancée who's pregnant with your child is a pretty big lie."

Jack ate a slice of bacon as he considered Audra. "What if Wendell told you his engagement was a mistake? Would you take him back?"

Audra shook her head. "He'd be leaving more

than a fiancée. I couldn't let him walk away from his baby."

Jack pressed her. "Suppose he agreed to take care of his child, but he wanted to marry you? Would you take him back then?"

Audra frowned. "Why are you asking these questions? I thought we were going to keep our summer romance light?"

He didn't understand his persistence, either. Audra wasn't Kerry. She hadn't cheated on her boyfriend. It was the other way around. She was the injured party. Still, he wanted to know whether Wendell was history.

Jack shrugged. "Just curious. Would you give him another chance?"

Audra met his gaze. "What would you do if your ex-wife returned? If she told you she'd made a mistake. She's still in love with you and wants you to forgive her. Would you give *her* another chance?"

Jack tensed. He pushed his plate aside. "Do you think our situations are the same?"

"I didn't say that. Your wife didn't just leave *you*."

Jack's eyes never wavered from Audra's. "I know. She left our daughter, too. For that, I could never forgive her. What does that make me?"

Audra leaned toward him. "Your situation doesn't define you. Other people can't do that, either. Only you can define you."

Jack crossed his arms. "Is that some sort of New Age crap?"

"No, it's not. How do you see yourself?"

Jack wanted to squirm under Audra's intense regard. It took some effort to remain still. "You and half the people in this town say I've become the Beast in that fairy tale."

"That was before I got to know you."

"And now?" Jack steeled himself for her answer.

"I see a loving father who's coping with his grief the best he can."

It wasn't pity he saw in her eyes. It was admiration. Jack didn't want pity, but he didn't deserve admiration. He wasn't anybody's hero. But Audra made him feel as though he could be.

CHAPTER 10

Audra's afternoon trips to Books & Bakery had become her drug of choice. Trinity Falls Fudge Walnut Brownies were her addiction. After purchasing a copy of Friday's *The Trinity Falls Monitor,* she lingered in the book stacks, considering the romances, mysteries, and sweeping epic fantasies. She paused when she happened across a familiar author, then moved on when she realized she'd already read that novel. The scents of sugar, chocolate, and coffee grew stronger as she neared the bakery.

How did Jack stand sequestering himself in Harmony Cabins day in and day out for months? She'd been like that in Los Angeles. But she couldn't imagine living that way anymore. She was tired of being afraid to try new things and go to new places. She'd changed her location and her perspective.

"You're just the woman I'd hoped to see." Doreen greeted Audra as she finally made her way to the counter.

Audra raised a hand, palm out. "First, I owe you

an apology. My name isn't Penny. It's Audra. I'm sorry I misled you about my identity."

"I understand that you don't want people to recognize you, but that's what I wanted to talk with you about." Doreen lowered her voice. "Rumor has it that you're in the music industry."

"The rumor's true." Audra slid onto a bar stool opposite the baker. The dining area was moderately full. Only one or two cozy tables were free. "Why are we whispering?"

"I thought your identity was a secret." Doreen poured her a mug of coffee.

"That was Benita's idea. Benita Hawkins is my business manager."

"Of course." Doreen nodded. "She was bossy as a child."

Audra's lips curved with amusement. "She still is."

"She doesn't return to Trinity Falls often. When she does, she doesn't stay long, but I can tell she hasn't changed." Doreen hesitated nervously. "Do you know any singers who might be willing to perform at our sesquicentennial celebration?"

"I'll ask around." Audra added cream and sweetener to her coffee. "Why don't you check with Benita?"

"I did." Doreen gave her a bashful smile. "When I told her our budget, she laughed."

That also sounded like her business manager. Nothing motivated Benita like the almighty dollar.

Audra sipped her coffee. "What's your budget?" Doreen named an amount that made Audra wince. She thought about the up-and-coming singers she knew. "I might be able to find someone who would perform for that. But it won't be a big-name star, and you'll have to pay expenses, travel, and lodging."

Doreen gave her a grateful look. "We can handle that. Thank you for agreeing to help."

"The performer will also need a band."

Doreen brightened. "The university has a concert band."

Audra's brows quirked. "Are they any good?"

"They earned first place in last year's regional concert competition."

Audra wasn't convinced. "I'll have to hear them before we make any final arrangements."

"Fair enough." Doreen sounded relieved. "Now what can I get for you?"

"How are the Trinity Falls Fudge Walnut Brownies today?"

"Just as moist and delicious as they are every day."

Audra could barely wait. "May I have one?"

"Coming right up. I've got a fresh batch in the oven." Doreen disappeared into the kitchen.

Audra perused *The Trinity Falls Monitor*. Her breath caught in her throat. A large photo of Jack stared up at her from page two beneath the title FOUNDER'S GREAT-GREAT-GRANDSON HEADLINES MAIN EVENT. She became lost in the article, learning about Ezekiel Sansbury's trials and triumphs while founding Trinity Falls, Jack's parents' contributions to the town, and Jack's efforts to protect his family's legacy.

"Mind if we join you?" Darius's voice interrupted her.

Audra looked up as he settled onto a bar stool beside her. "Not at all. I want to apologize for misleading you about my name. It's not Penny. It's Audra."

Quincy shook his head. "We understand."

"It was Benita's idea, wasn't it?" Ramona took the stool to Darius's right and Quincy sat beside her. "Jack told Darius she was your business manager and that she'd made your reservation to the cabins. She's always been a bossy know-it-all."

Audra silently agreed. Relieved, she turned back to Darius. "I was just enjoying your interview with Jack."

"Thank you." Darius gave her a slow smile that made her wonder how many hearts he'd broken.

Audra tapped the paper. "I feel as though I know him a lot better now."

Ramona rolled her eyes. "Don't feed his ego."

Audra smiled at the other woman's warning. "I also didn't realize he was your boss."

Quincy laughed out loud. "I don't think Darius acknowledges he has one."

Darius leaned forward to see his friend. "Since Jack's the publisher of the *Monitor*, I know he's my boss."

Audra looked around. "Where's Ean?"

Quincy inclined his head toward the opposite side of the store. "He's getting Megan."

Quincy and Ramona, Ean and Megan. Did Darius have someone special?

Doreen returned with a tray of Trinity Falls Fudge Walnut Brownies. "I thought you all would be here by now."

She placed one plate in front of Audra and gave the others to Darius, Ramona, and Quincy.

The final brownie was put to rest in front of an empty chair, presumably for Ean.

Doreen pinned Quincy and Ramona with a stern look as she filled their mugs with coffee. "It's already mid-July. We can't put off plans for your going-away party any longer."

Ramona cut a small slice of brownie with her fork. "Don't look at me. I've been trying to get him to help me with the planning for months."

Doreen tsked. "You're not supposed to plan your own send-off. That's what friends are for."

"That's what friends are for." Audra nodded at Doreen's sentiment.

Quincy forked up his pastry. "You're already planning the town's sesquicentennial. Don't worry about throwing a party for us."

Ramona gaped at him. "Speak for yourself. I want a party, *especially* if I don't have to plan it."

Who wouldn't? Audra took another bite of brownie, reminding herself to get one for Jack. Perhaps she could use it to lure him back to town.

Megan added her voice to the chorus. "Quincy, we're not going to let you leave next month unless you let us throw you and Ramona a party."

The bookstore owner joined Doreen behind the counter. Megan looked as though she'd stepped off the cover of *Forbes* magazine. Her emerald green skirt suit complemented her tall, slender figure. Her warm honey skin glowed.

Ean sank onto the stool beside Quincy. "Megan's right. And Mom isn't going to arrange the party by herself. We'll help."

"It must be hard, leaving friends who care so much for you." Audra spoke without thinking.

Darius drained his coffee. "We grew up together. You must have friends you're close to back in L.A."

How had she lost touch with her friends over the years? "My industry is too competitive for real friendships, but I'm enjoying yours."

Ramona looked around. "So what were you thinking? Flashing lights, streamers, a live band, confetti?"

Darius snorted. "Flashing lights? Are you going with a disco theme?"

Quincy sighed. "A live band? Really?"

Ramona turned to him. "Why not? Aren't we worth it?"

"No." Darius bit into his dessert.

Ramona glared at the reporter. "No one's talking to you."

Darius shrugged. "When has that stopped me from volunteering my opinions?"

Audra smothered a grin. "I like the idea of flashing lights. It's very retro."

Quincy rested his hand on Ramona's fist. "Calm down, honey. This isn't your wedding."

A flush pinkened Ramona's cheeks. "Are you proposing?"

Quincy grunted, retrieving his hand. He turned back to his brownie. "When I propose, we won't be surrounded by other people."

Ramona grinned. "You said 'when' you propose."

A blush darkened Quincy's brown cheeks. "No, I didn't."

Ramona poked a finger into his arm. "Yes, you did. I heard you."

"I heard it, too, dude." Darius turned to Audra. "Didn't you hear him?"

Audra sipped her coffee. "I heard the prelude to a proposal, the opening chords." Her gaze moved between Ramona and Quincy. "When he proposes, and he will, you'll recognize it for what it is. You won't need to ask."

The group stared at her in silence for a beat. Then Megan turned to Ean. "I want you to propose to me just the way Audra described. First the prelude, then the proposal."

Darius doubled over with laughter. Ean and Quincy frowned at Audra in unison. "Thanks."

"You're welcome." Audra swallowed her last bite of brownie, pleased with her contribution to the discussion. "Doreen, may I have another brownie for the road?"

"You sure can." Doreen's response was rich with amusement.

Darius shook his head as his humor dwindled. "You're dangerous." He turned to Quincy. "How's the faculty search going for your replacement?"

Quincy drained his coffee. "They're narrowing down the candidates."

"Will someone be in place before you leave?" Darius wiped his mouth with a napkin.

"I think so. They have strong candidates. One of them is a professor from New York University."

Darius arched a brow. "Why would an NYU professor apply for a position at Trinity Falls University? TFU can't match that salary."

Audra accepted her extra brownie from Doreen and rose to pay her bill. "Maybe the professor's tired of the rat race and is looking for a more comfortable community."

Ean nodded. "It's been known to happen."

* * *

"You haven't returned my calls." Simon's voice rang with petulant accusation.

Darius's worn gray swivel chair squeaked as he spun to face his father later Friday afternoon in *The Trinity Falls Monitor*'s building. He found the older man frowning in the threshold of his office cubicle. "Your message wasn't urgent."

Simon infringed farther into the close confines of Darius's workspace. "I didn't realize I needed to leave a life-and-death message to have my son return my call."

Darius dropped his pencil to his desk. "What do you need?"

"I'm running for mayor."

"You're circulating a petition."

Simon didn't seem to hear him. "I'd think you'd want to interview me for the newspaper."

Darius studied his father. Was he wearing a new suit? He didn't recognize the dark blue pin-striped outfit. "I don't want you to run for mayor."

Simon's brows knitted. "Why not?"

Darius saved the Word document he'd been editing for the newspaper's Saturday morning edition before returning his attention to his father. "Come with me."

He led Simon to a small, unoccupied conference room. Its dingy walls and ceiling afforded them more privacy than his cubicle. He closed the door behind Simon and watched his father make himself comfortable at the table. "Why are you doing this?"

Simon huffed a breath. "I've already told you."

"I want the truth this time." Darius leaned against the wall and crossed his arms.

Simon glared up at Darius, biting the inside of his cheek. "Trinity Falls deserves a true mayoral contest, not a one-person race."

Darius hadn't bought that four days ago when Simon had shocked him with his announcement in Books & Bakery. He wasn't buying it now. "You didn't care when the last three mayoral elections were uncontested. Why do you care now?"

Simon shrugged. "I just do."

This sounded more like his father. They were making progress. "What made you change your mind?"

Simon looked puzzled. "Is this the interview?"

Darius unfolded his arms and straightened from the wall. "I'm not interviewing you. And you're not running for mayor."

Simon stiffened. "Who do you think you are?"

"The better question is, who do *you* think you are?" Darius drew in a deep breath. The room was small and the air was stuffy. He had to get out of here.

Simon stood. "I'm your father. You owe me respect."

Respect? Is he kidding?

Darius stepped closer. "You know that your mayoral campaign would not be a good idea for this family."

"Who are you to tell me what to do? I can do whatever I choose."

"Not if it's going to hurt other people, although

I realize you're probably too selfish to even consider that."

Simon pointed a finger in Darius's face. "Watch your mouth, son."

Darius held his ground. "Before you go any further with your pursuit of public office, you'd better consider the things in your life that you don't want brought to light."

Simon searched Darius's expression. "What are you talking about?"

Darius's temper spiked. "Don't pretend not to know."

"I have no idea what you're talking about." Simon turned away.

The movement exposed his lie. Simon may not realize Darius was aware of his secret, but his father knew damn well his closet hid skeletons.

Darius glared at his father's back. "Yes, you do. You may not care about the embarrassment, but Mom would be mortified and so would other people. You have no right to do that to them."

"How would my campaign embarrass your mother?"

"In fairness to Mom, don't pursue this petition. She doesn't want you to run for mayor. You owe it to her to respect her wishes."

Simon spun back to him. "I've done nothing wrong."

"Is that the way you're going to play it?"

"If you have something to say, say it."

"I'm not playing this game with you."

"Are you interviewing me or not?"

"I'm not." Darius turned to leave.

Simon's voice stopped him. "You're not the only reporter on the *Monitor*'s staff. This will be the first contested mayoral race this town has seen in three terms. It's big news. I'm sure one of the others will jump at the opportunity to interview me."

Darius gripped the doorknob, then faced his father. "For the record, I won't sign your petition."

Simon shook with anger. "You're my son. Are you going to vote against your family?"

"Are you still pretending we have one?"

"What do you think is in my past?"

Darius stared at his father. "Was it really that easy for you to forget?" He walked out of the room without waiting for an answer.

Doreen gripped the coffeepot harder as she watched Simon advance toward the bakery counter at Books & Bakery Saturday morning. Her hand shook as she refilled Sheriff Alonzo Lopez's mug.

"Thank you, Doreen." Alonzo gripped Doreen's wrist in a firm but gentle hold.

Doreen glanced at the sheriff's mug, now filled to the rim with coffee. She gasped. "I'm sorry."

The sheriff released her wrist. "No harm done." His calm drawl soothed her.

"But I didn't leave room for your creamer."

Laugh lines around his dark eyes deepened. "I'll make room as I drink the coffee."

Doreen collected his empty breakfast plate. Her smile faded as Simon joined them. She glanced at the copy of *The Trinity Falls Monitor* he carried.

"Morning, Simon. What can I get you?" From the

corner of her eye, she caught Alonzo's sharp look. It made her regret her cool tone.

"A cup of coffee, please, Doreen." Simon settled onto the stool beside the sheriff. "Good morning, Alonzo."

Alonzo gestured toward the paper Simon rested on the counter between them. "I saw the article about you."

Simon's eyes lit with pleasure. "Did you, now? What did you think?"

Alonzo sipped his coffee. "It was interesting."

Doreen listened to the exchange as she set the dirty plate in the bucket beside the coffee station. She placed a mug in front of Simon and filled it with coffee.

"Would you like to sign the petition to add my name to the ballot?" Simon whipped out the sheet of paper he'd tucked into the newspaper.

Doreen couldn't read the look in Alonzo's eyes. "There's no soliciting in Books and Bakery."

Simon glanced at her. "Trying to stifle your competition, Doreen?"

Her lips trembled, but she managed not to ask, *What competition?* "This isn't about my campaign, Simon. The Trinity Falls Town Center has a no-solicitation policy." Doreen gestured toward the front of the store. "It's posted clear as day on each shop's door."

She could read the expression in Alonzo's eyes now. It was relief. The sheriff drank more of his coffee, then stirred cream into his mug.

Simon nudged the other man's arm. "I'll bring the petition by your office later, Sheriff."

Alonzo picked up his coffee. "I have this weekend off."

"Oh. That explains why you're not in uniform. Well, I'll bring it by Monday, then."

"The sheriff's department has a no-solicitation policy also." Alonzo drained his mug, then stood to take his bill to the nearby cash register.

Simon frowned. "How's a person supposed to get their petition signed?"

"I'm sure you'll think of something." Doreen attended to the sheriff's bill at the register. "Enjoy your weekend, Alonzo."

Alonzo accepted his change. "You do the same, Doreen."

Doreen closed the register as she watched Alonzo disappear into the bookshelves. He looked so different out of uniform—approachable, relaxed, sexy.

There's something about a man out *of uniform.* Doreen frowned. *Where did that thought come from?*

She turned to Simon. "I read your interview as well. It's clear to anyone that you're not taking this campaign seriously."

He waved the petition. "The nearly one hundred people who've already signed this form don't agree with you."

"You've collected a hundred signatures?"

Simon nodded with apparent satisfaction. "And there are one hundred more on the website."

Doreen lost her breath. He was almost halfway to the number of signatures he needed. "Public office is a huge responsibility."

"I know." Simon tucked the petition back into his newspaper.

"The Founders Day Celebration is separate from the mayor's office. That's why I'm leading the celebration planning committee instead of Ramona."

"I know that, too." Simon folded his arms on the countertop. "Can I have a slice of Boston cream pie?"

Doreen swallowed her impatience and turned to get Simon's pie from the display case. She set the dish and a fork in front of him. "If you're aware of these things, why would you talk about making the success of the sesquicentennial celebration part of your campaign platform?"

"Because the celebration is important to the town. It'll bring in money." Simon dug into the pie.

"But it shouldn't have a bearing on the campaign."

Simon shook his head and swallowed more pie. "I disagree."

Doreen crossed her arms. "That's interesting, particularly since you aren't on any of the committees. What are you doing in support of the event?"

"I got Jack Sansbury to agree to participate in the Founders Day presentation."

Doreen thought her eyes would pop out of her head. "That wasn't your doing. *Darius* convinced Jack to change his mind."

Simon grinned. "And Darius is my son."

The headache started right behind Doreen's eyes. "You're good at taking credit for what other people have done, aren't you?"

His answer was another shrug. "Leo's supporting my campaign."

Doreen's skin chilled. *My Leonard? The man I've been dating for more than a year?* "What are you talking about?"

"He signed my petition to be added to the election ballot." Simon brought the sheet back out.

Doreen skimmed the piece of paper until her gaze settled on line seventy-three. She blinked twice, but Leonard's name didn't disappear.

CHAPTER 11

Why was he torturing himself this way? Darius's blood boiled Saturday morning as he sat in his cubicle in *The Trinity Falls Monitor*'s building, re-reading the newspaper's article on his father's quest for the mayoral office.

"Now, Darius, if the story bothers you so much, why are you reading it?" Helen Gaston's voice came from behind him.

Darius almost jumped from his skin. His chair squeaked as he spun to face his visitor, almost colliding with her in the process. "Ms. Helen." He rose to his feet. "What makes you think I'm upset?"

Her faded brown eyes twinkled up at him in her elfish brown face. "My first clue was the way you clutched the edges of the newspaper in your fists, like this." She clenched her thin hands and scowled in a brief reenactment.

Ignoring her antics, Darius gestured toward the

guest chair beside his desk. "Do you have time to visit with me?"

"I'll make the time, young man." Ms. Helen settled onto the seat. "Why are you working on a Saturday? Are you making overtime?"

Darius returned to his chair, grateful for this distraction. "I won't be here long. What brings you to the paper?"

"I want to place an ad." Ms. Helen brushed the flowered print of her skirt, then settled her silver handbag on her lap.

"For what?"

She tilted her head. "Why are you asking so many questions? Are you going to write a story about it?"

Darius grinned at her quarrelsome words. "Why are you being so secretive?"

Ms. Helen smoothed her gray hair back toward the thick bun at the nape of her thin neck. "I'm looking for someone to write my memoirs, if you must know."

Darius's grin vanished. A chill of fear invaded his heart. "Ms. Helen, it's way too early to be thinking about writing your memoirs. You're going to be with us for a very long time."

Helen Gaston, or "Ms. Helen," as Trinity Falls residents called her, was a tiny woman who'd been ancient the day Darius had been born. Since then, time had stood still for her. She was a fixture in Trinity Falls, doling advice—solicited or not—and encouraging neighbors, both young and old, through triumphs and challenges. She'd been more of a parent to him than his parents had been. The idea of the town without her was inconceivable.

Ms. Helen rolled her eyes, though the blush on her brown cheeks revealed her pleasure in the compliment. "You're better off keeping your pretty words for your girlfriends, young man. They won't turn my head."

"If you're determined to write your memoirs, I'd be happy to help you."

"I appreciate your offer, but it looks like you have your hands full right now."

Darius followed Ms. Helen's gaze to the newspaper, still open on his desk. "What do you mean?"

Ms. Helen gave him a sympathetic look. "You can't mean to let this foolishness continue."

"What 'foolishness'?" He didn't feel good about pretending not to understand.

Ms. Helen's face softened into a smile. "I've read every one of your articles since you came back to write for the *Monitor.* I can tell how much you care about this town. I know Simon's your father, but you can't possibly agree with his decision to run for mayor."

He'd call his father's mayoral aspirations a lot of things, but "foolishness" was an understatement. "What can I do about it?"

"Stop him."

The muscles in the back of Darius's neck screamed with tension. "Ms. Helen, I've tried. He won't listen to me."

Ms. Helen leaned forward, placing a hand over Darius's. "I know you, Darius. If Simon didn't change his mind, it means you didn't try hard enough."

"Just because he runs for mayor doesn't mean

he'll win. Everyone knows Doreen's the better candidate."

"So you're just going to give up and hope for the best? That's not like you, Darius. You know you can't separate yourself from Simon's campaign."

Couldn't I? Darius remained silent.

"You didn't even write the article about his petition drive." Ms. Helen sighed. "I read the article. There isn't one part of it that's true. That kind of dishonesty could hurt the town, splitting it between those who believe Simon and those who know the truth. Do you want that for Trinity Falls?"

"No, I don't."

"Then what are you going to do about it?"

He wished he knew.

On Saturday night, Doreen welcomed Leonard into her home for dinner. Their menu was steak and potatoes, comfort food. The knowledge he supported Simon's campaign had weighed on her since she'd seen his signature on the petition that morning. Even now, the reality of what he'd done sat at the dining-room table with them like an unwanted guest.

Doreen sliced into her steak. "I was surprised you didn't come into Books and Bakery today."

Leonard scooped a forkful of mashed potatoes. "I had a lot of errands to run."

"So many that you had to skip lunch?" Did she sound as witchy as she felt?

Leonard gave her a curious look. "I ate lunch at home."

Doreen chewed and swallowed a bite of steak,

giving herself time to get her temper and her tone under control. "Simon came in today."

"Oh? What did he want?" Leonard seemed disinterested.

"To talk about his interview in today's *Monitor*."

Leonard ate more steak and potatoes before answering. "I read it."

"What did you think of it?"

Leonard shrugged. "It was OK."

Doreen almost choked on her iced tea. "It was OK that he took credit for things that *I* did?"

"No one's going to believe it."

"Why not? It ran in the paper." Doreen drew in a breath. "He also showed me his petition to be added to the mayoral ballot. Your name was on it."

Leonard looked up from his plate. "He asked me to sign it. I didn't think there was any harm in it."

Doreen's eyebrows shot up her forehead. "Do you really think Simon's qualified to be mayor of Trinity Falls?"

Leonard cut another slice of steak. "Just because I signed his petition doesn't mean I'm going to vote for him."

"Simon thinks you are."

Would he? Doreen desperately wanted an answer to that.

"I didn't tell him that." Leonard continued eating.

Doreen lowered her knife and fork. "Then why did you sign his petition?"

"If he wants to run for mayor, he should be able to. Who are we to decide who runs and who doesn't?"

Doreen pushed aside her half-eaten dinner.

Tonight the steak and mashed potatoes didn't deliver the comfort they usually gave her. "You surprise me, Leo. You don't have any trouble with Simon running for mayor. But you resent my campaign. Why is that?"

"I'm not in a relationship with Simon."

Doreen willed Leonard to meet her gaze. "You're supporting Simon's petition because you want someone else to be mayor."

Leonard finished his dinner. He set his knife and fork on the empty plate. "I'm not going to campaign for Simon, if that's what you're asking."

"But will you vote for me?" Doreen barely breathed while she waited for Leonard's reply.

Seconds stretched like minutes. What was taking him so long to answer? It wasn't a trick question.

Leonard leaned back on his chair. "I'll listen to what you both have to say, then make my decision. That's what I do for every election."

That's his response? He didn't say he'd vote against her, nor would he commit to supporting her. Doreen had no idea his nonanswer would hurt so much.

Dinner was over.

She stood from the table. "I appreciate your giving me the opportunity to earn your vote, although I'd think you knew me well enough to know I deserve it."

She choked on the words. They'd been friends for decades. They'd been lovers for a year. He wanted them to be something more. But she shouldn't have to choose between being his lover and being mayor.

Leonard stood. "Would you be running for mayor if Paul were still alive?"

Doreen braced her hand on the back of her chair to keep her balance. "Is that what this is about? You're comparing our relationship to what I had with Paul?"

"I have a right to know."

"What gives you that right?" The words ripped from her throat. Her body shook with outrage. "The fact that we're sleeping together?"

"Is that all our relationship is to you?"

"I'm through with defending myself to you." Doreen fisted her hands.

"I just want to know where I stand in your new life. What role do *I* play?"

"I've told you how I feel. I respect your right to decide if that's enough for you. But I will not continually apologize or explain myself to you."

Leonard nodded once. "Then I've made my decision. This semirelationship isn't enough for me. I need more."

His words took her breath away. Maybe she should have known this would happen. Instead, Leonard had caught her off guard as he turned and walked out of her home. Out of her life?

Saturday evening, Darius's mother let him into his childhood home. He watched Ethel as she locked the front door. His mother stayed fit with aerobics classes at the university. She was well-groomed, with minimal makeup. Not a hair out of place. Her leaf green sundress complemented her smooth maple skin. Only her fuzzy bedroom slippers seemed out of place.

"Is Dad home?"

"I don't know where your father is." Ethel didn't sound as though she cared, either.

Darius followed his mother into the great room. The space was large and tidy, well-maintained rather than cared for. The white walls were sparsely covered with flowers Ethel had dried and framed. The fireplace's maple mantel on the far wall displayed her collection of ornamental birds—glass, china, porcelain, and wood. Heavy red curtains covered the two large front windows. Was Ethel shutting the town out or closing herself in?

The room was devoid of family mementoes, no pictures commemorating his parents' wedding or anniversaries. There weren't photographs chronicling his birth or childhood. Had they ever been a real family?

Darius looked at his mother seated on the stiff red paisley sofa in front of the television. She was watching a cable network reality show.

He checked his Timex watch as he lowered himself onto the matching armchair. It wasn't yet five o'clock. "Will Dad be home for dinner?"

"I don't know. Hush." His mother pointed the remote at the television screen and pumped up the volume.

Darius raised his voice to be heard above the program. "How long has he been gone?"

"Darius." His mother turned toward him. Her scowl had been a familiar expression since childhood. "I'm watching my show. I don't know where your father is, and I don't care."

"How do you feel about his petition?" Darius knew the answer before she spoke.

Ethel's expression darkened. "How do you think

I feel? I don't want your father to be mayor of Trinity Falls. I don't even want him in the race."

"Why is he running?"

Ethel returned her attention to her program. "Who knows why he does what he does?"

"When did he decide to run?"

She glared at him again. "Why are you asking me all of these questions?"

"Because I want to understand what's going on." Darius leaned forward on his seat, rubbing the back of his neck. "I don't remember Dad ever donating to a fund-raiser, volunteering for civic events, or even signing a petition. Do you?"

"No."

Darius met his mother's gaze across the room. "What makes someone like that wake up one day and decide to become mayor?"

"I don't know." Confusion mixed with irritation in Ethel's black eyes. "But I don't need to understand. I just want him to stop."

Darius stood, crossing to the front windows. He nudged apart the curtains to check the street. Where was his father?

He turned from the window. Silence stretched as he considered his next step. "We should talk with Dad when he gets home. Maybe together we can convince him to drop his petition."

Ethel shook her head as Darius spoke. "That won't work. I'm done with talking. I tried talking to him. Simon won't listen. I told him that if he even campaigned for mayor, I'd divorce him. He still chose to start this petition."

Darius tensed. He'd known for a long time—decades—that his parents' marriage wasn't a happy one. If the town had a yearbook, their marriage would be voted "Least Likely to Succeed." But he still couldn't imagine them divorced. "You would divorce him? Where would you go?"

Simon's voice interrupted them from the room's entrance. "Yes, Ethel. Tell us what you would do without me."

Ethel rose from the sofa and turned her glare on her husband of more than thirty years. "You don't believe that I would divorce you?" She looked at Darius. "You both think that I'm bluffing? Try me, then."

Ethel dashed across the room, shoving Simon out of the way before racing up the stairs. Darius's heart broke at the sound of her sobs.

"This has gone too far, Dad." Darius gestured after his mother. "You can see Mom's miserable."

Simon stepped farther into the room. "Your mother's always threatening to divorce me."

"Your campaign for public office isn't a decision you can make on your own." Darius's muscles were screaming for him to shake Simon until his father's teeth rattled. "We need to make that decision as a family. It affects all of us. Mom and I don't want you to run. We want you to drop your petition."

Simon crossed his arms. "We've talked about this before. My answer's still no."

Darius rubbed the back of his neck, where the muscles were still knotted. "Are you going to let this decision destroy your marriage?"

"Your mother's not going to leave me."

"What if she does? Is that a risk you're willing to take?"

Simon frowned. "I've provided for my family. Now I've decided to do something for myself."

"You're being selfish." The urge to shake his father grew stronger and stronger.

"No, you are. This is what I want. You should support me, instead of trying to talk me out of it—which you won't be able to do."

"The interview you gave the *Monitor* is bullshit." Darius massaged the back of his neck again. "The town knows those initiatives you claimed to have proposed to the council came from Doreen."

"I would have proposed them if she hadn't."

Darius stared at his father, seeing a stranger. "Can you hear yourself? Drop the petition, Dad. You've done enough damage to your reputation and to the family. Don't tear the town apart as well."

"Stop asking me to drop my petition. I'm not going to."

"Why not?"

Simon's thin cheeks flushed. "Because it's what I want."

Darius considered the evasive expression in Simon's dark eyes, the flush on his thin cheeks and the hesitation in his voice. Realization dawned on Darius. "Who talked you into doing this?"

Simon's eyes widened. "No one. This was my idea."

"I don't believe you."

Simon shrugged. "Believe what you want."

It was so obvious. Darius should have realized it sooner. Someone else was behind Simon's decision to run for public office. Who was it, and what were they after?

"How can you read the Sunday paper on your laptop?" Audra's question broke Jack's concentration.

He half sat, half lay on his dark plaid sofa with his computer balanced on his lap. Jack looked up from the screen and the online version of the *Monitor*'s Sunday paper. His lips twitched with humor. "That's the third time you've asked that question."

"Actually, it's only the second." Audra was curled up on the recliner, positioned catty-corner to the sofa.

Jack surrendered to a smile. "My answer's still the same. The *Monitor*'s online edition isn't as large as a major metropolitan's Sunday paper. Besides, an online newspaper subscription is more convenient."

"You mean it fits your hermit lifestyle. I prefer the feel of newsprint in my hands." Audra shook the newspaper she was reading.

Jack grunted. "Don't fear technology."

"You've offended me." Audra hummed to herself as she skimmed the pages of the metropolitan newspaper's Sunday edition. "Remember, if I hadn't gone into town to get a newspaper after our morning jog, you wouldn't have had Doreen's fresh Trinity Falls Fudge Walnut Brownie."

Jack stared at Audra. It was a pastime in which he enjoyed indulging. He took in her pixie features, winged eyebrows, high cheekbones, full lips, and stubborn chin. Her warmth reached out and wrapped around him. Today she was dressed in a rainbow of colors: a pink-and-orange striped T-shirt and orange shorts.

He nodded. "Doreen's brownies are a benefit of going into town."

"That's an understatement." Audra sounded distracted. Her smooth caramel forehead was wrinkled.

Jack sat up on the sofa. "What's wrong?"

Audra looked to him, then back to the newspaper. "There's an article about Trinity Falls in this paper."

Jack frowned. "Why would a newspaper in Cleveland run an article about us?"

Audra hesitated. "It's not exactly about the town. It's more about the town's founding family."

Jack's blood ran cold. He closed his laptop and stood from the sofa. He extended his hand toward Audra. "Let me see."

It was all there in black and white. The article moved quickly past his family's founding of Trinity Falls in northeastern Ohio at the base of the three waterfalls. It then took its time covering Jack's life.

Where did the reporter get his information about his marriage to Kerry? When the article turned to Zoey, Jack saw red.

CHAPTER 12

Jack crushed the edges of the newspaper in his fists. The words became a hazy red blur. "Where did they get this information about my daughter?"

"Jack, I'm so sorry." Audra stood beside him.

The cold darkness grew toward him. Jack crossed the family room, needing space. "Her medical records are private."

"Perhaps they did an Internet search."

He pulled his right hand over his close-cropped hair, crushing the newspaper in his left. "Details like these wouldn't turn up in a basic search."

"Maybe they went deeper than a basic search." Audra's suppositions exacerbated Jack's frustration.

"I need to know." Jack pushed the words through clenched teeth. The veins above his temples throbbed aggressively. "How did they get this personal information about my family?"

"You have every right to an answer."

Jack turned back to Audra. He strained to focus on her through a fog of emotion. "But?"

"I don't understand why you're so angry."

"How would you feel if this happened to you?"

"You're angry about more than the invasion of your privacy."

Looking into her champagne eyes, Jack saw more curiosity than concern. A sense of calm hovered near him, just out of reach. He fought it. "They don't have the right to discuss my daughter."

"Then who does?"

"What?" He struggled to understand her.

"No one talks about Zoey. You haven't said much about her, and the only thing people in town say is that she died too young."

"You've asked other people about her?" A pulse pounded in his inner ear. He could barely think through the buzzing.

"Yes, I did. Zoey existed, Jack. Why don't you want people to know about her, to talk about her?"

His gaze lowered to the newspaper in his fist. "She's not their business."

"Not talking about Zoey is hurting you." Audra closed the distance between them. "As a songwriter, I've taught myself to express my feelings in my lyrics. It's cathartic. I think it would help if you did the same thing."

"I disagree." Jack gritted his teeth.

She placed her small hand over his damaged heart. "Tell me about Zoey."

Audra's words were a command. They allowed no resistance. A chain of images played across Jack's memory: bringing his baby girl home, teaching her to ride her bike, helping her with her homework, taking walks in the woods, fishing at Pearl Lake.

"She was my daughter." His voice broke.

"What did she like to do?" Audra stepped closer. Her words were as soft as a lullaby. Her warmth did battle with the ice pressing against his chest.

"I read to her."

"You told me. Fairy tales." Audra smiled and Jack allowed the calm to settle over him.

"Every night before she went to sleep." He'd tuck her in, then settle into the chair beside her bed to read to her—fairy tales, Bible stories, children's books. At first, Zoey would pepper him with questions, which he'd do his best to answer. The questions dwindled as the minutes flew by and sleep overcame her.

"What else?" Audra's expression softened. She dropped her hand from his chest.

"Zoey hated bedtime. Kerry would make her hot cocoa to help her sleep." Jack chuckled. "She'd sip the cocoa one drop at a time so she could stay up later."

"Smart girl." Audra's laughter was magical. It had the power to vanquish the cold darkness.

Jack took her hand to lead her back to the sofa. He pulled her down to sit beside him. "It drove Kerry nuts, but I had a hard time keeping a straight face." He chuckled again. "I'd forgotten about that."

"Tell me something else." Audra leaned against him. "Tell me how she made you feel."

Jack sobered. "Is this more of your songwriting tricks?"

"They're not tricks."

"I'm not good at talking about feelings."

"Give it a try."

"This is stupid."

"Come on." Audra nudged him with her shoulder.

Jack pressed his head against the sofa's back and closed his eyes. "She made me happy. She gave my life a purpose. She made me feel . . . heroic." Seconds ticked as he waited for Audra's reaction. In her silence, he felt dumb.

Audra's sigh quavered. "That was beautiful."

"She made me feel as though I could do anything. Bring a fairy tale to life, make a gourmet meal." His throat worked as emotions threatened to constrict his muscles. "Find a cure for cancer."

Jack kept his eyes closed. But he felt Audra rise from the sofa to settle on his lap. His arms tightened like a vise around her waist. His body shook with silent grief.

She wrapped her arms around his shoulders and whispered into his ear. "I'm so sorry, Jack. I only meant to remind you of the happy times you shared with Zoey. Don't distance yourself from those memories."

Jack drew her closer. Her attempts to remind him had worked. But those happy times only made him miss his daughter more. How could he ever forgive himself for failing his little girl?

Monday morning, Darius propped his hip on the corner of Opal Gutierrez's desk and waited for her to arrive at work. His pulse beat a maddening tattoo in his temple. He gripped Saturday's newspaper in his fist, covering the article about Simon and the half-page color photo that accompanied it. He'd waited two days to confront the reporter over the story she'd written about his father. Instead of defusing his temper, the delay had increased it tenfold.

"This is a sexy surprise." Opal's voice preceded her into the cubicle. She stopped less than an arm's length from Darius and lowered her voice. "It would've been even better if this were your bedroom."

Darius ignored her suggestion. "I read your article on my father's petition."

Opal turned her back to him, bending low to store her purse in her desk's bottom drawer. Her raven hair swung forward. Its straight strands masked her thin, tan features. "No need to thank me. Take me to dinner and we'll call it even."

"I'm not thanking you. I'm not taking you to dinner, either."

She straightened, facing him as she shrugged out of her navy blazer. Her coal black eyes sent him a sizzling look. "You may change your mind once you see what's on the menu."

Darius wasn't interested in her games. "Why did you let my father take credit for things you know he didn't do?"

Opal stilled. "What?"

Darius lifted the newspaper in his hand to help jog her memory. He wanted an answer, damn it. "When you interviewed him Friday, you let my father take credit for other people's work."

He tracked her as she maneuvered herself farther into her cubicle.

"Hey, I was taking notes. He was the one making the claims." Opal took her seat behind her Formica desk and crossed her long legs. Her short navy skirt rose midway up her thigh.

"And you didn't think to question him on anything he said?" Darius struggled with his irritation.

"It's not my job to vet his answers."

"Yes, it is."

Indignation snapped in Opal's eyes. "How?"

"You're supposed to interview the subject. You're a newspaper reporter, not a Dictaphone."

"Did you talk to Daddy about his lies?"

"Yes, I did. Now I'm talking to you."

Opal leaned forward on her chair. She aimed a finger at his face. "You're pretty high and mighty, lover. If you're God's gift to journalism, why are you here at the *Monitor,* instead of at *The New York Times?*"

"Why are you?"

She threw herself back against her chair. "Back off, Knight. Liu already read me the riot act."

Opal sounded as though she expected Darius to feel sorry for her. He didn't.

"Liu spoke with you?" Darius mentally crossed Loretta Liu, the *Monitor*'s managing editor, off his hit list.

"She woke me Saturday morning, then spent fifteen minutes screeching at me and threatening my job. She put me and the entire weekend copydesk on permanent detention."

"Good." Darius was satisfied his editor would keep a closer watch over Opal's work. He straightened from the other reporter's desk.

Opal caught his wrist. "Why are you so upset about the story?"

Darius shook off her hand. "It's not accurate."

"Give me a break, Darius. Do you have some sort of hero worship for Doreen Fever?"

"She's done a lot for the town." Darius turned to leave, but Opal's next question stopped him.

"Why don't you want your father to run for office?"

"I never said that." He met her eyes over his shoulder.

Opal gave him a shrewd look. "It's written all over your face."

"Are you claiming to have reporter's intuition now? Pity you didn't use it Friday."

"Are you saying I'm on the right track?"

"No, I'm not." Darius's tone was as icy as the anger he held in check.

"It would make a good story." Opal lifted her arms as though framing a photo. "'Hometown Hero Votes Against Father in Mayoral Election.'"

Darius's blood ran cold. "Try sticking to the facts. It would be a refreshing change for you."

Opal's black gaze frosted over. "What does your family have to hide, Darius?"

He returned Opal's heated glare with a cool regard, then left her cubicle. The trouble he'd predicted had started even before Simon's petition passed. What would happen to his family once his father's campaign began in earnest?

* * *

Doreen checked the next agenda item for her Monday meeting with one of the town council's subcommittees. It was the Founders Day Celebration invitation to State Representative Isaac Green. She hated the idea of Representative Green attending the event, but it would be a mistake not to invite the elected official.

She looked at the three council members seated across the table in the Trinity Falls Town Hall small conference room. They seemed bored.

Doreen tapped the agenda with her clear plastic pen. "We need to let Jack know we've invited Representative Green to the Founders Day Celebration."

"No, we don't." Council member Christopher Ling's tone was flat, as though he didn't want to debate the issue.

"Why not?" The air conditioner blasted the small, blue-carpeted room. Doreen pulled her rose linen blazer more tightly to her.

"Doreen, I believe you're being hasty." Nessa leaned back on her seat. Her round brown eyes were clouded with concern. The dark brown skin around her mouth was tight. "Representative Green may not even attend the event."

Doreen faced Nessa. "But he might. I don't want to leave this to chance."

CeCe Roben snorted, drawing her fingers through her pencil-straight auburn hair. "I would be more concerned about pissing off Jack unnecessarily. It took you long enough to convince him to participate. Why risk having him change his mind when we don't even know whether there'll be a problem?"

"It's common courtesy." Doreen swept her hand to encompass the council members. "Wouldn't you want to know?"

Christopher shrugged. "What's the worst that could happen? They'd see each other on the stage. What's the big deal?"

"The big deal is Isaac Green was sleeping with Jack's wife while they were still married and their daughter was dying." She shouldn't need to remind him of that painful scandal.

CeCe folded her hands on the table. "The situation would be very awkward. I understand your concern. But I still say we can afford to wait, at least until we hear back from Green's office."

These meetings with members of the Trinity Falls Town Council's Events Subcommittee were intended as updates. She wasn't seeking approval.

Doreen sat straighter on the blue-cushioned swivel chair. "I've followed up with Representative Green's office twice. I haven't heard from anyone." Yet another reason she disliked the state representative. "I don't want to wait too long to tell Jack. He'll need time to prepare."

Nessa glanced around the table. "Do we really believe Jack will honor his commitment to the event if he thinks his ex-wife and her new husband will be in attendance?"

Doreen's resentment stirred at the insult to Jack. "I think Jack deserves the opportunity to make that decision."

Nessa's eyebrows arched. "I don't. Besides, Kerry

may not accompany Representative Green to Trinity Falls. The situation would be uncomfortable for her as well."

Doreen could only hope Jack's ex-wife would show that level of sensitivity. "We can't take that chance."

CeCe shook her head. "I'm sorry, Doreen. I, for one, vote against our telling Jack the sesquicentennial committee invited Representative Green to the Founders Day Celebration."

There was a general murmur of agreement around the table.

The council members were wrong on this count. Luckily, Doreen didn't have to listen to them. "I'm sorry. I somehow gave you the impression this decision was open to a vote. I'm not asking for your permission. I'm keeping you informed."

Christopher exchanged glances with the other two council members before returning his dark gaze to Doreen. "You aren't mayor yet, Doreen. You can't make decisions like this on your own."

CeCe chuckled. "That's right. And, since Simon is petitioning to run against you, your election isn't guaranteed anymore."

Doreen counted to ten, then drew a calming breath. "Thank you for your input. I do realize I'm not mayor. That's why I consulted with Ramona. She agreed that I should tell Jack that Representative Green may attend the event."

"Why did you speak with Ramona before meeting with us?" There was a hint of censure in Christopher's tone.

Doreen tilted her head to the side. "She's the mayor."

CeCe waved a hand dismissively. "But we're the council's Events Subcommittee."

Doreen inclined her head. "Representative Green's invitation to the sesquicentennial came from the mayor's office."

"You're quite right, Doreen." Nessa lifted her hands, palms out. "Your group is in charge of the event. You don't need this committee's approval."

"Thank you." Was she imagining things or was the councilwoman's tone patronizing?

Nessa returned her hands to the table. "I just hope Jack proves to be more reasonable than his past behavior would indicate."

Doreen dropped her gaze to the table. She dreaded her coming confrontation with Jack.

"Leo signed Simon's petition. And then he broke up with me." Doreen sat at Books & Bakery's kitchen table with Megan, baking and drinking coffee before the store opened Tuesday morning.

Megan blinked. "I can't believe it. Why?"

Doreen lowered her mug. "Why did he break up with me, or why did he sign the petition?" Their conversation seemed surreal, as though other people were having it.

Megan covered Doreen's hand with her own. "Doreen, I know you're worried about Simon's petition, but there's no reason to be. Even if his name is added to the ballot, Simon is not a viable challenger to your campaign. Leo knows that."

"No, he doesn't." Doreen stared into her mug of

coffee. "He signed the petition because he doesn't want me to be mayor. He wants me to be his wife."

Megan blinked again. "Leo proposed?"

Doreen balanced her elbows on the table and propped her head in her palms. "Yes, but I told him I need more time. I need to know who I am without Paul before I can be myself with him."

Megan came around the table to hug Doreen's shoulders. "Give Leo time, Doreen. He'll soon realize he's being an idiot. Ean didn't want you to run for office at first, either. Now he's your biggest supporter."

Doreen met Megan's eyes. "I announced my decision to run for office seven months ago. If Leo hasn't come to his senses by now, he's not going to. Instead, he's signed Simon's petition to hurt my campaign."

The bell chimed on the industrial oven. Doreen grabbed a mitt from the wall. She pulled out the brownie tray and set it on the counter to cool.

Megan replaced it with several trays of cookie dough. "I can't understand why you're worried about Simon. You were prepared to run against Ramona. She would have been a much stronger challenge to your campaign than Simon. So why are you concerned about him?"

Doreen crossed back to the table and sat. "I could handle losing to Ramona. I didn't agree with some of her plans for Trinity Falls, but she's a good mayor."

Megan followed Doreen. "I agree."

"But losing to Simon would mean that all of my hard work, all of my efforts to help improve the community, mean nothing to anyone."

Megan's hand closed over Doreen's wrist. "You shouldn't feel that way."

"Why not?"

"First, Simon hasn't filed his petition."

"Yet."

"Second, if he's allowed to campaign, you're going to defeat him, so stop worrying about Simon and let's figure out what we're going to do about Leo."

"There isn't anything to do. He broke up with me."

"He'll come around, Doreen. Just give him time." Megan checked her watch. "Come on. We need to open the store."

Doreen followed Megan out of the kitchen. "He wants me to choose between him and the mayor's office. I don't know why I can't have both."

"This is the twenty-first century. You *can* have both." Megan's voice was tight with indignation.

"Not in Leo's world." Doreen peeked around Megan at the sight of a customer waiting outside. "Is that Alonzo?"

Alonzo tipped his brown felt campaign hat at them from the other side of the front door. Megan turned the lock to let him in.

"Morning, ladies." The sheriff crossed the threshold, tucking his hat under his arm. He looked very official in his short-sleeved tan shirt, black tie, and spruce green gabardine pants.

"Good morning, Alonzo." Doreen's worries eased under the warmth of her old friend's regard.

"Are you making Books and Bakery part of your morning routine?" Megan's tone teased him.

Alonzo nodded toward Doreen. "I could get used to Doreen's breakfasts."

Doreen led him back to the café, while Megan went to her office. "That's nice to hear, Alonzo. But the scrambled eggs and bacon you order aren't anything fancy."

Alonzo's husky chuckle further lightened her mood. "You haven't had my eggs and bacon, or my coffee."

"Tired of your own cooking?"

"And my own company." A dimple appeared at the right corner of Alonzo's mouth.

"I can understand that." Doreen remembered those lonely mornings after Paul had died.

She continued behind the counter as Alonzo settled onto one of the stools. She poured him a mug of coffee, careful to leave room for cream this time.

"Thank you." Alonzo's gaze was direct but wary. "I need to tell you something."

Doreen returned the coffee to its warmer, then searched his eyes. "What is it?"

Alonzo held her gaze. "Simon again asked me to sign his petition. I—"

"I understand, Alonzo." Doreen looked away. "If Simon wants a chance to campaign for office, we don't have the right to stand in his way."

"I didn't sign his petition."

Doreen's head snapped around in surprise. "What?"

"I don't want to call Simon Knight 'Mayor.'" Alonzo stirred cream into his coffee. "But I thought you should know he's accusing you of exerting undue influence on your customers to convince them not to sign his petition."

"Thanks for letting me know." Doreen studied Alonzo's proud, tan features, his kind coffee eyes. "Why haven't you ever married?"

Alonzo sipped his coffee. "Never found the right woman."

"You're only a few years older than me. Are you telling me you've never been in love?"

His gaze wavered. "I didn't say that."

"Morning, Ms. Doreen." Darius interrupted them.

Doreen reluctantly turned away from Alonzo. "Good morning, Darius. The usual?"

Darius settled onto the seat beside the sheriff. "Yes, ma'am."

She filled Darius's mug with coffee. "Two orders of bacon and eggs coming up."

Darius sensed Alonzo's tension beside him. It didn't take a mind reader to know he'd interrupted something important. "Morning, Sheriff."

Alonzo pulled his gaze from the kitchen door through which Doreen had disappeared. "Morning. I was surprised you hadn't written the *Monitor* article about your father."

"It would've been a conflict of interest." Darius was satisfied with his cover story. It wasn't a lie.

"Is that right? I think you would've done a better job, though." Alonzo drank more coffee.

Darius inclined his head. "Thanks."

"Saw you heading out of town again Saturday. You left later than usual."

"You don't miss much, do you?"

"Wouldn't be much of a sheriff if I did." Alonzo

met Darius's gaze. "You've visited this person every weekend for years. Must be very special."

"Is there a question in your future?" Darius enjoyed the game of wits with the sheriff.

Alonzo shook his head. "Just an observation."

"I have a couple of questions for you."

"Is that right?"

"Why would a person return to his hometown after more than forty years? And why wouldn't he go after the person he'd come back for?"

To the casual observer, the sheriff appeared relaxed. But Darius noticed the tight grip with which his companion held his mug.

"You'd have to ask that person." Alonzo's gaze flickered, but he didn't look away.

"I just did." Darius picked up his own mug and savored his coffee. "I'm glad Quincy finally found the courage to admit his feelings to Ramona. He's a changed man now, much happier. What do you think?"

"Yes, he is."

"They say confession is good for the soul, Sheriff." Darius's words echoed in his own mind. Maybe confession would be good for Simon's soul as well. Should he dare force the issue?

CHAPTER 13

"Doreen invited me to Quincy and Ramona's going-away party." Audra's delivery seemed deceptively casual.

Jack packed their breakfast dishes into the dishwasher. He watched Audra scrub the pan she'd used to cook their breakfast this Tuesday morning.

"Would you like to go together?"

"Yes, I would." She tossed him a smile as she set the pan on the drain board.

Audra and Jack had fallen into a morning routine: a five-mile run, breakfast, then a kiss before work. He was getting used to it. Perhaps, too used to it.

"Thank you."

"For what?" Audra dried her hands on a kitchen towel.

She'd changed into a vivid orange T-shirt and warm purple shorts after their jog. When she returned to L.A. in two weeks, he'd miss the color she'd brought into his life. He'd have to soak it in while she was here.

"For helping me talk about Zoey." Jack turned away from her soft champagne eyes. "I'm still not comfortable talking about my feelings, but it's easier now than it's ever been."

"I'm glad." Audra laid her hand on his shoulder. "I'd love to hear more about her, whenever you're ready."

Jack's skin warmed under Audra's touch. "What about you?"

"What do you mean?" She let her hand drop.

Jack resisted the urge to put her hand back. "Is there anything you'd like to share with me?"

"Like what?"

Jack held her gaze. "Wendell."

"I've told you all there is to say about him."

"Would you take him back?"

"He's with someone else, Jack." She turned away from him and left the kitchen. "Do you honestly think I'd have a relationship with him when he's engaged to a woman who's having his baby?"

That wasn't an answer. "Some people wouldn't let that stop them." Kerry hadn't.

"I'm not one of those people." Audra curled up on the sofa. "Wendell's pregnant fiancée isn't the only reason I ended our relationship. I realized he was only dating me for my industry connections. He never cared about me."

Jack sat beside her. "If he doesn't care about you, why is he still calling you?"

She pulled on her right earlobe. "He probably wants my help with some other scheme."

"Would you take him back?" Jack wanted a straight answer.

"No. I don't want anything to do with him ever again."

His muscles relaxed. "Good."

"Why is that good?"

"Because the idea of you reuniting with him makes me want to throw up." What had made him say those words out loud? Maybe getting in touch with his feelings hadn't been a good idea. For the first time in his life, he felt as though he'd said too much.

Audra's eyes widened. She searched his face. "We're not supposed to get attached, remember? This is only a summer romance." Her voice was soft, uncertain.

But Jack had come too far to back off now. He drew a finger down her arm. "Whatever the season, as long as we're together, I want to be the only man on your mind."

Jack leaned in and took her lips with his. His heart kicked when her body softened against him. He drew her onto his lap and deepened the kiss, pushing his tongue past her lips. He tasted her sigh as she let him in. Jack explored her mouth, stroking her tongue with his.

He'd told her the truth when he said he wanted to be the only man on her mind. He hadn't realized he'd felt that way until the words had fallen from his tongue. But ever since she'd sashayed into his life, wearing only a black plastic trash bag, Audra Lane had been the only woman on his mind.

With his hands, Jack feathered the soft curve of Audra's cheek, traced the graceful lines of her

back. He loved the silken texture of her bare arms.
If they were to have only these few short weeks, he
wanted to know her everywhere. He needed to
imprint her touch, taste, and scent on his mind
to get through the long, lonely nights without her.

Audra's slender arms wrapped around his shoulders. Jack broke their kiss and pressed his face into
the curve of her neck. He breathed deeply, filling
his lungs with her scent, soft and sweet. It brought
images to mind of the time they'd spent together:
fishing, hiking, dancing, loving. His body throbbed.
His muscles tightened. Just for now. Just for the
summer. He'd have to make these memories last.

He stroked his tongue over the long, delicate
arch of her neck. Jack felt a flare of possession as
Audra trembled in his embrace.

"I love the way you feel."

"I love what you do to me. You cast a spell on
me." Audra's words were breathless.

Jack sought her lips again. This time, he took the
kiss deeper, moving beyond her feel and flavors,
and seeking her essence. Audra moved under him.
Her shallow breaths and racing pulse resounded
through him. Her fingers drilled into his muscles
through his shirt.

With his own breathing ragged, Jack freed her
mouth and sat up. "Too many clothes."

"Yes." Audra stripped off his T-shirt and reached
for his shorts.

"You too." Jack's hands shook as he helped
Audra remove his clothing and hers as well. "You
take my breath away."

Audra wrapped her arms around his neck. "You
make my head spin."

Jack kissed his way to her shoulders, then lower to her breasts. He drew her left nipple into his mouth as he teased her right one, rubbing it between his fingers.

Audra's body undulated beneath him. Her movements were driving him to the edge. Her breath came thin and fast, like music to Jack's ears. He smoothed his hand lower, past her waist, lingering near her hip. He used his knee to nudge her legs apart, then stroked a finger intimately between her folds.

"*Jack.*" Audra gasped as her hips lifted from the sofa. She pinned him with her gaze. "I need to touch you."

Jack's muscles almost spasmed. Her small hand pressed against his chest and he let her push him onto his back. Audra straddled him. She took his hand, trailed her tongue across his palm, then placed it on her breast. The heat in her eyes nearly melted his bones.

Jack sighed, palming her breast and caressing her soft skin. "Kiss me again."

Audra's warm body settled over him like a sensual blanket. She covered his mouth with hers.

Jack parted his lips and let her in. His mind spun as the taste of her had a different type of tension throbbing through him. He wrapped his arms around her waist, then slid one hand down to stroke and knead her derriere.

Audra released his lips to rain kisses across his chest, licking and nipping his pecs. She strummed the muscles at his abdomen, taking an inordinate amount of time at his hips. There wasn't an inch of Jack's body that didn't feel her touch. His erection grew increasingly painful as her fingers moved closer, then farther away from his manhood.

Jack exhaled on a groan. "Audra, you're killing me."

Her breath came closer, brushing over the part of him that strained to join with her. "I wouldn't want to do that."

Audra covered him with her mouth. Jack's toes curled. His hips tensed. He moaned long and deep. He felt greedy that he wanted more, yet anxious to love her the same way.

She worked his breadth and licked his length, sucked his tip over and over and over again. His hips moved to the rhythm she set with her mouth and her hand. His heart pounded in his chest. Sweat broke out on his upper lip. *"Audra."*

She leaned away from him, licking her lips. "Now we need that condom."

Audra stretched her lithe body toward the floor to claim the condom from his shorts pocket. As she rolled the rubber over his rock-solid erection, Jack reached forward to tease between her thighs. Moaning, Audra closed her eyes. Her hips pumped in response. Pleasure softened her pixie features.

Jack wanted nothing more than to join with her and give them both the release their bodies cried for. But not yet.

"It's my turn to love you." Switching places with her, Jack raised up on his knees and hooked her legs over his shoulders.

Audra's eyes widened. "What are you doing?"

Jack cupped her hips. "Loving you."

Audra's breath rushed from her lungs. She shut her eyes again as Jack palmed her hips, opening her to his tantalizing tongue. He focused on her most sensitive flesh, kissing her, licking her, tugging her with his lips. Blood swooshed in her ears. Her muscles trembled in his palms. Her body moved like a puppet in Jack's capable hands. She wanted to race to the finish. She wanted these sensations to go on and on. Her body was flooding with desire. She moaned and panted her pleasure.

Oh, God, this feels so good! What he was doing to her—loving her, learning her—no one had ever made her feel this treasured, this desirable ever before.

Her skin moistened with perspiration. Her hips rocked in time with his long licks and deep kisses. Her muscles pulled tighter and tighter, deeper and deeper. Then her body went stiff. Audra screamed as she climaxed under Jack's thorough attention.

Her muscles were still shaking as Jack lowered her legs. He surged into her with one deep thrust. The sensation was achingly sweet, painfully intense. Audra pressed her head back against the sofa cushion and opened her mouth to scream again. Jack covered her lips with his. She raked his back with her short nails, feeling her body tossed under echoing waves of erotic pleasure.

Jack worked her body with a hard and fast rhythm. Audra met his demands and made her own. She'd never felt this free, this confident, this adventurous with anyone else. They rocked together as the pressure built inside her again. Audra gripped Jack's hips, urging him even deeper. Her body strained to meet his. His groan echoed in her ear. Her back arched and lights exploded behind her eyes.

Jack ripped his mouth from hers. Then he climaxed, holding her tight as their bodies shook. They shared their release, flying over the edge together and landing, wrapped in each other's arms, as one.

Quincy lowered his voice. He leaned closer to Darius as they sat beside each other at the Books & Bakery food counter Wednesday morning. "Are people signing your father's petition because they think that he'll make a good mayor, or because they want a real election?"

Darius almost lost his appetite for his half-eaten breakfast of scrambled eggs and bacon. "At least you waited until Doreen went into the kitchen before you asked."

Quincy frowned. "I know better than to ask when she's around."

"Those doctoral studies are finally paying off, huh?"

Quincy ignored the insult. "So what do you think?"

"I think you should change the subject."

"All right." Quincy cut into his blueberry pancakes. "Did you do anything special this weekend?"

"No." Darius dug into his breakfast, willing his appetite to return.

"You're not going to tell me about her, are you?" Quincy's look was chastising.

"Who?"

"Stop playing dumb. You've been visiting a woman in the next town every weekend for the past five years. All this time, I've respected your privacy.

But now I'm leaving town. Are you going to tell me about her or not?"

Darius swallowed his final bite of toast. "No."

Quincy's sigh was heavy with exasperation. "Man, I'm leaving Trinity Falls in three weeks. At least tell me the name of your mystery woman in Sequoia."

"You make it sound as though we're never going to see each other again." Darius eyed his childhood friend. "You're moving to Philadelphia. You're not going off planet."

"Come on, Darius. Who is she? Your secret will be safe with me."

"That's good to know. How's the search going for your replacement?"

"Fine." Quincy sighed again. "I can take a hint."

"That's a first." Darius mumbled into his mug of coffee.

Quincy ignored him again. "The search committee offered the position to the professor from New York. She accepted."

Darius lowered his coffee mug. Curiosity stirred in him. "Why would she leave NYU for Trinity Falls University?"

Quincy forked up the rest of his pancakes. "You can ask when you interview her for the *Monitor*."

"What do you know about her?" Darius bit into his bacon.

"She has an impressive CV." Quincy referred to the professor's curriculum vitae. "She graduated from Penn a couple of years after I did. But she got her Ph.D. from NYU."

"*Curiouser and curiouser.* TFU is a good school, but it's a stepping-stone. It's not a destination—unless you have ties to the area."

Quincy finished his coffee. "I don't think she has family here."

"What's her name?"

"Peyton Harris."

The name didn't ring any bells for Darius, either. But he did love a good mystery, and this sounded like one. "I'm looking forward to meeting her."

"She'll be here next Tuesday."

"That soon?" Darius pushed away his empty plate.

"She needs to find a place to stay." Quincy propped his forearms on the counter. "Classes start in the middle of August. That's less than a month away."

"You're still here." Darius drained his coffee.

Quincy's grin was smug. "Ah, but that's because Ramona loves the thrill of apartment hunting. She enjoys the exploration and stress. We're looking at a couple of places this weekend. Care to join us?"

Darius recognized the not-so-subtle trap. He stood, smiling tauntingly. "No, thanks. I've got other plans."

Quincy's smile morphed into a frown. "How did you meet her?"

"You just won't give up, will you? That's admirable." Darius started to walk past his friend to the register.

Quincy stopped him with a hand on his forearm. "All kidding aside, man, I'm worried about you." He released his grip. "After I leave, who's going to keep your perpetual moodiness at bay?"

Darius had wondered the same thing. He and Quincy had been friends their entire lives. They were more like brothers. Quincy's family had been his refuge when his dysfunctional parents had threatened to overwhelm him. As much as he teased the other man, he'd miss the hell out of him, once he was gone.

"You aren't my only friend, you know." Darius tried a cocky tone. "Ean's back and Jack's still here."

"Ean's with Megan, and Jack's still grieving. Why don't you think about moving to Philadelphia? There are some good newspapers there."

Darius was shaking his head before Quincy finished his pitch. "I'm happy with the *Monitor*."

"What's keeping you here?"

"Trinity Falls is home. You, Ean, and Ramona may want more, but I'm fine here. Ean came back after trying the big city." Darius pulled out his wallet. "Who knows? In a couple of years, you and Ramona may move back, too."

Quincy stood. "Why are you being so secretive about this woman? Is she good for you?"

Darius cocked an eyebrow. "This from the man who waited fourteen years to tell his friends he was in love with the mayor?"

"That was different. Ramona was with Ean." Quincy frowned. "Is your girlfriend married?"

Darius snorted. "Give me some credit."

Quincy lowered his voice again. "I don't know, man. If you can't even introduce her to your friends, you may not want to keep seeing her. This may not be a healthy relationship for you."

Darius laughed. "I'll keep that in mind, Mom."

"Yuck it up, Darius, but I'm serious. I won't be here much longer to watch your back."

Darius patted the other man's shoulder. "I hear you, Q."

He appreciated Quincy's concern. But there were some things you couldn't tell even your best friend.

Doreen's smile froze. Leonard had just entered the café area with the Heritage High School English teacher Wednesday afternoon. Why was his hand riding the small of the skinny woman's back? Why was he standing so close to her? Doreen's heart contracted as she watched him settle her at a table in the center of the dining area.

Ramona interrupted her description of the Philadelphia apartments she'd arranged to view with Quincy. She followed Doreen's gaze. "What is Leo doing with Yvette Bates?"

"That's what I'd like to know." Doreen's heart was ready to jump from her chest. She tracked Leonard's progress to her. "Why are you here with Yvette?"

Leonard's brown gaze was cool. "We're here for lunch."

Doreen wasn't in the mood for games. "Lunch with a friend, or is she something more?"

Leonard shot a quick glance at Ramona before turning back to Doreen. "Can we speak in private?"

What game is he playing?

Doreen looked at Ramona, who sat as though enthralled by their show. She struggled to keep her voice low. "If you wanted to keep our business private, you shouldn't have come here with another woman. You broke up with me five days ago. Are you already dating?"

Ramona gasped. "You two broke up? Why?"

"Do you mind?" A spark of temper showed in Leonard's eyes when he met Doreen's gaze. Good. "You don't know what you want, Dorie. You're your own worst enemy. You want all or nothing, but all or nothing of what? Do you even know?"

Doreen unclenched her teeth. "I know exactly what I want."

"So do I. I want a wife."

Ramona gasped again. "Leo proposed to you?"

Doreen ignored Ramona's interruption. "Your definition of a wife is someone who sits at home, waiting for you with dinner on the table."

Leonard's expression twisted as his temper built. "I want someone I can share my life with."

"But you aren't willing to share hers."

Ramona's hum interrupted their exchange. "She's got you there, Leo."

Doreen shook her head. "Ramona, please."

Leonard turned his temper to Ramona. "Mind your business."

Ramona sipped her coffee, but never took her attention from Doreen and Leonard. Doreen looked around and realized Ramona wasn't the only customer using her and Leonard as entertainment. Even Yvette watched them with a dismayed expression.

"Come on." Doreen led the way into the kitchen.

"I told you," Leonard muttered.

Doreen took a position beside the ovens and glared across the room at Leonard. "I had no idea you were such a selfish person."

Leonard pressed an index finger to his chest. "I'm selfish? You're the one who's walking away from our relationship because you don't have time for me."

"I'm not going to give up who I want to be. If that's not the woman you want to live with, then go ahead and have *lunch* with Yvette." She nodded toward the dining area, just beyond the kitchen door.

Leonard tossed his arms. "So that's it? You're walking away from me? From us?"

Doreen battled the tears burning her eyes. "You broke up with me."

"I'm in love with you, Dorie."

Doreen crossed her arms. "You've got a strange way of showing it."

"How long am I supposed to wait for you?"

She shook her head. "You're in love with who you want me to be. But I've finally figured out who I want to be. I won't let anyone else take that decision away from me. Not even you."

She held his gaze for what seemed like an eternity. She willed him to change his heart, to be supportive, excited, happy for her. Leonard finally broke eye contact and turned away. Doreen leaned against the kitchen counter, watching Leonard leave. She lowered her head and slapped away the tears that dared to trail across her cheeks.

"Doreen?" Ramona stood in the kitchen doorway. "Leo's gone."

"What?" Doreen straightened from the counter.

"He and Yvette have left Books and Bakery. Are you all right?"

"I will be." She hoped. Doreen turned toward the cabinet above the counter. She selected a coffee mug and filled it with water.

"Do you want me to get Megan?"

Doreen gulped the drink before turning to Ramona. "Why?"

"She could get someone to cover the bakery for you so you could go home."

Doreen finished her water. She put the empty mug in the dishwasher before crossing the kitchen. "I'll be fine."

Ramona laid her hand on Doreen's shoulder. "You did the right thing, standing up for yourself that way."

"I know." But why was she having second thoughts?

CHAPTER 14

"How's my favorite songwriter?" Benita's overly chipper voice and flattering comment put Audra on instant alert Wednesday afternoon.

She gripped the cell phone and looked away from her guitar and draft lyrics. "What's wrong?"

Benita sighed. "OK. I won't try to bullshit you. The producer wants something to work on now."

Audra sat straighter on the overstuffed sofa. Her gaze swept the cabin's great room. "His contract says I have another two weeks before I have to deliver the songs."

"I know. I know. But he's anxious to get started on the album." A keyboard clicking in the background accompanied Benita's reply.

"I don't have anything for him." It was a strain, but Audra managed to keep her temper from her voice.

This wasn't the first producer she'd ever worked with who'd agreed to a contract, then forgot the little details, like payment dates and delivery deadlines. It hadn't been an inconvenience in the past. Audra usually beat her deadlines. But this time, it was a problem. She'd never had to deal with writer's block before. Hopefully, she'd never have to deal with it ever again.

A printer whirred on the other end of the cellular phone line. Benita's response was barely audible beneath it. "He only needs one song, just something to get him started. Don't you have just one song?"

"No, Benita, I don't." She stood and wandered to the front window, tipping the sheer green curtain aside. The scene that waited for her felt like home after only two weeks. "You should remind the producer we have a contract. He can cool his heels because he won't see anything from me for another two weeks."

"That's what I told him."

"Then why are we having this conversation?" Audra turned away from the window. She walked to the kitchen for a glass of water.

"Because after I told him he would be in breach of contract to request early delivery of any of the songs, he offered to pay you a bonus for each song you delivered before your deadline."

Audra had to laugh. Obviously, the producer knew the way to Benita's heart was paved with Benjamins.

She pulled a glass from the cupboard and poured herself ice-cold water from the pitcher she stored in the refrigerator. "I appreciate your looking out for my financial best interests, but I don't want to rush the process. The quality of the songs would suffer."

"'Rush the process'?" Benita snorted. "You've been at Harmony Cabins for almost two weeks. I thought for sure you'd have at least one song completed by now. What have you been doing?"

Audra took a healthy swallow of water. "I took your suggestion. I've been meeting new people and trying new things." And having great sex.

Her manager sighed. The tapping in the background sounded like a pencil hitting Benita's desk. "OK, but now it's time to get some work done."

Audra rinsed her glass and turned it upside down on the drain board. "I have been working, Benita. I'm almost done with a song."

"Why didn't you say that? When will you be done?"

"I don't want to rush this. I want to make sure we're ready."

"Of course. Of course. When?"

Audra shook her head. She never should have said anything. Now Benita was rushing her to submit the song. "Tell the producer I'll send him the song when it's ready and not a day before. All right?"

Silence greeted her on the other side. Audra refused to be the one to break the impasse. She had a contract, darn it, and she had another two weeks to fulfill it.

"You've changed." Benita's voice was pensive.

"What are you talking about?"

"You used to be more accommodating, more willing to please. Now you're assertive, less willing to take shit from anyone—me, the producer, probably your parents as well."

Audra frowned. "I don't think I'm any different."

"How are things with you and Jack?" Benita's abrupt shift of topic caught Audra off balance.

"We're fine." Audra's mind raced to remember what she'd told Benita about her impressions of the property owner.

"The last time we spoke, you said he was being surly. Do you want me to talk with him? Get him to leave you alone?"

"No." Audra forced a measured tone. "I can handle him."

"Yeah, you've changed."

Audra sensed Benita's verbal nod. "I feel as though I'm the same."

"But you're not. I like it." Drawers opened and shut in the background. A stapler crunched. "I'll tell the producer to keep his jockeys on. We'll talk more next week. In the meantime, remember this is a working vacation. Get those songs written."

Benita ended the call as she always did—without saying good-bye. Audra stared at the receiver in her hand. Was Benita right? Had she changed?

If so, it was Jack's influence. She'd spent the most time with him. Audra smiled as she returned to the great room and her music. Maybe they were having a positive influence on each other. That would be a wonderful memento of her time at the cabins when she returned to Los Angeles. Her smile faded with that thought.

Jack left his car in front of Audra's garage and jumped the three steps to her porch Friday night. She was singing again. Her voice, accompanied by her guitar, floated through her half-open window.

Jack paused outside her door and listened for a while. She really did have a beautiful voice.

Was Audra ready for Quincy and Ramona's going-away party, or had she been so distracted by her music that she'd forgotten about the event? Jack knocked twice on her cabin's front door and prepared himself to wait. But when Audra answered his knock, he received a very pleasant surprise.

"You're right on time." Audra offered him a smile and pulled the door wider.

She wore a short-sleeved wine-red minidress. The color was similar to the gown she'd worn to the Grammy Awards. Her curly, dark brown hair floated above her shoulders.

Jack entered the cabin, turning to keep his eyes on her. "You look beautiful."

"Thank you. So do you." Her eyes glowed.

She collected her purse before preceding Jack onto the porch. After Audra locked the cabin, Jack escorted her to his silver Toyota Tundra. Should he put his hand on her back, her elbow? Before he could decide, they'd arrived at his vehicle. Jack helped her into his truck, then circled to the driver's side. He got behind the wheel and guided them off the Harmony Cabins property.

This evening would be more stressful than jogging, hiking, or fishing. It was a *real* date, not just a picnic or a dinner cooked together. He hadn't dated in twelve years. Even the word had the power to make him feel as clumsy as a high-school student taking his sweetheart to the prom.

Was it his imagination or were the first few minutes of the ten-minute drive into town awkward? Audra's warmth filled the close confines of the truck's cab. He breathed her scent—soap and vanilla. It made him want to turn the truck around and take her to bed.

"Thanks for coming with me. It's been a long time since I've socialized. I'm out of practice." He was out of practice with a lot of things. What do you talk about on a date with a beautiful woman?

"Thank you for inviting me." She sounded distracted. "Trinity Falls is so beautiful."

Jack glanced over and saw her staring out the window at the trees, bushes, and a clear blue sky. He smiled, feeling more relaxed.

There was a rustling sound as she turned to face him from her passenger seat. "How long have you known Quincy and Ramona?"

"We grew up together."

"Is that the reason you decided to break your moratorium on socializing?"

His lips twitched with a smile. He enjoyed her sassy mouth, even when she was just talking. "Trinity Falls is a tight-knit community. But people—especially young people—don't stay. They want the attractions and excitement of a bigger city."

"You've stayed."

"This is home." It was getting easier to express his feelings, at least with Audra. But it still wasn't easy.

"I love it here."

Enough to stay? Jack frowned. *From where did that thought come?*

Jack turned onto Main Street and pointed his truck toward the high school. "You were singing when I came to pick you up. You have a beautiful voice. I still think you should perform your own songs."

She laughed again. "And I've told you, I'm not comfortable singing in public."

Jack stopped at a traffic light. "Will you sing for me?"

Her teasing look caressed his body and set his blood on fire. "I thought I already had."

A horn sounded behind them. The light had turned green. Jack swallowed hard, shaking his head to clear the mental images, then drove his truck across the intersection.

"How are your songs coming? Will you make your deadline?" His voice sounded rusty.

"I should." There was a smile in her voice. "But I don't want to talk about work. I don't want the real world to intrude on our fairy tale."

"I'm just trying to get to know you better." He pulled into the parking lot at Heritage High School.

She leaned across the bench seat and kissed him, then whispered against his lips. "I'm more than my job."

"Tell me." His tongue was thick in his mouth.

"I'd rather show you."

Jack groaned. His abdominal muscles tightened almost to pain. "We won't stay long."

Audra was charmed by Heritage High School's gymnasium. It had been transformed into a ballroom to host a gathering of friends—a very large gathering of friends. At least a dozen round tables were arranged across the gym's floor. Each was set with a white tablecloth and ten chairs. Two buffet tables loaded with food framed either side of the room.

Audra raised her voice to be heard above the music playing through hidden speakers. "How many people were invited to this party?"

Jack entwined his fingers with hers. "A lot."

She let him lead her to the center of the room, where friends surrounded the guests of honor. Conversations stopped as people turned to watch them.

Audra kept looking forward. "Why are people staring at us?"

Jack's grip tightened on her hand. "Most of them haven't seen me in almost two years."

"This is weird." She really meant it.

"Jack!" Ramona stepped out of the group and wrapped her arms around him. "I'm so glad you came."

Quincy stepped forward to give Jack a man hug. "I didn't think you'd make it."

A confusion of voices and half-finished sentences spun around Audra. The excitement was contagious. She couldn't stop smiling. From the corner of her eye, Audra noticed a camcorder coming toward her. She was about to ask what was going on when Ramona wrapped her in a hug.

"Thank you." Ramona gave Audra a hard squeeze.

"For what?" Audra hugged her back, despite her confusion.

"For convincing Jack to come to our going-away party." Ramona looked over her shoulder toward

Ean, Megan, Darius, Quincy, and Jack. "I know how much it means to Quincy to have him here."

Audra was moved by the love in Ramona's expression as she looked at Quincy. "I didn't have to convince Jack to come. *He* invited *me*."

Ramona blinked her surprise. "Then that makes his being here even better."

Audra jerked her head toward the hovering camcorder. "What's going on?"

Ramona chuckled. "Belinda offered to videotape the party, since Quincy's parents couldn't make the trip from Florida." She waved toward the camera lens. "Hi, Mr. and Ms. Spates."

Belinda Curby, owner of Skin Deep Beauty Salon, lowered her video equipment. Her brown face glowed with enthusiasm. "I got the camera for Christmas, but I haven't been able to really use it. This is a lot of fun."

Belinda weaved her way closer to the group of friends surrounding Quincy. "Darius, say something to the camera."

Darius lowered his drink. His smile looked strained. "Belinda, this is the second time you've asked me that. Shouldn't you be taping Quincy? The video's for his parents."

Just then, an older woman joined the group. "Well, Jack Sansbury, does a person have to leave town to shake you out of the woods?"

Jack bent over to embrace the tiny newcomer. "Ms. Helen, I'm glad to see you're still alive."

Audra's gasp was drowned by Ms. Helen's laughter. "So am I, you rascal." Ms. Helen reached up to slap Jack's chest. "What is this I hear about a woman staying at the cabins? Do you need a chaperone?"

"No, ma'am." Jack offered his hand to Audra. "Audra Lane, I'd like to introduce you to Dr. Helen Gaston."

Audra shook the older woman's small, frail hand. "It's a pleasure to meet you, Dr. Gaston."

"Don't pay Jack any mind, hon. He's been away from civilization so long he's forgotten that everyone calls me Ms. Helen." The older lady looked Audra over with a critical eye. "Your name is familiar to me. Who are your people?"

Audra hesitated, unsure what Ms. Helen meant. "I'm from California."

"Where in California?" The older lady wasn't easily put off.

"Near Los Angeles."

Ms. Helen mulled that over. "We won't hold that against you. How long are you staying?"

"I'll be here for the Founders Day Celebration."

"Good." Ms. Helen nodded once with decision. "Enjoy Trinity Falls. You know what they say, 'You only live once. But if you do it right, once is all you'll ever need.'"

Ms. Helen excused herself to join the buffet line. Audra, Jack, and his friends followed her. There were chicken dishes in a variety of spices, vegetables, salads, fruits, and carbohydrates. The desserts looked to have come from Books & Bakery. Audra hadn't realized how hungry she was until all of that food was laid out in front of her. The music changed three times while she was filling her plate. The songs were all popular club anthems, Ne-Yo, Beyoncé,

Pink, and Alicia Keys. She wiggled her shoulders during a particularly engaging bridge.

Jack leaned forward to whisper in her ear. "Do you need more room so you can dance your way through the buffet line?"

"I can't help it. Reflex." She glanced toward the open floor behind them. "Will there be dancing later?"

"I don't know." He shrugged the broad shoulders she intended to wrap in her arms later.

After filling her plate, Audra followed Jack, weaving her way around other hungry guests with loaded dishes. She stopped frequently to observe neighbors who greeted Jack with stunned pleasure. Some people she recognized as Books & Bakery regulars. Many others she hadn't seen before. Either way, she'd never remember all of their names.

Jack finally guided Audra to a table toward the front of the room, where Quincy and Ramona already sat with Ean, Megan, Darius, and Ms. Helen.

Doreen sat on Audra's other side. She leaned in closer and lowered her voice. "You've been here just two weeks. In that time, Jack has cut his hair, shaved his beard, and bought new clothes. You've brought him back to the community."

"I didn't have anything to do with his coming tonight," Audra whispered back. "He wanted to be here."

"And he wanted to be here because of you."

Across the table, a young woman stopped to say hello to Ms. Helen, then lingered over Darius. There was a lot of hair twirling and even more giggling before she moved on.

Audra returned her attention to Doreen. "I don't deserve any credit. This is all Jack."

Another attractive woman came to pay her respects to Ms. Helen before exchanging words with Darius. This visitor found a number of times and various ways to touch the reporter. Ms. Helen eventually shooed the young woman away.

Audra speared her mac and cheese as she looked around the room. Several people turned away as though embarrassed to be caught staring. Others smiled and nodded their approval. Of what?

"You're good for him." Doreen picked up her silverware, then froze as something across the room surprised her.

Audra followed Doreen's gaze. Leonard was in the buffet line, laughing with another woman. Audra hadn't met his companion. She was attractive, tall, and thin. She appeared to be around Leonard's age, though her bright pink summer dress and flirtatious manner made her seem much younger.

Audra's gaze skipped back to their table and the empty seat between Ms. Helen and Doreen. She'd assumed it was for Leonard. "Isn't Leo joining us?"

"Apparently not." Doreen dug into her food with jerky movements.

"Who's he with?" Not that Audra had the right to ask. She watched Doreen stuff a forkful of green beans into her mouth and chew. Could she even taste it?

Doreen washed down her food with ice water before answering. "Yvette Bates. She's one of Heritage High's English teachers."

Audra glanced toward the food line again, then

turned back to Doreen. There was hurt in the woman's warm brown eyes. "Did the two of you break up?"

Doreen lowered her gaze. "A week ago tomorrow."

Audra's jaw dropped. "And he's already dating?"

"He's looking for a wife. I guess there's no time to waste."

"I'm sorry." Audra watched Doreen move her food around her plate.

Across the table, Quincy, Ean, and Darius exchanged brotherly banter. Even Jack joined in the reminiscences from their high school escapades. Laughter rose from their table, seemingly oblivious to Doreen's dampened spirits.

"Is this seat taken?" A warm drawl interrupted their conversation.

Audra glanced up. She hadn't noticed Alonzo's approach. He was a handsome man with warm olive skin, wavy black hair, and laughing coffee eyes. He stood behind the empty chair next to Doreen, waiting to hear whether someone else had a prior claim to the seat. A chorus of "no" answered him. Audra wondered at the pleased expressions around the table. Perhaps she'd been wrong. Perhaps the others had noticed Leonard and his date at the buffet line.

As the sheriff and Doreen engaged in conversation, Audra turned her attention to Jack. His hot onyx gaze was waiting for her.

He leaned in close. "Are you having a good time?"

Audra could feel his body heat, smell his skin.

She sipped her ice water before answering. "Yes, I am. Are you?"

"Better than I thought I would. I'm glad you're here with me." His husky tone was foreplay.

"People are still staring at us."

"Does it bother you?" Jack folded her hand in his.

"A little."

"Don't let it. Ignore them."

Easier said than done. Audra looked around the table. Ean and Megan, Quincy and Ramona, neither couple seemed hungry, at least not for food. A steady stream of women continued to visit with Ms. Helen and flirt with Darius.

Belinda appeared, nudging the latest female visitor to the side. "Darius, say something for the camera."

Darius shook his head with a sigh. "Belinda, go bother Quincy."

Ms. Helen threw back her head with a laugh.

"Everyone, may I have your attention, please?" Councilwoman CeCe Roben interrupted the festivities, looking very professional in a navy blue dress and pearls.

Audra shifted on her seat to face the podium in the front of the room. Her knees grazed Jack's thighs. His heated gaze caused the breath to lodge in her throat. He gently squeezed her hand, then turned his attention to the councilwoman.

Able to breathe again, Audra tried to ignore the streams of electricity that coursed from Jack's palm up her arm to her breasts.

CeCe gestured toward their table. "We're here to bid farewell to two of our most prominent and well-regarded residents, Ramona McCloud and Doctor

Quincy Spates." She waited for the applause to die down before continuing. "Quincy is leaving after Founders Day, and Ramona will serve out her term as mayor, which ends in January. But before we celebrated our sesquicentennial, we wanted to celebrate our citizens. Quincy and Ramona, you've meant a lot to Trinity Falls. Come back and visit. Often."

Applause and choruses of "Hear, hear!" followed CeCe from the microphone. There were Grammy Award winners who could benefit from the council president's speechwriting abilities—succinct and from the heart.

Doreen pushed away from their table and stood behind the podium.

"Don't make us cry!" Darius begged from his seat.

Doreen brushed aside his comment with a chastising wave. Laughter echoed around the gym. Audra watched Jack's enjoyment. His white teeth flashed in a grin. His broad shoulders shook in a silent chuckle. Her heart tripped when she thought of Doreen's words: *"You've brought him back to the community."* That wasn't true. Jack had made the choice to rejoin his friends and neighbors. She was glad she'd been here to witness it.

Doreen spoke over the fading chuckles. "Quincy, you've always been such a good friend to my son, Ean. I felt like a second mother to you, all the time you spent at our house, eating our food." More laughter halted Doreen's words. "Ramona, you put your dreams on hold because the town needed you. Trinity Falls is a better place because of your dedication and efforts."

The applause was even more thunderous as Doreen returned to her seat.

Darius leaned toward the older woman and raised his voice. "I asked you not to make us cry."

Ms. Helen patted his shoulder. "It's almost over."

An expression of horror crossed Darius's face as he turned toward the podium. "What is he doing?"

CHAPTER 15

Simon stepped behind the microphone in the front of the gymnasium. "Good evening, everybody. How's everybody doing?"

A harsh expletive jerked Audra's attention from the podium. On the other side of the table, Darius shoved back his chair and rushed to the back of the room.

Simon continued speaking. "I wanted to say a couple of words, too, since Doreen Fever spoke. Equal time and all that, since we're going to be competing against each other for the mayor's spot." His laughter bounced out of the mic and circled the room.

Behind her, Audra watched Darius exchange words with Wesley Hayes, the part-time bookstore clerk, part-time disc jockey, and full-time high school student-athlete. Wesley stood between a flat control panel and a tall compact disc player. He seemed surprised by Darius's appearance. The young man's braids swung as he shook his head. Darius gestured adamantly at the audiovisual controls, then toward the podium.

Oblivious to the drama in the back of the room, Simon kept on talking. "Quincy, I applaud you for going after your dream. You were in love with Ramona for a long time, even while she was dating Ean, your best friend. The whole town knew it. Even Ramona knew it. The only person who didn't know it was Ean. And he's a lawyer."

Silence exploded in the gym. Audra stiffened. The tension in the room was oppressive. She shot a look at the nearby guests. They seemed equally stunned. Quincy, Ramona, Ean, and Megan were frozen.

Simon was either unaware or uncaring of his audience's discomfort. "I think everyone in this room is thinking the same thing. Why'd it take you fourteen years to tell her, son? Fourteen years. Really? It only takes nine months to have a baby." He chuckled at his own wit. "And another thing I was wondering—"

The microphone went mercifully quiet, cutting off Simon's failed amateur comedy hour. Instead, Kelly Clarkson's "What Doesn't Kill You (Stronger)" blared over the sound system.

Audra strained to locate Darius across the room. He shook Wesley's hand before marching to the podium. He jerked his startled parent away from the microphone and practically dragged him from the gym.

Shocked, Audra looked at the other dazed expressions around the table. "That was horrible."

Ms. Helen shook her head. Her eyes were glued

to the exit through which Darius had hauled Simon. "How did an idiot like Simon Knight manage to have a son like Darius?"

Jack shook his head. "That's a good question."

Ms. Helen scowled at Doreen. "You'd better not let that jackass win the election."

Audra considered Quincy, Ramona, Ean, and Megan. "Are you all right?" She could only imagine how mortified they were by the experience.

A muscle flexed in Ean's jaw. "Consider the source."

Quincy shrugged, but the movement seemed stiff. "Yeah. That's just Simon being Simon."

Ramona had blood in her ebony eyes. "I'm going to kill him."

Megan leaned over to rub her cousin's forearm. "No, you won't. You don't want murdering a constituent to be one of your last acts as mayor of Trinity Falls."

Ramona frowned. "I don't?"

Jack sat back on his seat. "I'm glad Darius had the presence of mind to ask Wesley to shut off the mic."

Ms. Helen pressed a thin hand to her small chest. "Oh yes. It could have been much worse."

Doreen rubbed her forehead. Her eyes were shadowed with concern. "I had no idea Simon would think he had to have equal time at the podium after I spoke. I'm so sorry."

Alonzo covered Doreen's hand with his. "That wasn't your fault. You weren't making a political speech."

Others in the group voiced their agreement.

Several minutes later, Darius returned to their

table. Color stained his sharp cheekbones. His classic features were stiff. He folded himself onto his chair before looking at Quincy, Ramona, Ean, and Megan. "I apologize to everyone, but especially to you. That was—"

"Knock it off," Quincy interrupted him. "We're not so simple that we're going to hold you responsible for what your father does and says."

"Ask me to dance." Ms. Helen demanded Darius's attention.

Darius stood again. "Ms. Helen, would you give me the honor of this dance?" His grateful smile was close but not quite up to his usual wattage.

Ms. Helen put her hand in Darius's and let him escort her to the makeshift dance floor. The music changed again. Beyoncé's "Angel" was taking a turn on the CD player. The dance floor grew more crowded as people—young, old, and otherwise—joined Ms. Helen and Darius.

Alonzo stood. He offered his hand to Doreen. "May I have this dance?"

Doreen smiled her surprise. "I'd love to."

Ramona and Megan both tugged their grudging partners from the table. Audra looked at Jack.

He gave her a bashful smile that oozed sex appeal. "I suppose you want to dance."

"Yes, I do." She returned his smile.

"It's been quite a few years since I even attempted it."

"I remember a night not so long ago."

His onyx eyes twinkled. "It's coming back to me."

Audra placed both hands on the hard muscles of his left thigh. They flexed beneath her palms. Her body reacted. She dropped her voice. "Consider it foreplay."

"In that case . . ." Jack stood.

They found a spot on the edge of the dance floor. Jack wrapped his arms around her waist and she twined hers behind his neck. His heat seeped into her wine-red dress. Audra felt safe and warm in his embrace. She could stay like this forever.

In fact, tonight everyone seemed under a spell in Trinity Falls: Ean and Megan. Quincy and Ramona. The expression on Alonzo's face as he held Doreen in his arms revealed more of his feelings than he'd probably intended.

Nearby, Leonard's mask of dislike as he glared at the couple startled Audra. She sensed Doreen's ex-lover knew he'd made a mistake in bringing a date to the party.

"Are you having a good time?" Jack whispered in her ear.

Audra shivered at the sensation, promptly forgetting Leonard. "I am. This is one of many nights I'll always remember."

Jack drew her closer. "And the night's not over yet."

Hours later, Jack pulled onto the graveled driveway in front of Audra's garage, then followed her to her cabin. If someone had told him two weeks ago, he'd spend the night dancing—and enjoy it—he would have had that person drug tested. But that's what had happened tonight. It hadn't been as much fun as dancing on Audra's patio, though.

Audra let him inside. "I've been to a lot of

functions, but Quincy and Ramona's going-away party tonight was definitely my favorite."

Her cell phone rang before he could agree.

"Who would be calling you this late?" Jack closed and locked the door behind them.

"It may be ten P.M. here, but it's only seven in California." Audra dug her cell phone from her purse. A look of annoyance creased her forehead before she tossed her phone onto her sofa. It stopped ringing.

"Who was it?" Jack knew the answer.

"Wendell." Audra drew her fingers through her thick dark hair.

"He's still calling you?" That sounded like jealousy threatening to darken his mood.

"I've told him to stop."

The thought of another man pursuing Audra didn't sit well with Jack. It made him feel like that fairy-tale beast Audra had compared him to weeks ago. His reaction was a problem. He was falling deeper under her magic, and that scared him to death. Jack fisted his hands. What would he do when it was time to say good-bye?

He took a deep breath, then another. *Let tomorrow worry about tomorrow.* He wanted to love Audra tonight. He wanted to give her so much pleasure that she wouldn't remember any lover before him or imagine any after him. Wasn't that how he felt? He couldn't imagine any other woman in his arms. Ever. He was falling deep. He was falling hard.

Jack closed the distance between them. "I don't want to think about Wendell."

"Neither do I." Audra spoke on a sigh that went straight to his blood.

Jack lowered his head to kiss her. Once again, her taste shot through his system like pure alcohol, making his head spin. He held her loosely in his arms. Audra's palms rested on his chest. Still kissing her, Jack walked her backward toward her bedroom, shedding their clothes as they went.

Audra smiled against his lips as she unbuttoned his shirt. "I love a man who can multitask."

Jack chuckled as he helped her take off his shirt. There was something sexy about teasing each other while making love.

He unzipped her dress. "You haven't seen anything yet."

Audra kicked off her shoes on her way into her bedroom. She shimmied out of her underwear. Jack watched her movements as he stripped off the rest of his clothes. He could watch her anywhere, all the time. In a crowded room or when it was just the two of them. Reading the paper or making love.

Jack pulled a condom from his wallet and tossed it toward her nightstand. It slid to a stop on the table's surface.

Naked, he went to her, stopping only a breath away. With his fingertips, he traced her lips and touched her hair. "Do you know how beautiful you are?"

Her smile was soft. Her skin was flushed. "You make me feel sexy and beautiful."

His hand followed where his gaze traveled over her body—breasts, waist, hips, arms. "It's not just the way you look. It's the way you move." He bent his head to nuzzle her neck. "The way you smell. It's who you are. You drive me crazy."

Audra crawled onto her bed, tugging Jack with

her. "You're my Prince Charming. I was sleeping before I met you." Her gaze dipped to his mouth. "You woke me with a kiss."

Jack shook his head as he followed her onto the mattress. "I'm no one's idea of Prince Charming. But you make me feel as though I could be."

Audra drew his head down for another soul-searing kiss. He pulled her closer into his embrace. Her lips were sweet beneath his. Her breasts were soft against his chest. Her hands smoothed down his back, stopping just above his hips.

They were a contradiction, the feelings building in him with her touch. He wanted to take her fast and hard. At the same time, he wanted to be gentle and move slowly. He'd never been with a woman who touched so many parts of him. Audra challenged his mind, healed his heart, and made his body throb and ache.

Jack drew her down to the mattress beside him. He kissed her longer, his tongue playing with hers. With his fingertips, he traced her side, from the swell of her breast to the curve of her hip. He wanted her to burn for him, just as she was making him burn.

He raised his head. "Tell me what you like."

Audra searched his eyes. "With you, everything."

"Good answer." He smoothed his hand over her breast, gently pinching her puckered nipple. "Do you like that?"

"Yes." Audra's breath was short.

He drew his fingertips down her body to her navel. Audra's stomach muscles quivered. "And that?"

"Very much." Her voice shook.

"And this?" He laid his hand on her nest of curls. He kissed her mouth, quick and hard, before he moved down her body.

Jack kissed and suckled her breasts until their nipples pebbled in his mouth. He licked his way down her torso, stopping to tease her navel and nip at her waist. Her skin was sweet and scented, smooth and soft. She was his fantasy with the power to draw him from the cold cave in which he'd been sleeping and back to the land of the living. He surged back up and over her.

Breathing hard, Audra shoved against him, causing them to roll across the bed until she lay on top of him.

"Tell me what you like," Audra whispered into his ear.

Jack grinned up at her. "Everything you've ever done to me."

Audra smiled back. "Good answer."

She straddled him, leaning closer to kiss his neck. A cool breeze from the air-conditioning brushed over her heated skin. She feathered her lips over his molded pecs and six-pack abs. The man was a work of art. She took her time, exploring his clean lines and fine angles.

Her ministrations left him with a thin sheen of perspiration and a great deal of heavy breathing. She did that to him. He gave her the courage to be the woman she wanted to be: assertive, strong, confident. Unafraid to give pleasure—or to take it.

Audra sat up. She met Jack's heavy-lidded gaze and knew he was feeling as hot and restless as she was. She stretched toward the nightstand for the condom. Her fingers shook as she tried to tear open the packet.

Jack covered her hands with his. "Let me." He took the packet from her, opened the foil, and offered her the condom.

Audra sheathed him, smoothing the latex over his length. Jack throbbed in her hold. Audra slowly lowered herself onto his erection. His length and breadth stretched her deliciously. She closed her eyes and gave herself up to the sensation.

She controlled their rhythm, rolling her hips, loving the feel of Jack deep inside her. His hands gripped her thighs. His hips flexed and lifted as he matched her movements.

Audra arched her spine, letting her head fall back. Jack's hands covered her breasts, molding and shaping them. His fingers teased her nipples, causing the pulse between her thighs to deepen.

His hand slipped down her torso to the juncture of her thighs. He touched her there, pressing, rubbing, moving against her. Audra's body burned. Her hips sped up. The muscles in her thighs tightened.

Beneath her, she sensed Jack's increasing urgency and knew he was racing toward the fall with her. She clenched her inner muscles, squeezing him. She heard him groan, felt her desire flowing over him. Jack stroked her harder, faster. Audra's nipples tightened. Her thighs tensed. Jack surged up into her, again and again. Audra gasped as the tension exploded inside her. Jack lifted her one last time before she fell, limp, onto his chest. He gathered her close and their bodies shook with pleasure.

A long time later, Audra rolled to Jack's side. "My

Prince Charming. 'And they lived happily ever after.'"

Jack's laughter rumbled in his chest. Audra kissed his neck. She snuggled closer and went to sleep.

The next evening, Audra surveyed Trinity Falls Cuisine's beige-and-gray stone walls and wood trim. The lighting was low, creating a romantic ambience. "When you suggested we go out to eat, I thought you meant something more modest."

"Like McDonald's?" Jack sounded dubious.

Audra's cheeks heated. "Maybe."

"I'll pretend you didn't say that." He opened the menu their hostess had left behind. "You must have gone to fancier restaurants in L.A."

Audra had an unpleasant flashback to the business lunches she'd attended. "They're opportunities to see and be seen by other industry professionals. But I can't pronounce the food and I'm always hungry when I leave."

Jack chuckled. "And I bet the meals cost a pint of blood as well."

"You'd win that bet." Audra was pleased to recognize several proteins and carbohydrates on the menu.

"I still don't understand why you don't sing your own songs."

Audra considered the dinner choices. Her mouth watered as she went down the list: roasted chicken, wood-fired steak, rosemary salmon. "You've asked me that before. I don't know how else to explain it. I don't enjoy performing, especially in front of crowds."

"Have you ever tried it?"

"In high school. Stage fright doesn't begin to describe how I felt."

Audra gazed around the restaurant again. Ean and Megan sat at a nearby table. Quincy and Ramona were dining together at an intimate booth. The couples were absorbed in each other. Did they even remember where they were?

"This seems to be a big date spot. What are *we* doing here, Jack?"

"Having dinner." He didn't look at her.

Audra arched a brow. "Don't get cute. Are you sure this is a good idea?"

"There's no harm in two friends going out to dinner." Jack eased back onto his bench seating.

Audra leaned forward. Friendship. The word left her wanting more. "Is friendship all we have?"

"That was our agreement, wasn't it?"

"Yes, it was." Audra searched Jack's onyx eyes. There was no emotion, no uncertainty.

Is it that easy for him?

"I've wanted to try this restaurant." Jack allowed his gaze to travel the dining room. "It's a new place, only eighteen months old. But I didn't want to come here by myself."

Were his choices coming alone or inviting her? That wasn't very flattering. But could she blame him? They'd agreed to a no-strings-attached relationship.

So why am I looking for strings?

Audra swallowed a sigh. "I'm glad I could keep you company."

"Me too." Jack's smile didn't distract her, as it usually did. "Besides, you needed a break to help clear your mind before getting back to work."

"Maybe." She wasn't as sure about that.

Audra refocused on the restaurant's menu and her dinner selection. It wasn't an easy decision. The descriptions were enticing, and the entrées carried to other patrons were mouthwatering: salads piled high with colorful vegetables and well-seasoned entrées that reminded her that she was starving.

When their server returned, they accepted their drinks and ordered their entrées. Audra narrowed her selection to the roasted chicken. Jack chose the New York steak, with long-grain rice.

"How's your songwriting coming?" Jack asked the question as their server left.

Audra squeezed her lemon garnish into her iced tea. "It's going really well. I'm almost done with two of the three songs."

"That was fast. It's only been two weeks." Jack drank his iced tea.

Audra was momentarily distracted by another diner's dessert tray.

"I'd started one of the songs last month before my writer's block hit. Benita suggested a change of venue might help. It seems she was right."

"Don't tell her that." Jack chuckled. "She'll never let you forget it."

Audra nodded. "I've heard she's always been a know-it-all."

"Probably since birth." He drank more iced tea. "What caused your writer's block?"

Audra's humor was forced this time. "This is a

big change from the Jack I met, who wouldn't string five words together."

"What do you mean?"

"Your curiosity has developed with a vengeance." Audra sipped her drink. "First you wanted to know what this restaurant is like. Now you're asking about my writing progress."

"I've been curious about you since you walked into the main cabin wearing a garbage bag."

"You're not going to let me forget that, are you?"

"*I'm* never going to forget it." Jack hid a grin behind his iced tea. "So tell me about your writer's block."

Audra hesitated just a moment longer. "I guess Wendell's lies bothered me more than I'd been willing to admit."

"That's understandable." Jack thought of his ex-wife, Kerry, and knew how Audra felt.

"I tried to go on as though nothing had happened, but I'd introduced him to my industry contacts. That made him part of my world. Every event I'd go to, he was there. Every restaurant and nightclub, I'd have to see him."

"You didn't stop going out, did you?"

Audra took a drink of her iced tea. "No, I wouldn't let him win. But winning isn't everything. And the strain was getting to me. He wanted to act as though we were still friends, when, in reality, I loathe him."

Jack's eyebrows shot up his forehead. He could understand her animosity, but he'd rather she didn't feel anything at all for the other man. "So breaking up with him gave you writer's block?" He didn't like that idea, either.

"No. Being made to feel like a clueless idiot gave me writer's block. I doubted myself."

"Why?" Jack followed the movement of Audra's right index finger as she traced the condensation on her glass.

"I'd pretty much ignored my personal life. I didn't go out much. In fact, if it wasn't career related, I didn't go out at all. I was so focused on building my career."

Jack was beginning to see more of the woman who'd invaded his every waking and sleeping moment. "Your drive explains your success at such a young age."

Audra laughed. "There are people who are much younger than I am in this industry, and much more successful. It's a young person's game these days."

"That must make the competition even harder."

"Yes. And it gave me tunnel vision to everything that wasn't related to my music. I was an easy target for Wendell."

Jack frowned. "What do you mean?"

Audra's sigh lifted her slender shoulders clothed in a buttercup yellow blouse. "I was dazzled by the first man who pursued me. It was even easier for him, because he was interested in music, too. We were together for five months. At first, I thought I'd found my soul mate. It turns out *he'd* found an easy entrée to connections that could help build his career. I ended our relationship three months ago."

"I'm sorry."

"I hope I've learned from the experience. Getting away from Los Angeles helped. But I won't mention that to Benita."

Jack's own disturbing memories brought a cloud. "I felt the same when I found out about Kerry's affair—angry and duped. Luckily, Kerry moved. But even having her almost two hundred miles away at the state capital in Columbus wasn't enough."

"Is that when you decided to buy the cabins?" Audra braced her elbow on the table and propped her chin on her fist.

"Zoey had loved Pearl Lake. We'd have picnics and go fishing at the lake as often as we could until she got too sick."

"Those are great memories." Audra's voice was a whisper, as though she didn't want to intrude on his thoughts.

"Yes, they are." Jack reached across the table to cup her hand. "Thanks for giving them back to me."

She turned her hand to link her fingers with his. "Thank you for sharing them with me."

Jack looked at their joined hands. Had he just made it that much harder to let go?

CHAPTER 16

What was bothering Doreen? Jack leaned back on his recliner and gulped his ice water. His guest perched on the plump sofa, catty-corner from him. She stared into her glass of water as though waiting for it to reveal her future. Her cream skirt suit, matching pumps, and pearl earrings were sure signs she'd attended church that morning. But judging by her rigid posture and the waves of tension emanating from her, the service hadn't eased her mind.

"I heard you had dinner with Audra at Trinity Falls Cuisine last night." Doreen's words were an abrupt departure from their previous less-than-stimulating conversation.

They'd progressed from the weather to last night's dinner. He was pretty sure neither subject had compelled Doreen to his cabin straight from church.

"Was my date with Audra part of the pre-service or after-service discussion?"

There was a saying in Trinity Falls, "All roads lead to church." It was the best place to hear the latest gossip about your neighbors.

Doreen sketched a smile. "Pre-service. You didn't think anyone could have made it through the entire sermon without sharing the news, did you?"

"I guess not." Jack drained his glass.

"That young woman has been a healing influence on you."

"Yes, she has." Thanks to Audra, he was almost human once more. Zoey was back in his life, at least her memory. And he gave a damn again.

"I'm going to be sorry to see her go."

So will I. "She has a life in L.A." If he repeated the words enough times, maybe he could accept them.

Doreen sipped her water. "And you have to continue rebuilding your life here."

The conversation was getting away from him. Jack set his glass on the coaster on the table beside him. "Doreen, we've talked about Ean's practice, the weather, and now my personal life. Why don't you tell me what's really on your mind?"

Doreen tipped back her head and drained her glass of water. Not a good sign.

She squared her shoulders before meeting his gaze. "Representative Isaac Green is going to attend the Founders Day Celebration. Kerry's probably coming with him."

Jack grew cold from the inside out. His muscles knotted. A pounding began above his right temple. Shadows reached for him. Kerry Dunn Sansbury, now Kerry Dunn Green, his ex-wife who'd had an affair while he'd sat vigil beside their daughter's deathbed.

"The hell you say." His voice was a raspy whisper as the cold darkness threatened.

"I'm sorry, Jack." Doreen's gaze was steady but watchful.

Jack surged from his armchair and crossed the room. He wanted space. He wanted air. He needed Audra.

"Why didn't you tell me this before?"

"I didn't know that Representative Green would be joining us. He only accepted our invitation last week."

Not good enough. "You could have told me you'd invited him."

"It's the town's one hundred and fiftieth birthday, Jack. Of course, local politicians are invited. But we want the founding family to be represented, too."

"And I want to be left alone." Too many raw emotions ripped through him——anger, betrayal, resentment——from injuries past and present.

"I'm sorry, Jack."

"Really? Then tell Green and my bitch ex-wife to stay home."

"I can't do that." Doreen's tone was flat, revealing neither regret nor resolve.

"Can't or won't?" He paced the width of the living room, trying to evade the cold darkness.

"Both." Doreen placed her empty glass on the coaster on the coffee table. "Representative Green will participate in the Founders Day Celebration. We've asked him to say a few words."

Jack stilled. "You want me on the stage with the bastard who screwed my wife while I watched my daughter die?"

Doreen stood. Her hands lay flat on the skirt of her cream suit. "Jack, we're not asking you to interact with him. But this is an opportunity for Trinity Falls to get the recognition we deserve from our state representatives. The attention could persuade them to direct industry our way. The town is coming out of the red, but this could help further secure our financial future."

All Jack heard was the buzzing in his ears. All he saw was a wash of red and memories he wanted to forget. "You knew I wouldn't come if Green was there."

"Jack, I want you to be a part—"

"You lied to me."

Doreen looked stricken. "I wanted what was best for the town."

"You lied to me."

Doreen held out her hands. "I didn't know Representative Green would attend. I didn't know you'd agree to participate. You've been so reclusive for so long."

"You thought only one of us would come?"

"That was a distinct possibility."

"Then choose."

"What?"

"Green or me. Choose."

Doreen stiffened. "Jack, I can't make a choice like that." She continued when he didn't respond. "The town wants both of you at the event for different reasons. You represent the town's founders, and he's our state representative."

"Choose."

"I can't. We all want you both to be there."

"Fine. I'll choose." He crossed his living room and pulled his front door open. "Keep Green."

Doreen gasped. "Jack—"

"Good-bye, Doreen."

She hesitated before crossing to the door. She stopped beside him. It was clear she wanted to say more. Jack didn't want to hear another word. She finally continued through the door. Jack closed it behind her.

He'd been a fool. He should have known the Sesquicentennial Celebration Committee would have invited every elected local, state, and federal representative Trinity Falls had. Because of his relationship with the town, Green would have topped the list. The little shit.

Jack paced away from the door to glower before the empty fireplace. What made him think he was ready to rejoin the community and have a normal life? Audra. Her warm light kept his demons at bay. How was he going to control them without her?

When Audra stood at Jack's cabin door later that afternoon, it took only one look at him for her to know something was wrong. His lips were tight. His eyes were cold.

"What's happened?"

"Nothing." He stepped aside so she could enter. *That's a good sign, isn't it?* Audra wondered.

"I can tell something's wrong, Jack." She locked his door.

His back muscles were stiff beneath his sage green T-shirt. "I don't want to talk about it."

Audra followed him into his kitchen. "You might as well. We can't ignore it when it's hovering between us like a great big bulk."

Jack stopped behind the kitchen island. He was making cold cut sandwiches. A bowl of salad stood at the other end of the counter. Audra turned to one of the cupboards and freed two salad dishes.

"Tell me what happened." She returned to the island to serve the salad.

Jack smeared mustard on a slice of toast. "Doreen stopped by this morning. She said Kerry was coming to the Founders Day Celebration."

Audra tensed. Now she understood Jack's mood. "She's coming back to Trinity Falls? Why?"

"The celebration committee invited her husband to make a speech during the event." His voice was tight. He laid the toast on top of the cold cuts, then cut the sandwich in half.

Audra frowned. "Who's her husband?"

"State Representative Isaac Green." Jack practically spat the other man's name.

Audra froze in the act of filling the second bowl with salad. She opened her mouth twice before she could voice her question. "Did Kerry cheat on you with an elected official?"

"Yes."

"Oh, my word." Her voice was faint.

"She married me for the prominence of my name and slept with Green for the prominence of his office." Jack carried the sandwiches into the dining room.

Audra followed with the salads. "I'm sorry Founders Day is going to be so awkward for you."

"What makes you say that?" He walked past her and back to the kitchen.

Audra set the salad bowls beside the plates of sandwiches and returned to the kitchen with him. "Won't you have to sit on the stage with the person who broke up your marriage?"

Jack poured two glasses of lemonade. "I'm not going to speak at the event."

Audra paused in the act of selecting silverware from a drawer. "Excuse me?"

"You heard me." He returned to the dining room.

It bothered her more than she thought it would that Kerry could still incite such strong feelings in him.

She marched back to the dining table and stood with her hands on her hips. "Jack, you have to speak at the celebration. Do you have any idea how few towns established by African Americans have survived? On August ninth, Trinity Falls will celebrate its one hundred and fiftieth birthday. This is extraordinary. As a descendent of the town's founding family, you have a responsibility to address its residents."

"Damn it, Audra!" Jack dragged his hands over his close-cropped hair and paced into the living room.

Audra dropped her arms and followed him. She softened her tone. "I know this situation is unfair, but you'll regret it if you don't represent your family on Founders Day."

"It's my decision to regret." Jack stared into the cold fireplace. His words carried much less heat.

"Don't allow Kerry to continue to have power over you. She's moved on. You should, too."

"I don't give a damn about Kerry."

Audra closed the gap between them. She rested a gentle palm on his taut back. "All of your reasons for initially agreeing to represent your family still exist—your grandfather, your father, Zoey."

The muscles under her palm shook as though electrically charged. Had she been unfair in evoking his daughter's name? Perhaps, but Zoey was a member of the founding family. His words would represent her as well.

"And one very good reason not to make the speech also exists." He faced her. "I don't care anymore what Kerry did to me and our marriage. But I'll never forgive her or Green for Kerry not being there when Zoey needed her mother."

Audra nodded, ashamed that she hadn't realized Jack wasn't holding a grudge against Kerry for himself. He was still hurting for Zoey. She could understand that. Although she'd never met mother or daughter, Audra also resented Kerry for putting her selfish pleasures above Zoey.

"I'm sorry Zoey's mother wasn't there for her. But her father was." Audra laid her hand on his chest. "Honor her memory and the memory of the rest of your family by being there for them now."

Audra returned Jack's tortured gaze. A battle raged within him. She never moved a muscle. But her eyes pleaded with him, *If not for the town or yourself, then for Zoey.*

Slowly his tension eased. His sigh was long and heavy. Jack drew her to him, wrapping his arms around her waist. "You have a way of ripping out all the ugliness from my heart and leaving only what's good." He whispered the words into her hair.

Audra inhaled sharply. Her body shook with shock. "You've come a long way from five words and no emotion to a declaration like that."

"You've changed me."

She leaned back to look up at him. "So you'll give a speech at the Founders Day event?"

His onyx eyes delved deeply into hers. "Yes."

Audra tapped his chest. "Zoey would be proud."

"I'm considering withdrawing from the mayoral race." Doreen had less trouble voicing the thought than seeing Megan and Ean's shocked expressions.

They'd just finished the Sunday dinner Megan had cooked. Doreen sat on the plush red armchair, watching her son and his girlfriend, who sat together on the matching sofa to her left.

"Why?" Ean broke the stunned silence.

"You saw Leo at the party Friday with Yvette Bates." The image still hurt two nights later. Doreen's gaze drifted to Megan and Ean's fingers intertwined and resting between them on the sofa. She felt a pinch of envy.

Megan inclined her head. "And we saw *you* dancing with the sheriff."

Doreen dismissed the comment. "He was just being nice."

Ean grunted. "If he'd wanted to be nice, he would've brought you a drink."

"Don't make more of it than it was, Ean." Doreen had enough on her mind without dwelling on Alonzo's dance—and her reaction to it. "I never intended for the campaign to come between Leo and me."

"Why does it have to?" Ean's question was softly spoken.

"It doesn't." Megan crossed her legs. "Leo's the one putting it between you."

"But I was the one who decided to run. Maybe I was wrong." Doreen was afraid. Of what? Failure, being alone, the unknown? All of the above?

"Do you love him?" Megan's question startled Doreen.

She hesitated. "I don't know."

Leonard had proposed to her in December. She'd asked him to wait. He'd agreed to give her time to consider his proposal, but she'd had other things on her mind. Ean had come home. She was campaigning for mayor. She hadn't had the time to search her heart.

She hadn't taken the time.

"Do you want to be mayor?" Ean asked.

"I do." Doreen didn't hesitate with that answer.

Megan frowned. "Why would you give up what you want for something you're not certain of?"

Doreen pushed out of her chair and crossed the room. Sun poured into the living room through the sheer white curtains. The house was still fragrant with the scents of the pasta dinner they'd shared less than fifteen minutes before.

She stopped at the wall separating the living and dining rooms. "Suppose Simon wins? Then I would have lost Leo and the election."

"Simon doesn't even have enough names to be added to the ballot." Ean's voice carried from the sofa behind her.

"Yet." Doreen turned to him. "Suppose he gets them?"

"How can you consider leaving the town to Simon Knight's mercy?" Ean seemed incredulous.

Her son had a good point. Could she bow out of the race and leave the mayor's office to Simon? Was her relationship with Leonard too high a price to pay?

Megan interrupted her thoughts. "Don't misunderstand. It's not a matter of your protecting us from having Simon for mayor. The fact is, you're the leader we need now."

The added pressure terrified her. "But what if I'm not fully committed to the office?"

Megan scooted forward on the sofa. "Are you making this decision for you or Leo?"

"I can't put my career above the people I care about." *Can I?*

Megan shook her head. "But you shouldn't give up your dreams, either."

Doreen gestured toward Ean. "You understand what I'm talking about, don't you? You came back from New York because you missed your friends and family."

"My circumstances were different, Mom." Ean spread his arms. "I left Trinity Falls to pursue my career, but it turned into a nightmare. That's when I came home. You're giving up your dream before it's even started."

Doreen turned away from the truth of Ean's words. "I don't want to disappoint either of you, but maybe this isn't the right dream for me."

Ean's voice followed her. "Why not? Because it's not what Leo wants?"

Doreen returned to her seat before meeting Ean's gaze. "You're criticizing Leo because he's trying to tell me what to do, but so are you."

Megan rested her elbows on her thighs. Her voice was earnest. "That's not a fair comparison, Doreen. Leo's trying to talk you out of doing what you want to do. We want you to make your own decision."

"Of course you want me to stay in the election." Doreen frowned at Megan. "It was your idea that I run for mayor."

Megan shook her head. "I asked you to consider it because I know how much Trinity Falls means to you. You've been active in the community since before I was born. And you've had great ideas on how to improve it."

Doreen crossed her arms, fighting the persuasion of Megan's words. "But even Ean pointed out, I don't have to be mayor to continue to have an impact on Trinity Falls."

Megan and Ean exchanged looks before he spoke. "No, you don't."

Megan's gaze bore into Doreen again. "This is about what you want, Doreen. We'll support whatever you decide to do."

Ean faced his mother again. "I understand how Leo feels. Remember, at first, I didn't want you to run for office, either. But I changed my mind when I realized this is what you want. I care about you, Mom. I want you to be happy."

Doreen read the unspoken question in Ean's eyes.

If Leonard cares about me, wouldn't he want me to be happy, too?

CHAPTER 17

"I'm done." Audra made the announcement into her cell phone Monday evening. She added a little happy dance.

"Hallelujah." Benita's sarcasm wasn't welcome.

"Hey, I beat the producer's deadline by a week." Audra tipped aside the sheer green curtains hanging in her front window.

July's evening sky was painted an achingly warm blue. The modest front lawn rolled like a carpet toward the spread of evergreen and poplar trees that circled the cabin like playful overgrown children. A gentle breeze tickled the leaves on their branches. In the distance, sunlight danced off the lake like diamonds on the water.

"Your medal's in the mail. What time is it over there?" Benita seemed distracted. Was her business manager reading e-mail or going through snail mail during their call?

"It's three o'clock, and I'd rather my check was in the mail." Audra turned away from the window.

"I'll e-mail the files to the producer tonight. I want to listen to them one more time before letting them go."

"Good. Copy me on that e-mail."

"I always do." Audra rested her hip on the arm of the dark plaid sofa. "I wrote an extra song, too."

"Since when do you give away work?"

"I'm not. This song is just for me." And perhaps one other. Restlessness drove Audra to her feet again. Her bare feet crossed from the cool wood flooring to the gray Berber area rug as she toured the room. "My muse was flowing, just as it had when I first started my career. It was great. You were right about my getting out of my comfort zone."

"Of course I was right," Benita sniffed. "I'm always right. You should accept that in the future, instead of arguing with me."

Audra ignored the other woman's interruption. "Or maybe it's Trinity Falls."

"What's Trinity Falls?"

Audra hesitated before responding. "The songs I wrote here are different."

"Not too different, I hope. The producer contracted you for Audra Lane songs. You weren't channeling someone weird, were you?"

"These songs are crisper, happier, more abandoned." Audra only half listened to her business manager's grousing as she relived the adrenaline rush of breaking through her writer's block.

"OK, that should work." Benita resumed clicking her keyboard.

"I can see myself coming back here." Audra settled again on the sofa.

"Where? The cabins?"

"Yes. And Trinity Falls. I like it here." Jack's image came to mind. "I like it here very much."

"It's a nice place to visit. Can't see how people live there, though."

"I can." Audra shifted to lie across the sofa. Its thick cushions sighed around her. "The people are so warm and welcoming. The town's beautiful and charming." She smiled as she thought of the quaint shops in the Trinity Falls Town Center and the characters who owned them.

Benita grunted. "You say that now. By the end of the week, those Pollyanna glasses will come off and you'll be screaming for L.A. There's nothing. To do. In Trinity Falls."

"There's plenty for me."

"Then you're boring, just like the town."

"Maybe." Audra was in too good a mood to be offended. She'd completed all three songs and intended to spend the remaining twelve days in Trinity Falls playing. Would Jack be able to play, too?

"So, does that mean you're not cutting your vacation short?" Benita clicked more keys. Audra thought a printer powered on in the background.

"Benita, if this had been a vacation, I wouldn't be speaking with you."

"Good, because the three-hour time difference with these calls is driving me nuts."

Audra thought of Jack. "I'm going to stay through Founders Day."

"Suit yourself." There was a shrug in Benita's voice. "Personally, I'd take my vacation somewhere else, like Paris, New York, London . . . but you paid for that cabin."

Yes, she did. And she was definitely getting far

more than her money's worth. Audra rolled into a sitting position. "Are you coming for the Founders Day Celebration?"

"Indeed, I am. I'm only staying for the day, though. Not a minute longer." A stapler crunched on Benita's end of the line. "The only reason I'm coming is that my cousin's been hounding the whole family about it for more than a year."

"Who's your cousin?"

"Dr. Helen Gaston. Have you met her? Everyone in town calls her Ms. Helen."

Audra grinned, thinking about the charismatic older woman with whom Darius had spent the evening. "I like her. I'm surprised you're related. She seems so nice."

"Ha-ha." Benita rustled papers on the other end of the line. "Look, hon, as much as I'm enjoying your conversation, I've gotta run. Listen to those songs again. Copy me on the e-mail. Have fun on your well-deserved vacation. Look for me August ninth."

After delivering her to-do list, Benita hung up. Audra shook her head in amusement. Had Benita ever waited for her to say good-bye before hanging up? She couldn't recall.

But now that she was done with her contract, there was someone else she wanted to say hello to. Audra punched in Jack's cell phone number.

"Hello, beautiful." Jack's baritone was even sexier over the phone.

Audra savored the delicious shivers his greeting gave her. "I've finished all three songs."

"Congratulations." There was a smile in his voice.

"Thank you." Completing her songs had never felt so wonderful. "Are you free for dinner?"

"It's already on the stove."

Audra smiled. "I'll be right there."

Doreen's doorbell chimed Monday evening. She turned from the refrigerator, where she'd been contemplating a lonely dinner. Was it Leonard? She shut the fridge and made her way to her front door. What if it was? How should she react? Should she offer him dinner or ask why he wasn't mooching a meal from Yvette? A glance at the security peephole only raised more questions.

"Alonzo?" Doreen stepped back, pulling the door wider. Leonard must be having dinner with Yvette. Her heart dropped.

"Evening, Doreen. Is this a bad time?" The sheriff's warm, slow drawl preceded him across her threshold.

"Not at all." She found a smile. "I didn't think you knew where I lived."

"I knew."

Doreen locked the door before leading him to her living room. "Can I get you anything? I have iced tea, lemonade, and, of course, plenty of water."

"Iced tea would be good." Alonzo seemed awkward, standing in the center of her living room. His black T-shirt stretched wide across his broad chest. His cream khaki shorts hugged his hips before falling loosely to his knees.

Doreen excused herself. Within minutes, she'd returned to the living room with two glasses of iced tea and lemon. Alonzo hadn't moved from the center of the room.

She handed him one of the glasses, then settled onto the sofa behind her. "Have a seat. What brings you by tonight?"

Alonzo dropped onto the love seat to the right of the sofa. He took a long drink of iced tea. "Sorry to stop by uninvited. I should've called first."

He seemed nervous. Doreen studied him closely. The smile lines bracketing his mouth and creasing the corners of his eyes, and the gray strands weaving through his raven hair, were his only signs of aging. Otherwise, Alonzo looked the same as he had in high school—tall, dark, and exotically handsome. At sixty-six years old, he had the physique of a man thirty years younger.

Doreen met his coffee brown eyes. "You don't need to check with me before you come over. You're always welcome. Although I'm surprised it's taken you this long to find me."

Alonzo held his glass suspended by both palms. "I've known which house was yours, Doreen, ever since I moved back to Trinity Falls. But I didn't think it was right for me to come by."

"Why not?" Doreen took one last sip of her iced tea before placing her glass on a coaster on the coffee table.

Alonzo's nervous laughter shook his shoulders. "I'm surprised you never realized this."

"What?"

Alonzo met her puzzled gaze. "You really don't know?"

"Why are you being so myster—"

"I've been in love with you since high school."

Doreen's jaw dropped. Had she heard him correctly? "What did you say?"

Alonzo rose from the love seat and crossed the room. He stood with his back to her. "You and Paul were right for each other. You made each other happy. That's the reason I never tried to come between you."

Doreen struggled to keep up with Alonzo's words. He spoke so fast. "You and Paul were friends."

His shoulders slumped. "We were best friends . . . before I fell in love with you."

Doreen's hand pressed against her chest. A chill went through her. "Did he know how you felt?"

Alonzo faced her. "No. I never told him. But you're the reason I never returned to town after college. You're the reason I never married. How could I promise before God to love another woman when I was already in love with you?"

"Alonzo, I never knew." Doreen's head was spinning.

"You weren't supposed to."

"It's been more than forty years."

"I know. It's been killing me." His dark gaze burned her. "I've tried to love other women. But I realized there's no other woman like you."

"But, Alonzo, I'm with Leo now."

"Leo isn't right for you."

Doreen stood, wiping her damp palms on her brown walking shorts. "Leo and I are having a disagreement. We'll work it out."

Alonzo pulled his right hand through his thick

dark hair. "I'm sorry Paul died. He was a good person. The community misses him, and I know his death broke your heart. I wanted to give you time to grieve him before making a case for myself. But Leo dove in like a vulture."

"That's not fair. Leo was a good friend and support through Paul's illness."

Alonzo shook his head. "Think what you like. I don't mean to upset you. But I'm not hiding my feelings any longer."

There was a buzzing in Doreen's ears. Was this really happening? Alonzo closed the distance between them. She took an instinctive step back.

"I'm with Leo now, Alonzo. I can't . . ." Her voice trailed off as Alonzo lifted her left hand, rubbing its bare third finger.

"You're not wearing a ring." His voice was low, soft, and persuasive, causing the muscles in her lower abdomen to flutter like hummingbirds.

Doreen tugged her hand free. "He *has* asked me to marry him."

"Is that the reason he brought Yvette to Quincy and Ramona's going-away party?" Alonzo used his right index finger to lift Doreen's chin when she lowered her gaze. "Leo realized he was a fool to try to make you jealous with Yvette. But I'm not going to quietly step aside this time. I'm taking a page from Quincy's book and fighting for what I want."

Alonzo lowered his head and settled his mouth on hers. Doreen gasped her surprise. Alonzo moved in, slipping his tongue between her lips.

His kiss was a dark, demanding drug. This wasn't the tentative caress of a secret admirer making his

plea. It was the impatient seduction of a would-be
lover taking a stand. Doreen's world tipped off its
axis. But instead of pushing him away to set things
back to order, she clutched Alonzo's muscled shoulders to keep from slipping away. He wrapped his
arms around her waist, tucking her more tightly
against him. Alonzo finally released her, allowing
her to catch her breath.

"I won't hide my feelings anymore, Doreen. Will
you?" His voice was husky. His brown eyes had darkened almost to black.

Alonzo didn't wait for her response. Instead, he
walked past her and out her front door. Doreen
watched him leave. They'd been friends since childhood. But now, after that kiss, she was seeing him as
something more.

How could she not have known Alonzo had such
strong feelings for her? Had anyone else known?
Should she tell Leonard?

But one question would keep her up all night:
*Why did I wait for Alonzo to end that kiss rather than
pulling away myself?*

Jack gathered his courage and his dishes before
he rose to clear the table after dinner. "Now that
you've finished your songs, how much longer are
you staying?"

Audra preceded him into the kitchen. "I'm staying for Founders Day, remember?"

Jack swallowed his sigh of relief, but couldn't
contain his smile. "What are you going to do for the
next twelve days?"

Audra bent to load the dishwasher. "Do you have any suggestions?"

"A few." Jack handed her his plate and silverware.

"Fishing, hiking, canoeing?"

"Those too." He rested a hip against the laminate counter, and, with his gaze, traced the curve of her hips in the powder blue shorts. "For a big-city woman, you've connected well with our town. It's like you've been here for years, instead of only three weeks. I'm impressed."

Audra straightened, closing the dishwasher. "That says more about the people of Trinity Falls than me. Everyone has made me feel like a part of the community, as though I were home. It'll be hard to say good-bye."

Jack didn't want to talk about Audra's leaving. "Trinity Falls has always been a friendly town. It's trite, but it's true."

"Before we get too far sidetracked, have you spoken with Doreen?"

"About what?" Jack knew what she was asking, just as she knew he hadn't made up with Doreen.

Audra gave him a skeptical look, settling her hands on her hips. "You need to let her know you'll still speak during the Founders Day Celebration."

Jack took one step forward and placed his hands over hers. "I will."

"When?"

"Soon."

Audra shifted their hands so she could hold his. "The celebration is in twelve days. When are you going to tell her?"

Jack dragged one hand over his close-cropped hair. "I'll tell her tomorrow."

Audra's smile soothed him. "You'll feel better once that's behind you."

Jack started to say he'd feel better once Founders Day was over, then remembered Audra would be leaving the next day. He'd never longed for something yet dreaded it so much at the same time.

CHAPTER 18

Darius tugged his office telephone toward him Tuesday morning. He tapped in Quincy's old Trinity Falls University phone number from memory. It now belonged to the new history professor. He couldn't think of her as Quincy's replacement. No one could replace his childhood friend. As he waited for her to answer, Darius reviewed his Microsoft Outlook calendar for dates on which he could interview the faculty member for a feature article for the *Monitor*.

"Peyton Harris."

Darius's hand froze on his computer mouse. Dr. Harris's warm, rich voice entered his blood like pure alcohol.

"Hello?" she prompted when Darius didn't respond. Her voice was sharp.

He pulled himself together. "Dr. Harris, I'm Darius Knight. I'm a reporter with *The Trinity Falls Monitor*. Welcome to—"

"I'm not doing interviews."

Darius had heard that line before. Ean had tried it about nine months ago when Darius wanted to do a story on his childhood friend returning to Trinity Falls and opening a solo law practice.

He looked away from his computer monitor to give the phone conversation his full attention. "I understand your reluctance to be interviewed—"

"No, you don't." Her voice cooled.

Darius hesitated. Her attitude took him by surprise. "I know a lot of people are uncomfortable being in the spotlight."

"Then you'll respect my decision not to be interviewed—"

"I won't take much of your time, Dr. Harris." Darius's mind moved quickly. She sounded like she was going to hang up on him.

"This isn't about time, Mr. Knight."

"I can bring the photographer with me. We can do the interview and take the photo at the same time." Darius brought Quincy's old office to mind. It wasn't exactly photogenic, but they could make something work.

"No. No photos." Her response was fast and firm.

Darius's brows knitted. Why was she so opposed to a simple interview? What was behind her aversion to having her picture taken? "I was hoping to do a feature on you. We'd need a photo to go with the article."

"You won't need a photo. There will be no article."

"Dr. Harris, what's this about?"

"It's about the need for you to respect my wishes not to appear in your newspaper or any newspaper." She spoke in a precise, measured voice. "I won't grant any interviews to you or anyone else. There's no need for publicity."

Perhaps Darius should give up. For some reason, he couldn't. Was it the reporter in him, refusing to let go of a story, or the man in him, responding to the sound of her voice?

"Dr. Harris, you're new to Trinity Falls. We don't often have people move into our community." Usually, people moved out. "That alone makes you newsworthy. Add to that, you're the newest addition to our local university's faculty. Your neighbors will want to get to know you."

"I'm sure I'll meet them. They don't need to read about me in your paper."

Darius was at a loss. "It doesn't have to be an extensive article. We can cut out your childhood aspirations of walking on the moon and just cover your immediate past."

"I've given you the wrong impression, Mr. Knight." Her words were brisk. Clearly, his attempt at levity hadn't impressed her. "My decision is not up for debate. I will not grant you any interviews, nor will I allow you to take any photos of me."

The line went dead. Darius stared at his blank caller identification screen. What had just happened? No one had ever turned down his request for an interview. They may have needed some persuading, like Ean, but in the end, he'd always gotten the story. Why was Peyton Harris so opposed to the press?

Darius jabbed the buttons for Quincy's cell phone number. His friend answered on the third ring. "What's up?"

Darius rubbed his eyes with his thumb and index

finger. "What's the deal with the new professor? She doesn't want to be interviewed."

"Maybe she's read your work."

Darius shook his head at the weak insult. "I'm serious. Why is she blocking me?"

"I don't know. Why don't you call Foster to see if he could convince her to talk to you?"

"Good idea. I'll catch up with you later."

Darius ended the call, then launched his online contacts file. He located the number for Foster Gooden, the university's vice president for academic affairs. He didn't like pulling rank; but if that's what he had to do to get the article on the university's new faculty member, he'd put his connections to use.

"Are there any ugly men in Trinity Falls?" Audra whispered the question to Jack as Doreen and the Trinity Falls University concert band director approached their table at Books & Bakery Tuesday afternoon.

Jack scowled. "I'm sitting right here, Audra."

"I'm sorry." The humor in her voice contradicted her apology. "I don't know what I was thinking."

Jack grunted. "That's why I came to Books and Bakery with you today."

"Jealous?"

Jack grunted again.

Vaughn Brooks didn't fit her image of a university band director. He appeared to be in his late thirties. Standing a little over six feet tall, he was built like a football tight end. He was bald, with nutmeg skin and a neat goatee. A plain white T-shirt stretched across his chest. Knee-length blue jean shorts emphasized his long, powerful legs.

Doreen stopped at their table in the far corner of the bakery section. "Audra Lane, Vaughn Brooks."

Vaughn accepted her hand. "I enjoy your work." His voice was deep and smooth, his smile friendly.

"Thank you." Audra shook Vaughn's hand. "I've heard great things about your band."

"I bet you have." He winked at Doreen before releasing Audra's hand. He took the seat across the table from the bakery manager, sitting next to Jack. Each spot had a mug of coffee, compliments of Doreen. "Thank you for agreeing to help us put together a surprise number for the celebration."

Audra slipped a look toward Doreen. "Unfortunately, as I explained to Doreen, none of the performers I contacted are available that day. But Electra Day's record label has given you permission to cover one of her most recent releases."

"Electra Day?" Vaughn's dark eyes widened. "Which song?"

Audra smiled at his excitement. "It's a song I wrote for her, 'Lifting Me Up.' Do you know it?"

Vaughn leaned back on his chair. A slow smile lit his face. "Do I know it? I love it. It's fast, upbeat."

Doreen clapped her hands together. "It's perfect for the celebration."

Audra had thought the same. "Will your musicians be able to learn it in time for the event? It's already July 29. They only have eleven days."

Vaughn nodded. "We're just doing four pieces. We learned the other three during the school year, and I told the kids to keep practicing over summer break."

Audra frowned. "When will they come back from break?"

Vaughn leaned into the table. "Most of my kids are local. The rest came back early for the concert. They moved into the dorms Sunday."

Audra smiled her relief. "Then it sounds like you can get started."

Vaughn nodded. "How soon can you get the sheet music to me?"

Audra pulled a folder from the oversized canvas tote bag on the floor beside her feet. "I have it now. It's a pretty simple piece." She passed it across the table to Vaughn. "All you need is someone to sing it."

"Why don't you do it?" Jack made the question sound like a dare.

Audra met the challenge in his onyx eyes. "I'm not a singer."

"You sound like one." Jack's look said he wasn't backing down.

Neither was Audra. "Being able to hold a note and being able to sing are two separate things."

Doreen joined the debate—unfortunately, on Jack's side. "Audra, if Jack says you can sing, then you can sing. We'd love to include you as part of our Founders Day Celebration."

If they were alone, she'd reach over and pinch Jackson Elijah Sansbury really hard. But there were so many lunch patrons in the bakery area; too many witnesses to cause a scene. She glared at him, instead. "Doreen, I'm not a performer."

Doreen chuckled. "The Trinity Falls sesquicentennial isn't a 'Night at the Apollo.' It's just a small-town celebration."

Audra wasn't buying it. "The town's residents have been planning for and anticipating this event for more than a year. They deserve someone who can do the song justice."

"And who's better at that than the songwriter?" Vaughn added his voice to the pressure mounting against Audra. And he'd seemed so rational.

Audra gave Jack a look that said, *I'll get even with you.* He met her gaze with innocence. She shifted her attention to Doreen and Vaughn. "Doesn't the town or at least the university have a glee club or something, people who enjoy singing in public?"

"The university has a choir," Doreen offered.

"They perform classical and gospel songs," Vaughn explained. "As you know, those are very different types of music."

"Audra." Jack's voice was as compelling as a spell. "You can do this."

She made one last effort at resistance. "I haven't performed since high school."

Jack just smiled. "You're a different person now. You're more confident, more accomplished. This is a different situation. It's a chance to be part of something big and historical. No one's here to judge you. We just want to enjoy your music."

Audra looked from Jack to Doreen and Vaughn. There was hope in their eyes. Jack was right. This was a momentous opportunity. She didn't want to sit on the sidelines if she could be a part of it. "All right. I'll share the stage with you."

Jack gave her his slow, sexy smile, the one that curled her toes against her sandals. "Thank you."

Doreen leaned over to hug her. "Audra, this is wonderful. Wonderful! Thank you so much."

"The kids are going to be pumped." Vaughn's grin brightened his lean features. "Thank you."

Audra wished she could share their enthusiasm. Maybe later. Right now, her mouth was dry from nervousness. Trinity Falls had moved the boundaries of her comfort zone. Permanently. Audra didn't know whether she deserved the look in Jack's eyes—admiration, gratitude, and something indefinable.

The university felt different now that Quincy had left campus. Darius allowed muscle memory to lead him to his friend's former office, now the office of the stubborn Dr. Peyton Harris. Classes wouldn't start for another three weeks. Campus was deserted, except for staff members, and the handful of students and faculty on summer programs. Quincy had spent four years of his career on this campus, and—except for his undergraduate and graduate studies—his whole life in Trinity Falls. Darius would miss being able to see his friend every day. Still, he was happy for Quincy. He had a great opportunity at the University of Pennsylvania, and he'd won Ramona's heart, the woman of his dreams. Ean also had found his soul mate in Megan. Darius was pleased for both men.

He stopped in the office's open doorway. It was probably safe to assume the woman seated behind the wood laminate desk was Peyton Harris. She'd sounded taller on the phone.

Darius knocked twice in rapid succession. "Dr. Harris?"

Peyton popped out of her chair like a fawn flushed from the bushes. She stared at him, wide-eyed with surprise. "Who are you?"

Darius crossed into the office, mistaking Peyton's question as permission to enter. "I'm sorry. I didn't mean to startle you. I'm Darius Knight from *The Trinity Falls Monitor.* We spoke earlier this morning."

The room was cleaner than it had been in the four years Quincy had called it "home away from home." It was brighter, less cluttered, and no longer stank of stale coffee.

"What are you doing here?" Peyton squared her slight shoulders beneath an oversized navy blue T-shirt, bracing her fingertips on the surface of her well-organized desk.

She couldn't be more than five feet tall. She was small and fine-boned. Her bright brown hair was a riot of curls bobbing just above her shoulders. Her honey-and-chocolate-cream complexion housed a few freckles. Her full, bubble-gum pink lips were tight with displeasure, and her caramel eyes snapped up at him.

"I wanted to talk with you about your interview for the *Monitor.*"

Her eyes narrowed. "I told you I won't grant any interviews to anyone for any publication."

"I heard you over the phone." Darius stepped farther into the room. He stopped when he sensed a spike in the professor's tension level.

"Then why are you here?"

Darius tried a winning smile. Its power had melted the hearts of much colder women. "I wanted to give you a reason to change your mind."

"I have no intention of changing my mind." Her voice left Darius without any wiggle room.

Darius puzzled the best way to reach her. "Why don't you want to do the interview?"

"I'm not newsworthy." Peyton's caramel gaze was quelling. "I'm a history professor at a liberal arts university. There are thousands of us across the country, four at this university alone who are just like me."

"No, not like you." He hadn't meant to say that out loud, but it was the truth.

"What makes me different?" Peyton's voice was sharp.

For starters, two of those professors were men. The third was a woman, but her hair wasn't a cloud of curls that would warm his fingers. Her skin wasn't a warm chocolate cream that begged to be tasted, and her eyes weren't pools of caramel in which he could drown. But somehow, Darius didn't think it was a good idea to tell the formidable Dr. Harris any of that.

There were other things that made her unique. "To start, you left a coveted position at New York University to teach at a school with less than a quarter of NYU's enrollment, much less prestige, and in a sleepy little town."

Peyton crossed her arms. "I'll remind you that you also live in this sleepy little town."

"I was born and raised here." And, God willing, he'd die here. "Trinity Falls is better known for people leaving. Not many people choose to relocate here."

Peyton cocked her head. She gave Darius a considering look that made his muscles tremble. "If that's the case, since you're still here, you're more of a story than I am."

"Perhaps, but let's start with your story."

"Let's not."

"You still haven't told me why not."

Peyton's winged brows lowered. "I don't have to justify myself to you. I told you, I don't want to do the interview. I don't have to do it, and I'm not going to. My reasons are none of your business."

Darius considered her. Angry color highlighted her sharp cheekbones. Her caramel gaze steamed. "I'm just curious. After you turned down my interview request this morning, I called Foster Gooden."

Peyton stilled. Was she breathing? "You called my VPAA? Why would you do that?"

"I wanted his help in persuading you to do the interview." Darius wasn't proud of what he'd done, but he'd wanted the story.

"What did Dr. Gooden say?"

"That if you didn't want to do the interview, he wasn't going to force you." Now Darius's curiosity was at fever pitch.

"Well, then, this subject is closed. I need to get back to work." Peyton's relief was palpable.

"The thing is, Dr. Harris, I'd like to understand why you're opposed to the article. Most faculty members jump at the opportunity to get publicity for their work." Darius needed the answer to his question. He wanted to understand the "why."

"I've asked you to get out." Peyton's voice carried an edge.

"I've interviewed every other faculty member at the university."

"I want you to leave me alone." Aggression built with her tone.

"If you don't want to do the interview, I won't force you—"

"You can't force me. I won't let you."

"I just want to understand why."

Peyton circled her desk and crossed to him. She grabbed Darius's upper arm and marched him toward the door. "I won't tell you again. Get. Out."

Peyton caught him off guard. The top of her head didn't even reach his shoulder. Playing football in college, Darius had tackled and been tackled by men more than twice her size. What made her think she could take him on? He could have slipped her hold at any moment. Yet he allowed the pissed-off, pocket-sized professor to drag him to her door—and then shut said door in his face.

Darius stared in shock at the sealed entrance before walking away from Peyton's office. He shook his head in confusion. If nothing else, this encounter convinced him the former New York University professor wasn't going to change her mind about an interview.

But he'd still like to know why not.

The bell above the main cabin's door chimed Wednesday morning. Jack welcomed the distraction from his bookkeeping—until he looked up from the registration desk and saw the stranger crossing the lobby. He dragged a rolling suitcase across the hardwood floor.

Jack stood. "Can I help you?"

The sesquicentennial had lured former neighbors back to Trinity Falls. It also had attracted a few strangers, but no one had reserved a rental. Few people knew Harmony Cabins existed.

"Give me a cabin." Without looking at Jack, the stranger stood the suitcase on its end, then pulled his wallet from the back pocket of his white mesh shorts.

"I don't have any." Something about the man rubbed Jack the wrong way. It might have been the matching white mesh shirt worn over a black T-shirt. White canvas shoes completed the odd outfit. The guy couldn't be from anywhere near here.

The would-be guest stared at him in incredulity. "What do you mean you don't have any? I just passed four of them on my way over here."

"They aren't available."

"Are you telling me they're all booked?" He gestured behind him. "Why don't you have a No Vacancies sign up, then?"

Jack crossed his arms, growing tired of the smaller man. "They're being renovated."

"What the hell does that mean? Do you know who I am?" He held up his gold American Express card. "I'm Wendell Weber, music producer."

Jack froze.

∽◦ CHAPTER 19 ◦∼

This was Audra's ex-boyfriend? The man on the other side of the counter was average height and weight. His tan features were clean-shaven except for the soul patch hanging from his bottom lip. His diamond stud earrings were the size of nickels.

"Did Audra know you were coming?"

"She's mentioned me?" Wendell puffed his chest forward.

What had she seen in this guy? "Not in favorable terms."

The music producer's grin disappeared. "Who are you?"

"Jack Sansbury."

Wendell looked him up and down. "You got something going on with her?" When Jack didn't respond, Wendell continued. "You own this place or something?"

"Yes." Jack didn't like Wendell's smile.

"Well, good for her." His expression sobered. "Which cabin's she staying in? I want to talk to her."

No. Way. "Guest information is confidential."

Wendell rolled his eyes. "Come on, you know I know her. Just tell me where she's staying."

"That's the policy." Which he'd just made up.

"Then give me a cabin."

"They aren't available."

"I came all the way from L.A. for this? This is bullshit. Where am I supposed to stay?"

"In L.A."

"Funny." Wendell was surly. "This place got any hotels?"

"Yes."

Wendell scowled. "You wanna tell me where they are?"

Against his better judgment, Jack pulled out a map. He drew one circle around the town's hotel and another around the bed-and-breakfast.

"We're here." He drew an X near Pearl Lake.

Wendell studied the map for several moments. He rapped twice on the counter. "Thanks, man. Tell Audra I'll call her later."

Jack watched the other man drag his wheeled suitcase back across the lobby and through the door. He'd dreaded the day Audra would return to L.A. It seemed L.A. had come to her.

"I heard you were thinking of pulling out of the mayoral race." The challenge in Ramona's tone echoed in her strides as she entered Books & Bakery's kitchen Wednesday afternoon.

Doreen straightened from unloading the dishwasher and watched the younger woman strut to the chair at the small table in the corner. "News always travels fast in Trinity Falls."

"I never thought I'd hear this news: Doreen Fever backs away from a fight." Ramona sat and crossed her long dancer's legs, readjusting the skirt of her lemon yellow summer minidress. She'd gathered her thick raven tresses into a ponytail. Her café au lait features bore the barest hint of makeup.

"I'm not afraid of Simon. I know I can beat him."

"That's not the fight I was talking about." Ramona swung her top leg, letting her strappy yellow sandal dangle from her toes.

"Then what is it?"

"Leo."

Doreen's heart popped into her throat. She swallowed to push it back into place. "Did he ask you to talk with me?"

Ramona's arched eyebrows lifted. "Doreen, we're not in the fifth grade. What makes you think I'm passing notes? You're both grown. If you want to talk with each other, just talk."

Doreen stared absently at the white-tiled kitchen floor. "I thought he might have . . ."

"What?" Ramona prompted. "Come to his senses? Have you come to yours?"

Doreen's gaze shot back up to meet Ramona's. "What do you mean?"

"You said you got into this race because you care about Trinity Falls. You cared so much that you were prepared to challenge me for my job—and you know I would've beaten you."

"Actually, Ramona, I don't know that." Doreen's response was dry.

Ramona waved a dismissive hand. "We can argue that another time. It's not relevant to this discussion."

"Then what *is* your point? Why are you here?" Doreen let her impatience show.

"To help you find your spine." Ramona uncrossed her legs and sat straighter on her chair.

Doreen's jaw dropped. "Excuse me?"

Ramona ignored the interruption. "Megan and Ean were too nice to say anything Sunday when you dropped this bomb on them. But someone needs to hold a mirror in front of your face."

Doreen inhaled a sharp breath. The scents of sugar and coffee were familiar. "I haven't lost my spine."

"Yes, Doreen, you have. What happened to the woman who filed her application for the election, despite Leo? You told him, if he couldn't handle your being mayor, he could find the door. What happened to that woman?"

"That was before." Doreen cringed. Had she really said that? She turned from Ramona and continued unloading the dishwasher.

"You mean before Leo tried to play you by bringing Yvette to Quincy and my going-away party?" Ramona's snort was incongruous with her sophisticated appearance. "Oh, please. The English teacher dating the high-school football coach? Can you think of anything more clichéd?"

"Maybe this sounds silly to you, but I'm still finding myself, Ramona. I'm not sure who I am, who I want to be, who I should be. You're young and confident. You've always had your family's support to be who you wanted to be." Doreen shrugged. "I don't expect you to understand."

Ramona's ebony eyes twinkled at her. "You're wrong, Doreen. I understand perfectly."

Doreen arched an eyebrow at the town's mayor. "I find that hard to believe."

"You shouldn't." Ramona stood to join Doreen at the counter. "I've tried many identities, looking for the one that most suited me. I tried to be a New Yorker. That lasted seven months. I thought I could be mayor. That's barely lasted one term."

Doreen waved a hand to interrupt the younger woman. "Ramona, you're a good mayor."

"You'll be a better one."

"But is that who I should be?" Doreen expelled a deep breath. "If my choices are between being mayor and being Leo's wife, I'm not certain I want to choose a lifestyle in which all I have are a bunch of policies and bureaucracy, and council members breathing down my neck."

Ramona leaned a hip against the kitchen counter. "But the choice should be yours. Don't let Leo or anyone else define you, Doreen."

"That's not what I'm doing."

"Yes, you are. Stay in the race. *You* have to decide who you are. Don't allow other people to make that decision for you. I'm speaking from experience."

Doreen watched her friend with new eyes. "Aren't you trying to define me by telling me to stay in the race?"

Ramona shook her head. "I'm not telling you who you are. I'm telling you who you *aren't*. You're not a quitter."

"No matter what I do, I'm quitting something, either the race or my relationship with Leo." Doreen rubbed the frown between her eyebrows.

"Being mayor is a natural progression in your community involvement. Leo should know that. He's known you for more than sixteen years."

"Yes, but—"

"No 'but.' Why would you change who you are?"

Doreen hesitated. "Because I'm afraid of losing Leo."

Ramona arched a neat brow. "Do you really want a lover who'd use scare tactics to keep you?"

Doreen's eyes widened. *When you put it like that . . .* "No, I don't."

"Good." Ramona heaved a sigh as she straightened from the kitchen counter. "My job here is done."

Doreen smiled. "Yes, it is. I'm not quitting. Leo can accept me as I am, or he can find the door."

Ramona shrugged her slender shoulders. "Frankly, if he's causing you all this trouble over the election, I don't think Leo's the right man for you."

Doreen watched the other woman strut through the door, much as she'd entered the room minutes before. Ramona was the second person to tell her Leonard wasn't right for her. But since Alonzo had an agenda, could she trust his judgment?

Audra rocked to a stop in front of Books & Bakery. She blinked twice. When her vision didn't clear, she had to accept that her eyes weren't playing a trick on her. Wendell Weber had come to Trinity Falls.

Shit.

His blindingly white shorts outfit was more suited to the Hamptons than Trinity Falls, Ohio. He was climbing out of his rental car and hadn't seen her yet. Audra had two choices: pretend she hadn't seen him and continue to her car, or confront him.

She ground her teeth and marched across the Trinity Falls Town Center parking lot. "What are you doing here?"

Wendell blinked away his surprise. His reaction confirmed that he hadn't expected to find her at the center. It was just her bad luck he had. "Is that any way to greet an old friend? We haven't seen each other in months."

He'd brought everything she disliked about Los Angeles with him: the stench of smog, the feeling of being crowded, the bitter taste of deception.

Audra unclenched her teeth before they cracked. "How did you find me?"

"Your mother told me where you were." His smile grew even wider. "Running into you in this crowded parking lot means we were meant to find each other."

Audra was going to be sick.

She'd noticed additional people arriving for the town's sesquicentennial celebration. The pedestrian traffic at the town center had increased. Books & Bakery was even more crowded, especially during lunch.

Audra's grip tightened on her Books & Bakery pastry bag. "There are laws against stalking. You've wasted your time coming here."

"Your mother likes me." Wendell cocked his head. "You didn't tell her about Tammy, did you?"

Audra glared in silence. No, she hadn't been able to tell her mother about Wendell's pregnant fiancée and the total depth of his deception. She'd been too ashamed. Then why had she been able to confide in Jack?

"Go back to Los Angeles, Wendell." She crossed the parking lot to her rental car.

Wendell followed her. "Where are you going?"

"Back to my cabin."

"Good. I'll join you."

Audra spun to face him. She stepped back when she realized how close he'd been. "No, you won't. Go back to Los Angeles. I don't want you at the cabins. I don't want you in Trinity Falls."

"I've been to your cabins."

That brought Audra up short. "You have?"

"Yes. I met the property owner. Is something going on between you?"

"That's none of your business."

"Maybe it is."

She saw the spite in his small brown eyes. Audra grew cold, then burned with anger. "You and I have nothing to discuss. Lose my number. Lose every memory you have of ever knowing me. I'm serious, Wendell. I never want to see you again."

It was a battle of wills as they stared each other down. Audra wasn't giving in. She'd stand in this parking lot, glaring at Wendell until the next sesquicentennial if that's what it took to get him out of her life.

Wendell blinked first. "Fine. If you want me to go away, I will. On one condition."

Of course he had a condition. "What?"

"Convince Electra Day to let me produce her next album."

Audra's jaw dropped. "What? No way." She dug her car keys from her purse.

"Don't be that way, Audra." He clamped a hand on her shoulder.

Audra glared from his touch to his eyes. "Get your hand off me."

Wendell stepped back, lifting both hands in a sign of surrender. "Come on, Audra. I'm having a little trouble getting my production company started. All I need is one big name to help me get off the ground, then I'll be fine. You've worked with Electra. She trusts you. If you tell her I can turn her next album into a hit, she'll listen to you. Then people will see what I can do, and other big names will follow."

"What a load of bullshit."

"No, it's not."

A warm breeze riffled through her hair. Audra brushed back the tousled strands. "Wendell, my name got your foot in the industry's door, but you need talent to keep the door open. You obviously don't have any."

His tan features twisted into an ugly mask of rage. He stuck a finger in her face. "Now *that's* a load of bullshit."

She slapped his hand away and held her ground. "You made a lot of promises, but you didn't deliver on the quality of your work."

"Who said that?" His tone was rough.

"Everyone." The word was delicious, tripping off Audra's tongue. Was it wrong to feel such glowing satisfaction? "People love to gossip."

His dark eyes searched hers. "You won't help me?"

"Even if I could, what makes you think I would?"

"You know, Audra, I'm not the only person whose happiness could be taken from them."

Audra stepped forward. "Are you threatening me?"

He shook his bald head. "No, I'm just making an observation."

"Is everything all right?" Sheriff Alonzo Lopez's question interrupted their standoff.

"Yes, thank you, Sheriff." Audra broke eye contact with Wendell and attempted a smile for the lawman.

Alonzo looked approachable in his Smokey-the-Bear-like uniform. One large paw incongruously gripped a dainty lavender Books & Bakery pastry bag.

Alonzo inclined his head in greeting toward Audra before turning to Wendell. "Welcome to Trinity Falls. Are you in town for the sesquicentennial?"

Wendell's frown was part irritation, part confusion. "What?"

Alonzo remained unruffled. "Town's celebrating its one hundred and fiftieth birthday."

"I'm happy for it, but this is a private conversation." Wendell waved a hand between him and Audra.

"And this is a public parking lot." Alonzo's reply was slow and easy.

Audra glared at Wendell. "We're done talking. Go back to Los Angeles."

Wendell crossed his arms. "I think I'll stay for the town's celebration."

"You have a place to stay?" Alonzo asked.

Wendell scowled at the sheriff's interruption. "You only have one hotel and one bed-and-breakfast, and they're both booked."

Alonzo jerked his head toward the road in front of the town center. "You'll have to try the hotels in

Sequoïa. It's one town over, but they might be full, too."

Wendell glanced at Audra. His smile didn't reach his eyes. "Or I could stay with you."

"Over my dead body." Audra deactivated her car alarm, which automatically unlocked her car. "Have a good afternoon, Sheriff."

Audra climbed into her car and pulled out of the parking lot. She was anxious to get Wendell in her rearview mirror. Hopefully, he'd be decent enough to listen to her and leave town. But in the meantime, he'd told her he'd met Jack. Audra had a shiver of unease.

What did Wendell tell him?

Jack looked at his watch. Only four minutes had elapsed since his last time check. Why was he pacing Audra's porch like a lovesick puppy? He had cabins to renovate and accounting ledgers to update. He couldn't spend the afternoon wearing a path in front of Audra's cabin. But he couldn't concentrate on work, either. His mind kept going back to his meeting with Wendell Weber—what kind of name was that?—and what the other man's arrival in Trinity Falls meant to his final eleven days with Audra.

The air was thick and heavy. Jack leaned against the porch railing. Even in the shade, he felt as though he were standing in a microwave. He wiped sweat from his brow and checked his watch again. Only seconds had passed. Jack had had enough. He straightened from the railing and jogged down the porch stairs. He followed the graveled path from Audra's cabin. His mind wandered as he traveled his customary trail home. *Where is she? Who is she with? What is she doing?*

The familiarity of his main cabin pulled him from his musings. Jack mounted the stairs. His limbs felt heavy from the day's heat and frustration. He crossed the porch and pushed open the front door.

The sight of the woman in front of the registration counter brought him up short. "Can I help you?"

Kerry Dunn Green looked at him over her shoulder. She tossed back her straight, dark brown hair. "You shouldn't leave your door unlocked."

The buzzing started in Jack's ears. His heart raced as he was yanked back in time. "What the hell are you doing here?" He pulled the door closed behind him.

"I was leaving you a note." She glanced at the counter. "But I guess I don't need to now. Isaac and I were invited to participate in the Founders Day Celebration." She turned to Jack.

His gaze dropped to her stomach. The ground seemed to shift. "You're pregnant."

"Yes. Six months." Kerry's ginger brown cheeks pinkened. She settled her hands on her rounded stomach.

Jack would have considered the gesture protective if his ex-wife had had a maternal bone in her body.

"You got pregnant less than a year after Zoey's death?" He leaned against the door and crossed his arms. "Do you expect me to congratulate you?"

"No, I don't." Kerry's response was resigned.

Jack wasn't appeased. Kerry hadn't been with

him as he'd watched their child die. Now she was having a child with another man. Did she think Zoey could be replaced? "I hope for this child's sake, she or he is a healthy baby. Maybe then, you'll keep her."

Hurt and anger flashed across Kerry's brown eyes. "That's not fair, Jack."

"No, Kerry, it wasn't." He straightened from the door. His tone made it clear it was Kerry's actions and not Jack's accusation that was unfair. "Why are you here?"

"I told you. Isaac and I are here for Founders Day."

"I mean, *here*." He stabbed a finger toward the ground. "In my cabin."

Kerry looked away. She drew her hand through her dark brown hair as her eyes bounced around the wide, barren room. "Why don't you have any chairs for people to sit on?"

"Because I don't want them to stay." Jack gave her a pointed look.

She shook her head as though exasperated. "I'm here because I didn't want the Founders Day Celebration to be the first time we've seen each other since . . ."

When Kerry's voice trailed off, Jack tried to fill in the blank. "Since your affair? Since your decision to desert your critically ill child? Since you—"

"Stop it, Jack!" She pressed a hand to her hair as though trying to keep her head from exploding. "I knew this was a bad idea."

"Yes, it was." Through strength of will, Jack kept his gaze from drifting again and again to Kerry's ripening belly. She'd come to see him, pregnant with another man's child, after she'd disappeared when their child had been dying. She must be mad.

"But I had to see you."

"Why?" Jack met her eyes with all the hate, hurt, and anger that had been building inside him since he'd discovered her deception.

"I wanted to explain why I wasn't there with you and Zoey."

They'd never talked about Kerry's reason for leaving. Jack hadn't seen the point. After he'd discovered her affair, Jack hadn't been able to stand to look at her. He'd just wanted her gone. And when she'd asked for a divorce, he hadn't been able to sign the papers fast enough.

"I know why."

Kerry's eyes widened with surprise—and hope? "You do?"

"Yes. You're a selfish bitch."

Her face stiffened with shock. Her cheeks flushed with anger. "That's not true."

"It's not what you want to hear, but it *is* the truth."

Kerry pointed a finger in his direction. Her words shrieked across the room. "It's fine for you to sit as judge and jury over me, but you don't know what I went through, knowing Zoey was dying."

Jack's eyebrows shot to his hairline. "I don't?"

"No!" she shot back. "I was her mother."

"In name only."

"You don't know what it was like for me."

"Enlighten me."

Kerry dropped her arm and her voice. "I was scared. I didn't know what to do. I was helpless and hopeless, watching her grow weaker and thinner. I felt overwhelmed, depressed, devastated."

Jack stepped forward, bracing his legs and locking his knees to remain upright. "If that's what it was like for you, Kerry, then I know exactly how you felt. It was the same for me. I needed you so I wouldn't feel helpless, hopeless, scared, and overwhelmed alone. But you weren't with me. You were with him."

"Jack—"

"You said what you came to say. Get out." Jack stepped back, clearing the path to his front door.

Kerry hesitated a moment before walking past him and leaving the cabin. He locked the door behind her, then sank against it. He dropped his head into his hands. He really needed Audra.

CHAPTER 20

Audra pulled her rental car into her cabin's garage Wednesday afternoon. Her muscles tensed. Jack was waiting for her on her porch. She closed the automatic garage door, then walked through the cabin. She braced herself before letting him in.

"I didn't know Wendell was coming." She stepped aside so Jack could enter.

He walked past her. "I knew Kerry was coming. But I didn't expect her to show up on my doorstep."

Audra's jaw dropped. She locked the front door before following Jack into her great room. "Your ex-wife came to see you?"

"Yeah. This morning was like an ex's reunion." Was he as calm as he sounded?

"What did she want?"

He shrugged shoulders clothed in an army green shirt. "She's pregnant."

Oh, my God. Jack's announcement was a sucker punch to her gut. How had Jack reacted to seeing his ex-wife carrying another baby, after she'd walked away from theirs?

Audra circled him to see his face. "How do you feel about that?"

Jack's eyes looked through her. "How should I feel?"

"You're the only one who can answer that." Audra's heart hurt for him, so much pain. Why had Kerry come to see him?

Jack paced past her, dragging a hand over his close-cropped hair. "Why are you always asking me how I feel? What does it matter?"

"Expressing my feelings through my songs has helped me. The only way you'll heal from Zoey's death is to stop running from your emotions. You have to deal with them."

Jack spun to face her. His onyx eyes glowed with anger. "She was my daughter. I will *never* forget her."

Audra's eyes widened in horror. "That's not what I said."

"You can't replace a child."

"No, you can't."

He turned his back to her again. "Then my feelings don't matter."

"I disagree." She'd been so close to getting him to open up about the pain he must be feeling.

Jack met her gaze over his shoulder. "Are you speaking from experience?"

"That's not fair. Why are you running away from your feelings?"

"Because they hurt." Jack clenched his fists. His arm muscles flexed under his short-sleeved shirt.

Audra briefly closed her eyes as Jack's pain sliced through her heart. She crossed to him, placing her hand on his back. "I wish I could take the pain away from you."

"I wouldn't wish this on my worst enemy."

She rested her cheek on his back and wrapped her arms around his waist. His body was warm. "What would you say to Zoey right now if you could talk with her?"

"I don't want to do this, Audra."

"Try." Her voice was a gentle nudge.

"What's the point?"

"Does there have to be one?" She kissed his back through his cotton shirt. "Pretend you're sitting with her right now. What would you say to her?"

Jack sighed. Moments ticked by before he broke his silence. "I'm sorry."

Audra frowned. "What?"

"I would tell her I'm sorry."

"For what?" Audra whispered.

"For not saving her. For not keeping our family together. For not being the hero she thought I was."

Audra forced him to turn around. She held his upper arms in a firm grip and shook him once. "None of those things are your fault—not her illness and not Kerry's leaving. You have nothing to be sorry for. And, of course, you were her hero. I'm sure you gave her courage when she must have been so scared."

Jack didn't look convinced. "How do you know that?"

"Because you give me courage."

One thick, dark eyebrow arched. "I don't think hiking in the woods is comparable."

"Of course not. What you had with Zoey is so

much more than what we have. That's why I'm certain your love gave her courage."

Audra didn't flinch under his searching regard. After a moment, Jack wrapped his arms around her and held her tight to him.

Audra closed her eyes and soaked up the strength she felt whenever she was around him. She hugged him even closer. "You are a hero. Remember that. Zoey would want you to remember, too."

Doreen greeted Audra with a Trinity Falls Fudge Walnut Brownie and a mug of coffee Thursday at Books & Bakery. "I've heard your rehearsals with the band are going well."

"I'm surprised how quickly they've picked up the music." Audra stirred cream and sweetener into the hot, dark beverage. She closed her eyes in pleasure as she took the first sip.

She opened her eyes and let her gaze drift across the room. It was just after one o'clock, but the lunch crowd was thick with residents, as well as tourists in for the activities leading up to Founders Day.

Doreen leaned a hip against the counter opposite Audra. "Vaughn is a great band conductor. Probably the best the university's ever known. He holds vigorous band tryouts to make sure he gets only the best musicians."

"I'm looking forward to the town's reaction to the band's performance. They're terrific. On the other hand, my singing's nothing to write home about." Audra grimaced.

Doreen laughed. "You're too hard on yourself. I've heard great things about your voice."

"I guess you'll judge for yourself next Saturday." Her heart grew heavy. "I can't believe tomorrow's August first. This summer's flown by."

"How's Jack?" There was a strange tone in Doreen's question.

Audra was thrown by the swift topic change. "He's fine. Why?"

Doreen glanced behind Audra. "His ex-wife has arrived. And don't look now, but she's headed your way."

Moments later, a voice spoke behind her. "You're Audra Lane."

Audra looked up. Why did people think they had to tell her who she was, as though she didn't know?

The woman who'd spoken to her was beautiful: tall, well-dressed, and exuding a mesmerizing confidence. Her fresh-from-the-salon hair flirted with her shoulders. Her photogenic ginger brown features glowed under expertly applied makeup.

Audra's gaze fell to the stranger's pregnant belly. "You must be Kerry Green." This *is* Jack's ex-wife? Beside this beautiful princess, Audra felt like a troll.

Doreen tapped Audra's hand. "I'll be in the kitchen." Her warm brown eyes finished the thought—*Call if you need me*—before she disappeared through the kitchen door.

Kerry maneuvered onto the bar stool beside Audra. Her movements were surprisingly graceful despite her advanced pregnancy. "I could pretend to be surprised that you know who I am, and you could pretend you'd just made a lucky guess, but we both know the truth."

"I wasn't going to pretend. Jack told me you were pregnant." Audra considered the state representative's wife. She'd obviously sought her out. What did she want?

"I've heard a lot about you. People are saying you're the one who finally got Jack to climb out of Harmony Cabins and return to Trinity Falls." Kerry's smile was bright, but her brown eyes were watchful.

Audra sipped her coffee. "What is it that you want?"

Kerry's expression dimmed. "I want to thank you for helping Jack."

"Listen, Kerry, I work in a very competitive industry. I can sense when someone's trying to pull a game on me." At least she used to be able to tell. Somehow Wendell had slipped under her radar.

Kerry's smile disappeared. She shifted on her seat, settling more comfortably against the back of the bar stool. "I heard you write songs." She made it sound like a hobby.

Audra channeled Jack, adopting his favorite response: silence.

Kerry continued. "I tried to speak with Jack yesterday. I know he's angry with me for not being with him and Zoey at the end."

"You mean when your daughter died." She wouldn't allow Kerry to hide behind euphemisms to minimize or escape her actions.

Kerry flinched. "I know what you're thinking, but I did the best I could."

"Personally, I think you could have done better."

"Zoey was our adopted daughter."

Zoey was adopted? Audra had had no idea. Jack

had never revealed by word or inflection that Zoey wasn't his biological daughter.

Michelle Mosely, one of the high-school students who worked part-time at Books & Bakery, emerged from the kitchen. Audra used the distraction to recover from her surprise. The young woman grabbed the coffeepot and refilled Audra's mug.

"Thank you." Audra glanced at Michelle's asymmetrically styled purple hair. Last week, it had been blue. "The fact Zoey wasn't biologically his doesn't matter to Jack. He couldn't have loved her more." And Audra loved him even more because of that.

Audra froze at the thought. She was in love with Jackson Elijah Sansbury, the grumpy, reclusive, rental cabin property owner. But she hadn't even known him for a month. How could she have fallen in love with him so quickly? She was returning to Los Angeles in ten days. Audra tabled that train of thought. She couldn't handle it right now. In self-defense, she tuned back into Kerry's conversation.

"I need your help." The other woman's declaration was the distraction Audra needed.

"With what?"

"I need you to make sure that Jack doesn't let his anger with me get in the way on Founders Day. It's only a little more than a week away." Kerry's expression was so earnest you'd almost think she was being reasonable.

Audra added more cream to her coffee. "Why are you here if you thought Jack's reaction to you would be politically awkward for your husband?"

A myriad of reactions crossed Kerry's features. "You're right. I'm concerned Jack might say something that would reflect badly on me and, therefore, on my husband. But I'm from Trinity Falls. If I hadn't come, the media would have been suspicious."

Audra arched an eyebrow. "One of those 'damned-if-you-do' and 'damned-if-you-don't' situations."

Kerry's manner cooled. "You could say that."

Audra collected the plate with her untouched Trinity Falls Fudge Walnut Brownie and stood. "I'm not going to plead your case to Jack. Your past is between the two of you. But I will wish you well with your baby."

"Thank you." Kerry's gratitude was automatic.

"He or she will be lucky if you're even half the parent Jack was." Audra turned to find Doreen on the other side of the counter.

The bakery manager handed her a Books & Bakery bag. "Here's the brownie for Jack."

"Thanks." Audra followed her to the counter, paying cash for both pastries.

"Thank *you* for what you said about Jack being a good parent." Doreen handed her the change. "I'm going to miss you. You've made a positive impression on this town, getting involved in the sesquicentennial and bringing our favorite son back into the fold."

"Your town has made a positive impression on me." Audra tried to smile, but the idea of leaving Trinity Falls—of leaving Jack—hurt more than she'd imagined it would three weeks ago.

Doreen cleared her throat. "Well, there's no reason you couldn't come back for a visit once in a while."

"No, there isn't." Though it wouldn't be the same. A vacation romance was no longer enough for her. But was it possible for Jack to give her anything more?

Jack watched Wendell saunter into the main cabin Thursday afternoon. He should have known the other man would be back. The music producer seemed like the type who had to have his way.

He lowered his laptop monitor and rose from his seat behind the registration desk. "Don't have any cabins."

"'No room at the inn'?" Wendell came to a stop at the counter.

Jack ignored the biblical reference, returning the other man's laughing gaze in silence. It was almost lunchtime. Audra would be back soon. He hoped Wendell wasn't planning on staying long.

Wendell leaned against the counter. "Don't worry. I booked a room in a hotel just outside of town. Thanks, anyway."

"Sure." Jack shoved his hands into the front pockets of his brown shorts.

"It seems that your sesquicentennial has overtaxed the town's one hotel and one bed-and-breakfast. And, of course, your cabins."

"Why are you here?"

"You know you're in the service industry, right? You're going to have to work on your customer interaction. Let's raise the volume on the friendliness quotient." Wendell's chuckles shook the smaller man's shoulders.

"Why are you here? Please."

"You may need a twelve-step program." Wendell straightened, scanning the room. "This is really pretty property."

"Thanks."

"I wanted to take another look at it—and at you." Wendell turned his full attention to Jack. "There's something going on between you and Audra, isn't there?"

Jack didn't respond.

"This time, your silence speaks volumes, dude." Wendell's grin was smug. "See, if you weren't making time with her, you'd say so. Frankly, I don't know what she sees in you."

Jack wondered the same about Wendell. He may have only known Audra for three weeks, but the music producer didn't seem to be her type. The music producer enjoyed the sound of his own voice. And, judging by his appearance, he liked to draw attention to himself. His gold hoop earrings, dark red mesh tank, and gold shorts screamed, *Look at me!*

The other man continued. "You're a small-town man with a couple of fixer-uppers. She has a Grammy. Did she tell you about that?"

Jack crossed his arms over his chest. No, Audra hadn't told him, but he'd already known. "You're saying I'm not good enough for her?" Why did the wannabe music mogul think his opinion mattered?

Wendell gave him his snake charmer's smile. "I want to make sure you know there isn't any 'happily ever after' for the two of you."

Wendell wasn't telling Jack anything he hadn't realized on his own. But knowing it and hearing it—especially from Audra's ex-lover—were two different things. At least that's how he explained the phantom pain around his heart. But he wouldn't let the other man know his words had hit their target. "Afraid of competition?"

Wendell's uproarious laughter was insulting. He'd probably meant it to be. "Dude, what competition? You're not even part of her world."

"You are?" Jack wasn't prepared for the sting of jealousy.

"You know I am." Wendell spread his arms. "I'm a music producer. She's a songwriter. She's like jelly to my peanut butter."

More like a cure to his disease. Jack gripped the edge of the desk beneath the registration counter. "Then why did she leave you?"

Wendell waved a dismissive hand. "Creative differences."

"You mean your lies."

Wendell's skin darkened with an angry flush. "Audra's a sucker for a sob story, too. I hate to break it to you, dude, but you're Audra's summer pity project."

Jack stiffened. "What?"

The malicious glitter returned to Wendell's dark eyes. "She probably heard about your daughter and felt sorry for you."

"How do you know about my daughter?" The pulse pounding in Jack's ears made it hard to think, hard to hear.

Wendell shook his head in a mockery of sympathy. "Dude, don't you know everyone talks in small towns? Trinity Falls isn't any different."

Jack forced himself to take one deep breath, then another. He wasn't Audra's pity project. He knew this because she'd told him so. Her words whispered across his mind, *"I'm sorry Zoey died, but I don't pity you. I admire you."* Wendell was trying everything possible to drive Jack and Audra apart. It wouldn't work.

He grabbed for a measure of calm. "What's your game, Wendell?"

"I'm not playing a game." Wendell waved his hand again. "But it's obvious that Audra's sorry for you. She's always trying to fix things for other people. Once she's fixed you, she'll move on."

"Did Audra 'fix' it so that you could have the career in the music industry you weren't able to build on your own?" Jack watched in satisfaction as Wendell's triumphant expression darkened. A muscle ticked in the other man's jaw.

"I made my career myself. No one did that for me." Wendell chewed the words. "It was my hard work and talent that got me where I am now."

Jack arched a brow. "If you don't need Audra's help, why did you follow her to Trinity Falls?"

"The same reason you want her to stay here, but that's not gonna happen, dude."

Shock shorted Jack's system. Wendell was right. He wanted Audra to stay in Trinity Falls. How had she sneaked past his emotional guard and made their make-believe relationship real? He was falling in love with Audra Lane. He hadn't felt this much fear since Zoey had died.

Wendell was still talking. "You'd better get over that little fantasy real quick. Audra may be playing house with you now, but she can't stay here, not if she wants to be at the top of her game. She has to be in L.A. She needs to mix it up with other artists, hang out in the clubs. This town doesn't have any kind of nightlife. What's she going to do here?"

"She's not going back to you." Jack spoke in anger born from fear.

"But she *is* returning to L.A. Who knows what'll happen from there?" Wendell licked his lips.

Jack couldn't let that pass. "You're deluding yourself."

"I think you are. Your ex-wife even left Trinity Falls, and she's from here. Audra's from L.A. What chance do you have of her staying? Hey, once her vacation is over, maybe you can become pen pals or something."

"Which is still more attention than she gives you."

Wendell stepped back from the registration counter. "I'll give you some advice. Wake up and smell the coffee. Audra is leaving. Make it easier on yourself, dude. Just rip off the bandage. Don't try to make her stay."

On that note, the music producer sauntered back across the lobby and out of the main cabin. Jack shook his head in amazement. Maybe Wendell was right. A quick good-bye would be less painful. Then he could try to heal—if that was even possible.

CHAPTER 21

"Afternoon, Darius." Alonzo's easy drawl announced his presence Thursday afternoon.

Darius automatically saved the news story he was drafting on his desktop computer before spinning his office chair toward his cubicle entrance. "Hi, Sheriff. What brings you to the *Monitor*?"

"Do you have a few minutes?" Alonzo removed his brown felt hat.

Darius checked his watch. It was just after three o'clock. He had almost two hours before the copy deadline. "Sure. Have a seat."

His curiosity was aroused. Had Alonzo ever come to the *Monitor*'s newsroom before? He watched the lawman settle onto the worn upholstered visitor's seat.

Alonzo rested his right ankle on his left knee. "I heard you've been to the university to interview the new history professor."

"That's right." Darius sat back, resting his wrists on the arms of his chair.

"And before that, you called her and Foster Gooden." There was a note of discomfort in Alonzo's voice.

Where was the sheriff going with this line of questioning? "I've spoken with the university's vice president of academic affairs before, Sheriff. Is there a problem?"

Alonzo sighed. "I know you're just doing your job, Darius. But Dr. Harris is calling it harassment."

Darius's head jerked back in surprise. "What?"

"I know you don't mean any harm, but the professor is very concerned. I offered to have a talk with you."

Dr. Peyton Harris had called the police about him. This, after throwing him out of her office Tuesday. Darius raised his hands in surrender. "Consider your message delivered, Sheriff."

"And she doesn't want you writing any articles about her, either."

That annoyed him even more than being frogmarched out of her office. "I can't write an article about her if she won't let me interview her."

Alonzo lowered his right leg to the ground. "Thanks, Darius."

Darius considered the sheriff. The older man's gaze was direct but guarded. "You know why she doesn't want to be interviewed, don't you?"

"Even if I did, I couldn't tell you."

"Look, Sheriff, I'm not going to write an article about her. I just want to know why she's so secretive about her past."

"If she wanted you to know, she'd tell you."

Darius leaned forward. "Is she a danger to the

town? Is she a fugitive from the law or in the witness protection program?"

"Darius, I can't tell you anything more than what I already have."

"You haven't told me anything."

"And I can't tell you anything more." Alonzo's eyes twinkled with humor.

Darius sat back. "That's not being diligent toward the community. The public has a right to know whether our newest neighbor is a threat."

"You're quoting the public's right to know, but you're the only one asking. Tell me, does your curiosity have anything to do with the fact that Dr. Harris is an attractive woman?"

"I hadn't noticed." Darius struggled to hold Alonzo's gaze as the sheriff silently laughed at him. "Mmm-hmm."

"You might as well tell me, Alonzo. Otherwise, I'm sure I'll find something on the Internet."

Alonzo's amusement disappeared. "I'd rather you didn't do that, Darius. This young woman has a right to her privacy. She's not hurting anyone. She's not a danger to anyone."

"I won't publish anything. I just want to know."

Alonzo gave him a long, silent look. "How would you feel if you were in her position?"

"I don't know what her position is."

"A lot of people in Trinity Falls are curious about the person you go to visit almost every weekend over in Sequoia." Alonzo cocked his head. "How would you feel if one of them started digging into your personal life?"

Darius's muscles strained with the effort to appear relaxed. "Your point is taken."

"I hope so." Alonzo stood. "I'd hate to have to execute the restraining order Dr. Harris requested."

Darius's eyes widened. "Restraining order?"

"I told her you were a sensible person and that I could reason with you. I'm glad you didn't make me a liar."

"Thanks, Sheriff." Darius couldn't believe his request for an interview would be cause for a restraining order.

"Don't mention it." Alonzo paused in the entrance of Darius's cubicle. "You know, Darius, you can always channel your extra energy toward convincing your father to pull out of the mayoral campaign."

Darius swung his chair to face the sheriff. "I've tried. He won't listen."

"Then maybe there's someone else he'd be willing to listen to."

Darius had realized long ago that the sheriff's easygoing manner and calm eyes masked a sharp intelligence. Dread settled on his shoulders. "Why do I have the feeling you've been checking into the person I visit in Sequoia?"

Alonzo settled his felt hat on his head. "Pure speculation. I've known your father for a long time, and I know you're not like him." The sheriff nodded before he disappeared.

Darius hoped Alonzo was right. He tried hard not to be anything like Simon Knight. He turned back to his desk and his gaze fell on his telephone. He lifted the receiver and dialed her phone number from memory before he had time to consider his actions. The call connected on the second ring.

"It's Darius. I need to see you tonight. I think it's time the three of us spoke with my father."

Doreen unlocked her front door and preceded Alonzo into her home Thursday afternoon.

"Thanks for your help with my groceries, Alonzo. Imagine running into you at the store." She locked the door behind him, then led him into her kitchen. Doreen lifted her bag onto the kitchen counter.

Alonzo set his two bags on the table. "Doreen, I have a confession."

"Mmm. What's that?" She started unpacking her groceries.

Alonzo hesitated. "I didn't bump into you at the store by accident. I know you usually go shopping after work on Thursdays."

Doreen turned from the bags to face him. A smile trembled on her lips. "In that case, I have a confession, too."

"What?"

"I didn't need all of these groceries. I just wanted you to help me with them and drive me home."

A slow smile eased the worry from Alonzo's proud features. "Really?"

"Really." Doreen chuckled. "We're acting like a couple of high school kids." And she thoroughly enjoyed the feeling.

A sudden frown appeared. "Can I still stay for dinner?"

"Of course. But for now, sit down and keep me company while I put away the groceries."

"Yes, ma'am." Alonzo settled onto a chair at the kitchen table.

Doreen tossed him a wry look for his response. "What do you want to talk about?"

"Have you decided whether you'll stay in the mayoral race?"

She hesitated before unpacking her fresh fruits and vegetables into the refrigerator's crisper. "Why are you asking?"

"I'd like to know who's going to be running the town for the next four years." There was a shrug in Alonzo's voice.

Doreen put the milk and juice on a shelf in the fridge. "Would it upset you if I ran for mayor?"

"No, it wouldn't." His voice was firm. "I don't have any qualms about your being mayor."

She shut the refrigerator door and faced him. "Why not?"

"A lot of reasons. First, I'm not Leo." Alonzo gave her a pointed look.

"I know." Doreen crossed to the table to unpack the remaining two grocery bags.

"Second, I know you, and I know you'd be good for this town."

Good answer. But not good enough.

"You said you were interested in a relationship with me." She continued putting away the groceries. "Aren't you concerned about the demands being mayor would make on my time?"

Alonzo chuckled. "I'm the guy who left town when you married Paul, remember? Doesn't that prove what your happiness means to me? I'm in love with the woman you are. Why would I ask you to change that?"

Very good answer. Doreen leaned against the kitchen counter, afraid her shaky knees wouldn't hold her. "That's a good point."

"It's also the truth. So, are you going to remain in the race?"

"Yes, I am." She stuffed the empty plastic grocery bags into the cabinet below the sink, then returned to her position at the counter. "Ramona convinced me that if being mayor is what I really want, I should run. I shouldn't let other people define me."

Alonzo's dark eyebrows stretched up his forehead. "Ramona, huh? Well, I'll be darned. She's right, but I never would have guessed she'd be the one to convince you to campaign."

Doreen tossed him a smile. "She wants to make sure there's someone to step in when she and Quincy leave Trinity Falls."

"It's more than that." Alonzo stretched his long legs, clad in his green uniform pants, in front of him, crossing them at the ankles. "She wants to make sure she's leaving the town in good hands."

Doreen blushed at Alonzo's words. "Maybe if we take this slowly . . ."

"It's been forty-two years. I have been taking this slowly."

Doreen's blush deepened. "I suppose you have—" The doorbell chimed, interrupting her. She checked her watch. It was nearing five o'clock in the evening. "Excuse me."

As Doreen passed him, Alonzo stood, trailing her across the living room. Doreen went up on her toes to check the front door's peephole. *Leonard. What does* he *want?*

She opened the door with more than a little reluctance. "Hello, Leo."

"I figured you'd be home from the grocery store by now. We need to talk." Leonard's dark eyes were grim with resignation. He stepped forward as though he assumed she'd welcome him into her home.

Doreen braced a hand against the threshold to bar his entry. "This isn't a good time. I have company."

Leonard's expression was blank with surprise. "Who?"

"Evening, Leo." Alonzo materialized behind Doreen. How had he appeared without her hearing him?

"Alonzo?" Leonard's voice strained with incredulity. His gaze moved from Doreen to Alonzo and back. "What's going on?"

Alonzo responded before Doreen could answer. "I could ask you the same thing."

"Bullshit." Leonard packed his irritation into those two syllables.

"Leo, we'll talk another time." Doreen rushed to control the situation.

She started to close the door. Leonard's arm struck out to keep it open. His reaction surprised Doreen. But with a subtle movement, Alonzo shifted his stance, putting himself between her and Leonard.

"Doreen asked you to leave." Alonzo's voice was cold and flat.

Leonard scowled at him. "I'm not leaving unless you do."

"Then we have a problem." Alonzo met the other man's challenge.

Doreen glanced at Ms. Helen's house across the street. She cringed, imagining her observant neighbor watching the entertainment through her front windows.

"For heaven's sake, get inside." She pulled her door wider. "I'm not having this conversation on my front porch." Once Leonard entered, she locked her door before turning to face both men.

Leonard confronted Alonzo. "What are you doing here?"

Doreen gasped at his aggression. "Leo!"

"Why are *you* here?" Alonzo didn't back down.

Doreen's eyes stretched wide. "Alonzo!"

Leonard led with his chin. "I don't want you sniffing around my woman."

Doreen's temper spiked. "*Your* woman?"

"That wasn't your first mistake." Alonzo's temper built like a storm gathering in her front room.

Leonard took a step back. "What are you talking about?"

"Your first mistake was taking Doreen for granted." Alonzo crossed his arms. "Your second was believing she was your woman."

Doreen set her hands on her hips. "Alonzo, I can speak for myself."

Leonard snorted. "What? Do you think she could ever be yours?"

What was wrong with them? Doreen stared from one testosterone faucet to another. Enough was enough. She stepped between Alonzo and Leonard, and shoved both men in the chest.

"How dare you talk about me as though I were some inanimate object you can tug between you?"

Alonzo stepped back, raising both hands in surrender. "Doreen, I'm sorry. I—"

She cut him with a look. "I'm not finished speaking."

Leonard smirked. "That's right—"

"Shut up, Leo." She switched her glare to the other man. "You have no right to even pretend to be jealous. You broke up with me two weeks ago."

Leonard stared in surprise. "No, I didn't."

Doreen crossed her arms. "Really? Then why have you been escorting Yvette Bates all over town?"

"I was trying to make you jealous." Leonard moved his hand dismissively.

Alonzo interrupted them. "Does Yvette know that?"

Leonard's expression darkened. "Why don't you shut up and mind your own business?"

Alonzo held his ground. "Doreen *is* my business."

"No, she's not." Leonard pointed a finger past Doreen toward Alonzo's face. "You came back to Trinity Falls too late. I got to her first."

"You don't deserve Doreen." Alonzo fisted his hands.

"And you do?" Leonard stepped forward, causing Doreen to stumble against Alonzo.

"Stop it!" Doreen threw up her hands.

Alonzo steadied her before moving her out of harm's way. "You played with Yvette just to hurt Doreen. You don't deserve either woman."

"I said stop it!" Doreen shouted to get their attention. "Get out of my house. Both of you!" They stared at her, frozen in surprise. Doreen marched to the door and ripped it open. "Out!"

Leonard jerked his head toward Alonzo. "I'm not leaving unless he does."

"Get! Out!" Doreen shook with fury.

Leonard recovered first. He stomped across the entryway and through the open door. "This isn't over."

Doreen met Alonzo's eyes from across the distance. Her voice was muted. "I want you to leave."

Alonzo held her gaze as he walked to her. "Forty-two years ago, I walked away without a fight. I'll be damned if I step aside now for Leo."

Doreen flinched at the way he sneered the other man's name. "I'm not a toy for the two of you to fight over."

"I'm not fighting over you, Doreen. I'm fighting *for* you. I can't lose you again. And I won't lose you to someone like Leo, who can't appreciate what he has with you." The yearning in his eyes weakened her knees.

Alonzo turned and walked to his car, parked at the curb in front of her house. Doreen locked her front door. Pride had demanded her show of strength to Leonard and Alonzo. They couldn't fight over her as though she were disputed property. She would decide who she wanted to be with—if she wanted to be with either of them.

"Does Noah know I'm coming?" Darius called to the woman waiting for him Thursday evening in the doorway at the end of the path. He still wasn't sure he was doing the right thing.

He felt like limp lettuce as he walked the short, curving path to the little wood-and-stone cottage in Sequoia, Ohio, a town neighboring Trinity Falls. Was it the heat, the strain of the coming visit, or both?

"He knows." June Cale let Darius into her home. "He'll be home from work soon."

The cozy little cottage reminded Darius of Doreen Fever's home. It was full of natural light, bright colors, and fat, fluffy furniture. Some of Darius's tension drained as he walked farther into the Cale home.

Darius glanced at June over his shoulder. At thirty-eight, she still looked like a college coed. Her short dark brown curls exploded around her makeup-free oval face. Her almond-shaped bright brown eyes lent an exotic look to her brown sugar features.

He shoved his hands into the front pockets of his gray Dockers. "Did you talk with him?"

"I wanted to wait for you." June gestured toward the foam green love seat, inviting Darius to sit. She took the armchair, leaving the matching sofa empty between them.

Darius's gaze circled the room again. It housed so many Cale family memories. Photos of Noah spilled across the fireplace mantel and clung to the pale yellow walls. They tracked his life from birth to young adulthood: first steps, first bike, prekindergarten graduation, First Communion, Confirmation, football. What was it like growing up in a home in which you knew you were loved, cherished even?

June interrupted his thoughts. "Can I get you something to drink?"

"No, thanks." Darius curled his fingers into his left palm to keep from drumming them against the armrest.

Their conversation hadn't been this stilted since Darius had formally met June and her son, Noah, five years earlier. But perhaps discussing the weather, their day, and preparations for Trinity Falls's upcoming sesquicentennial would calm June's nervousness, too.

They were running out of inane chatter when a key sounded in the front door. Darius sighed his relief even as he tensed in dread. He wasn't looking forward to this conversation or the confrontation that would come after.

"Ma, I'm home." Noah's greeting preceded his appearance in the living room.

Looking at him was like looking into a mirror sixteen years in the past. "Hey, Noah."

Noah studied his mother before switching his attention to Darius. "Hey, D. You want me to meet our father, don't you?"

Darius frowned his surprise. "How did you know?"

Noah leaned his left shoulder against the nearby wall and crossed his ankles. "It's Thursday. You never visit in the middle of the week, unless it's a big deal."

"You don't miss a trick, do you, kid?" Darius's lips curved in a reluctant smile.

Noah smiled in return. "It's about time you realized that. And don't call me 'kid,' old man. I'm seventeen." He shrugged. "I'll meet him."

"Wait a minute. I don't think that's a good idea." June's protest was immediate.

Darius had expected it. Simon had been a worse father to Noah than he'd been to Darius. He hadn't thought that was possible. In contrast, Darius had tried to be a better role model for his younger half brother, spending time with him, helping him with his homework, giving him advice, attending his football games, teaching him to tie a tie. But he couldn't replace Noah's father. And, although he wouldn't wish Simon on anyone, he'd always thought his sibling should at least meet the man who'd contributed to his birth.

Darius turned to face Noah's mother. "Why not?"

"Simon Knight may have provided Noah with his DNA, but he's not his father." June's frown was fierce.

Noah straightened from the wall. "Whether he's Father of the Year or just a sperm donor, I want to meet him. I want to know where I came from. I have that right."

June spread her arms to encompass their home. "This is where you came from."

"You know what I mean, Ma." Noah faced his mother. "The people I came from. All of them."

June's expression revealed her frustration. "Why? Where has Simon been for the past seventeen years? Darius found us. Simon didn't even try."

Noah shrugged. "I don't care. I want to know who my father is."

June spread her arms. "What difference will that make?"

Noah's expression was a study in stubborn determination. "It'll make a difference to me."

Darius gentled his voice. "Meeting his father

won't change the fact that you're a great mother and Noah loves you very much."

June turned on him. "You only want them to meet because you think seeing Noah will convince Simon to drop out of the mayoral race."

Noah crossed his long arms over his narrow chest. "Is that true?"

Darius met his younger brother's midnight eyes. "I want the two of you to meet, if that's what you want. But, yes, I'm hoping meeting you will change his mind about running for mayor."

"Because he'll be ashamed of me?" Noah's eyes snapped with accusation.

"No, because I want him to acknowledge you." Darius's response was firm and impatient. How could the younger man think his existence was something to be ashamed of? "If you make the first move, you can set the tone for your introduction. But if he lets someone else reveal your existence, the gossip will be nasty." He looked at June. "I don't want that for Noah. Do you?"

June clenched and unclenched her fists. The battle between protective and overprotective mother warred within her. "No, I don't want that for my son."

Noah nodded once. "When will we do this?"

Darius studied June's stark expression. She didn't want Noah and Simon to meet. But it was what Noah wanted and what Simon needed. He inclined his head toward her to acknowledge the difficult decision she'd made.

He switched his attention to Noah. "You'll meet our father tomorrow."

CHAPTER 22

Ramona's ebony eyes grew as large as saucers. "Leo shoved in the door?" The retiring mayor had joined Doreen and Megan Friday morning in the kitchen of Books & Bakery. She leaned forward on the dainty honey-wood chair, her mug of cooling coffee forgotten. "And then what happened?"

Megan gave her older cousin an exasperated look from the other side of the table. "If you'd stop interrupting, she could tell us that much faster."

Puzzled, Doreen looked from Ramona to Megan. Ramona looked almost gleeful. Megan looked stunned. "Ramona, you're missing the point. This wasn't fun for me. They made me feel like a pork chop between two starving dogs."

Doreen had invited the two women for a private conversation in her white-and-silver kitchen after Darius, Ean, and Quincy had left that morning. She'd put Michelle Mosely, the high-school junior, in charge of the bakery counter. Megan had asked

Wesley Hayes, the high-school senior, to watch over the bookstore area.

"Admit it." Ramona gave her a sly look. "You didn't feel even a tiny bit flattered that two attractive men were fighting over you?"

"Not even a little." Doreen huffed again. "They were sniping at each other as though I wasn't even in the room. It's my house!"

Ramona propped her elbow on the kitchen table and rested her chin on her right fist. "I used to love when boys would fight over me. It made me feel powerful."

"The key word there is 'boys.'" Megan leaned her forearms on the table. "Doreen's right. Alonzo and Leo should have known better. But in fairness, it did sound as though Alonzo was defending himself— and you."

An image of Alonzo crossing his muscled arms over his broad chest returned to Doreen. *"Your first mistake was taking Doreen for granted. Your second was believing she was your woman."*

Doreen shook off the thrill of attraction. "I don't need anyone to defend me." But did she want it?

Megan smiled. "Sometimes it's nice when they do."

Ramona crossed her legs, straightening the hem of her crimson sundress over her knees. "That's right. Give the guy a break, for Pete's sake. After all, he's been in love with you for more than forty years. Good grief! That's longer than I've been alive."

Megan crossed to the counter and placed a hand on Doreen's shoulder. "Put yourself in his place. Would you remain silent if the person you loved as deeply as he loves you was in a relationship with someone who was taking him for granted?"

Doreen's gaze dropped to the floor. She heard Alonzo's voice again: *"I'm not fighting over you, Doreen. I'm fighting for you."*

"No, I wouldn't."

Megan let her hand drop. "Alonzo must love you very much to have left you—and his home—the first time."

"Can you imagine?" Ramona swung her right leg above her left knee. "I couldn't have done it."

Michelle appeared in the kitchen doorway, interrupting their conversation. The unease in her tawny eyes drew attention from her spiked, lemon yellow hair. "Ms. Doreen, Ms. Bates is here. She wants to see you, and she doesn't look happy."

"Just when you thought it couldn't get any more interesting." Anticipation lit Ramona's eyes.

Doreen ignored Ramona. "Thanks, Michelle. I'll be right out."

Megan's expression showed her concern. "What do you think Yvette wants?"

Doreen propped her hands on her hips. "I have no idea."

"Why don't you speak with her in my office?" Megan glanced at Ramona. "Something tells me you're going to need the privacy."

"Something tells me you're right." Doreen removed her apron and hung it on a hook beside the sink.

Ramona stood. "Do you need backup?"

"No, thanks. I'm pretty sure I can handle this." Doreen left the kitchen, aware of Megan and Ramona following her.

Yvette Bates waited beside the cash register. Her pose was a study in disdain. The high-school English teacher was model slim, with subtly applied makeup and expertly styled dark brown hair. She appeared to be enjoying her summer. Her sun-kissed brown skin glowed in a skimpy peach tank top and matching shorts.

Facing her, Doreen felt dowdy and overdressed. "Hello, Yvette. How can I help you?"

"You can leave Leo alone." The other woman's words carried a matter-of-fact threat that would make a Mafia don proud.

Doreen offered her wannabe rival a smile. "Let's talk in Megan's office."

She led the way across the store, past special-interest book displays and fluffy armchairs. The rows of dark wood bookcases were packed with new releases and best-selling classics.

Business was brisk in both the book and bakery sections due to the out-of-town visitors, who'd come for the sesquicentennial. Wesley and Michelle had recruited their high school friends to help with the increased customer traffic. In fact, all the town center businesses had additional seasonal help.

Doreen held the office door open for Yvette, then pulled the door shut behind her. She gestured the teacher to one of the two blue fabric guest chairs as she sank onto the other.

"What makes you think I'm after Leo?" They might as well get this over with. They both knew this wasn't a social call.

Yvette's posture was rigid on the padded seat. "He told me he'd stopped by your house. That's why he was late getting to my condo."

Leonard had come to see her last night, knowing Yvette was expecting him? The thought made

Doreen's skin crawl. "Did he tell you he came to my house uninvited?"

Yvette ignored her question. "I'm sure it's hard, accepting that a man of quality like Leo would dump you and start dating another woman so quickly. But you have to get over that."

Doreen was speechless. She stared at the other woman for a beat, wondering what *she'd* ever seen in Leonard. He'd broken up with her because she'd wanted to pursue a very realistic dream. He'd admitted to dating another woman to make her jealous. But then he'd told his new girlfriend that it was *Doreen* who was stalking *him*.

Had Leonard fooled me, or had I just been a fool?

"Yvette, I'm not trying to hurt your relationship with Leo." Doreen used a very measured tone. "In fact, I wish both of you every happiness."

Yvette looked confused. "Are you sure?"

"I'm positive."

Yvette angled her head. "You sound sincere."

"That's because I am."

"Well . . . all right." The other woman stood.

"I'm glad we've cleared the air." Doreen walked with her to the door.

"So am I, especially since I intend to vote for you in November. I've heard things about Simon Knight that frankly make him seem untrustworthy."

"Men!" Doreen fought a smile. Leonard's new girlfriend intended to vote for her. How poetic.

She escorted Yvette to the bookstore's entrance, where they shook hands and parted with best wishes for the summer. The casual observer might even have mistaken them for friends.

Back at the café, Doreen sighted a familiar, leanly

muscled figure seated at her counter. Her busy morning was aging into a hectic afternoon. Doreen gathered her courage in both hands, strode through her crowded dining area, and tapped Alonzo on the shoulder.

He turned from his mug of coffee in surprise, then rose from his bar stool. He was handsome in his sheriff's uniform: short-sleeved tan shirt, black tie, and spruce green gabardine pants. He seemed almost as nervous as she felt.

Alonzo cleared his throat. "Doreen, I apologize for—"

She took his face in her hands and drew his mouth down to hers. She kissed him hard and quick, loving the taste of his lips on hers, then released him. "I'm the one who's sorry."

"For what?" Alonzo's voice was husky. His coffee-colored eyes were dark and dreamy. He made her forget where she was.

Doreen looked around the café. Her customers—both regulars and those here just for the sesquicentennial—regarded her with surprise and amusement. But she didn't regret her impulse. She'd do it again.

She took his left hand and smiled into his puzzled gaze. "Last night, I was blinded by pride. The truth is, I would fight for you, too."

Alonzo regarded her with a warmth that woke the butterflies in her stomach. "Will you have dinner with me tonight?"

She gave him a flirtatious smile. "For starters. We have a lot of catching up to do."

She thought she heard Alonzo groan. With a wink,

she walked past him and into her kitchen. *So this is female empowerment.* She liked it.

Darius rang his parents' doorbell Friday evening.

"Don't you have a key to your parents' house?" June sounded baffled.

"No, I don't." Darius met her gaze over his shoulder.

Noah exchanged a look with his mother. "That's cray."

Yeah, cray. Darius smiled at his half brother's use of the popular slang for "weird." Maybe not having a key to one's family home was odd for a normal family. But Darius couldn't think of anyone who considered Simon and Ethel Knight normal parents.

The front door opened, framing Ethel in the threshold. She scowled at him. "You didn't tell me you were coming for dinner."

"We're not staying."

His mother noticed June and Noah on the steps behind him. Her scowl deepened. "You brought company? Who are . . ." Ethel's dark brown eyes sharpened on Noah. She swayed. "Oh, my Lord."

Darius stepped forward to catch his mother. His hands banded her forearms. "Steady."

Her eyes pleaded with him. Her whisper rushed on a breath of air. "Is he your son?"

"You know he's not," Darius whispered back. He caught June and Noah's concerned gazes. "Come in."

Darius led them into his parents' great room. Ethel leaned heavily on his arm. June and Noah wandered past him. What did they think as they studied the white walls dotted with framed dried flowers, Ethel's collection of ornamental birds, and the heavy red curtains that guarded against the natural light?

Darius led his mother to her stiff red sofa. "Sit down, Mom."

Ethel ignored him. She stared fixedly at the younger version of her husband of thirty-three years. "How old are you?"

Noah faced her. "I'm seventeen, ma'am."

Ethel swayed on her feet.

Darius's heart leaped. "Mom, sit before you fall."

"Who was at the door?" Simon's voice accompanied his footfalls on the staircase.

With a surprising burst of energy, Ethel tore free of Darius' support. She marched across the room, meeting Simon at the threshold. "Your whore and her bas—"

"Watch your mouth!" A sudden flash of white-hot rage burned through Darius. He'd never spoken to his parents like that before. He hoped they'd never give him reason to speak like that to them ever again.

Ethel spun to face him, shock stamped on her face. Simon stared across the room as though he'd been confronted by ghosts. Darius didn't have a lot of moments with his parents for which he could look back and be proud. This evening wouldn't change that.

"Dad, you've met June Cale." Darius stood between her and Noah. His younger brother hadn't taken his eyes off Simon since the older man had entered the room. "But it's about time you met her son, Noah. Your sperm helped make this moment possible."

"June." Simon's voice was hollow.

Ethel grabbed a fistful of her husband's red shirt and shook him. "Did you know you had a son by her? *Did you?*"

Simon looked down at his wife. His arms hung limply at his sides. "I . . . Yes."

"*Aiiyee!*" Ethel pounded Simon's chest.

Darius stepped forward to stop his mother, but June caught his arm. She shook her head, cautioning him to let his parents work this out. Darius stepped back.

Ethel's tirade was painful to hear, painful to watch. "Everyone was talking, whispering about you sleeping with other women. But you told me you weren't having affairs. You're a liar!"

Her tears were the sobs of a woman betrayed. Darius's heart broke for her. She'd married his father because she was pregnant with Darius. And now she was left to wonder how many other children Simon had fathered.

Simon grabbed her wrists. "Ethel, calm down."

"*Calm down!*" Ethel's scream could shatter glass. "Did you pay her? Did you send her money?"

"No, he didn't." June's voice was kind but firm. "I took care of Noah on my own. Simon's never even met him. We didn't have contact with anyone in your family before Darius found us."

Ethel turned on Darius. Wide, wet streaks dampened his mother's face. Her eyes were red and puffy. She pointed a finger at him. "You. Did you bring them here to humiliate me?"

Darius shook his head, hating the pain he was causing her. "No, Mom. That wasn't my intent."

Ethel continued to glare at him. "Then what did you hope to accomplish?"

Darius pushed his fists into the front pockets of his pants. "Dad's plan to run for public office should be a family decision. Noah is family." He held Simon's gaze. "He's my brother and your son. You may not have acknowledged him, but I don't want him hurt if the media finds out about him."

Simon snorted. "The *Monitor* is the only paper that's going to cover the mayoral race. And you're not going to say anything that could embarrass your own family."

"I'm not the only reporter at the paper." Darius crossed his arms. "Opal Gutierrez interviewed you when you announced your petition. She'd love to get her hands on this story."

"Tell her you want to cover it." Simon shrugged.

Darius dragged a hand over his close-cropped hair. "That's sure to make her suspicious. And I'm not going to hide Noah for you. It's time you acknowledged him."

Ethel stuck her finger in Simon's face. "I'm through with your bullshit. I'm through with being humiliated by you because you can't keep your dick in your pants. I told you before that if you run for mayor, I'm leaving you. Well, that's just what I'm going to do now."

His mother spun and raced up the stairs. Simon stood and watched her. "Ethel!"

Darius gestured toward the staircase. "Aren't you going after her?"

Simon shrugged. "Your mother's too damn

emotional. Give her time to cool off. She's not going anywhere."

June adjusted her purse strap on her shoulder. "Frankly, Simon, I can't believe she's stayed with you as long as she has. You're a piece of work."

Simon reared his head in surprise. "What does that mean?"

"It means you're a pig." June sighed. "I knew you were never going to be part of Noah's life. You made that extremely clear. The only reason we're here is that he was curious about you."

"He's grown up well. He looks just like me." Simon's gaze was fixated on Noah.

"Any resemblance is only skin deep. Noah's a good and decent person." She crossed the room and got right in Simon's face. "If one harsh word about my son shows up in any paper, TV, or radio in connection with you running for mayor, I will come back to Trinity Falls and peel the skin off your ass like an orange."

Darius didn't doubt June's threat. Apparently, neither did Simon.

After a moment's consideration, his father nodded. "All right. I'll withdraw my petition."

"Good." June turned to Noah. "Has your curiosity been satisfied?"

Noah pulled his gaze from Simon. "Yes, ma'am."

"Take us home, Darius." June started toward the front door as though she expected Darius and Noah to follow her.

"Wait." Simon looked Noah up and down. "You must be about seventeen now."

"Yes, sir." Noah stood awkwardly in front of the

father he'd met for the first time in his life just minutes ago.

Darius moved to stand beside his younger brother.

Simon spared his oldest son a glance before returning his attention to Noah. "What college are you going to?"

"I haven't decided yet." Noah's shrug was a Knight mannerism. "I'm looking at a couple. I was thinking about Trinity Falls University."

Simon brushed that suggestion aside. "No, no. That's not good enough for a Knight."

June walked back to the group, putting a hand on her son's shoulder. "He's a Cale."

Darius arched an eyebrow. "A little late for paternal instincts, isn't it?"

He escorted June and Noah out of his parents' house and back into his car.

Noah settled onto the middle of the backseat. "I didn't think he was that bad."

Darius watched his brother from the rearview mirror. "You didn't grow up with him."

June buckled her seat belt. "How did you grow up in that house?"

"I didn't." He'd grown up in Ean and Quincy's homes.

"I used to envy you, growing up with both parents." Noah's voice was pensive. "But I think I was the lucky one."

Darius smiled without humor. "Yeah, you were."

June looked away, wiping a hand across her eyes. "Do you think he's telling the truth? Will he give up his petition?"

"I think so." Darius pulled away from the curb.

But had Simon's decision come too late to save his marriage? It seemed Darius had spent his whole life dreading, and yet expecting, his parents to divorce. Had it finally come to that? Only time would tell.

One thing he'd learn from this experience is that there are some stories the media should leave alone. His half brother was one of them. Dr. Peyton Harris's private life was another. He owed the professor an apology.

Nessa Linden wasn't happy to see Simon Saturday morning. He entered the councilwoman's home, anyway.

She locked the door before confronting him. "It's not a good idea for you to be here. I can't be seen endorsing your campaign."

"I'm not going to run for mayor."

"Because of your sons?"

Simon gave her a sharp look. "How did you know about that?"

She walked past him into her living room. "I underestimated Darius. I didn't think he'd have the balls to bring his brother into the equation."

"Everything's fallen apart." Simon chewed his inner cheek. "Ethel left me last night. I don't know where she is. I called Darius this morning and he blames me."

How had his life gone so wrong? Why did his son hate him? Where was his wife?

"You're right. You're no longer a viable candidate for mayor—if you ever were. And the sesquicentennial is only a week away." Nessa settled onto her black leather sofa. The full skirt of her cream sundress spread around her. "I'll have to think of something else."

"For what?" Simon paced her living room.

"For what I have in mind for Trinity Falls." She smoothed her cap of dark brown hair.

Simon stilled. "What are you planning to do?"

Nessa crossed her legs. "That no longer concerns you."

Simon chuckled without humor. He tucked his hands into his front pants pockets and rocked forward on his toes. "If you're planning to do something to hurt the town, you'd better hope Ramona, Doreen, and Megan don't hear about it." Or Darius, for that matter.

Nessa's dark brown eyes were cold. "How would they learn of it? We're the only ones who know I have a plan, and neither of us would say anything, would we?"

He heard the threat in her voice. Simon wasn't impressed. Nessa had a long way to go to match Ramona for intimidation.

"I'm no longer your concern, Nessa. I'll show myself out."

Simon needed a way to get back into his family's good graces. Taking his suspicions about Nessa to Darius would be a good start. But could he risk it? What would Nessa do if he told others she'd been the one behind his mayoral bid?

CHAPTER 23

Late Saturday morning, the sound of hammering led Audra to Jack. He stood on the grass as he repaired the railing of another empty rental cabin's porch. His long, leanly muscled legs extended from a baggy pair of army green shorts. The muscles in his back and shoulders flexed and relaxed under his sweat-soaked gray T-shirt. She was certain he heard her footsteps on the graveled path as she closed the distance between them. But he never turned, never looked up. Audra felt a chill of unease.

"Good morning." She raised her voice to be heard over his carpentry.

Jack spared her a glance over his shoulder before selecting another nail. "Morning."

Her brows knitted in a frown. Had she done something wrong?

Jack had stacked boards of cut maple wood beside his feet. His toolbox and a pile of nails were both within easy reach on the porch, but he hadn't brought any water. *Silly man.* The air was still and hot. The early August day was far too humid for him to be doing strenuous work without water.

Audra took one of her two bottles of water from her oversized canvas tote bag. She placed the still-cold bottle beside his toolbox, then stepped back. "Did you get my messages yesterday?" She'd left two—perhaps three—on his cell phone.

"Yes." Jack's attention shifted to the water bottle, then returned to his repairs.

"I stopped by your cabin yesterday, but you must have been out." The hammering was starting to strain her nerves. "I was hoping we could spend some time together before I leave next Saturday night."

Why was he still hammering? Why wouldn't he look at her while she spoke?

"Been busy."

A pain pierced her heart like a blade. He'd reverted to the stingy speech he'd used when they first met. "Are you too busy even for our morning run?"

Jack didn't respond.

Audra checked the time. It was just after ten o'clock in the morning. Vaughn Brooks and the Trinity Falls University concert band expected her at two o'clock for practice. She'd hoped to have lunch with Jack first.

She tried again. "Have I done something to offend you?"

His lengthy pause made her think he was going to ignore her again. "No, you haven't."

Audra sighed. "I prefer the unkempt mountain man. He may have looked scary, but at least he was honest. If I haven't upset you, why are you avoiding me?"

"I've been busy."

"Bullshit." The word whipped out as she lost her patience. Audra had the satisfaction of seeing Jack's back stiffen. "You're still jogging in the mornings, aren't you? You're still eating breakfast, lunch, and dinner. I've always joined you before. Why can't I now? Your schedule hasn't suddenly become so busy that you'd need to change our routine."

Jack spun to face her. "Change our routine? We don't have a routine. You're on vacation. Next Saturday, you're leaving."

Audra's heart raced as she stared into his onyx eyes. "I'm not looking forward to my leaving any more than you are. But I'm here now. Why don't you want to spend time with me?"

"Can't you understand I'm busy?" Jack's words were hard and harsh. He dragged a hand over his hair. "I'm not the one on vacation. I don't have time to entertain you any longer."

Audra took a shaky step back, then another. "I'm sorry. I hadn't realized I was monopolizing your time. I thought we were enjoying each other's company."

Jack steeled himself for the flash of pain that swept in and out of Audra's gaze. "And now the party's over. You can get ready to go home."

"Suppose I want to stay in Trinity Falls, specifically Harmony Cabins, a little longer?" Audra's voice was soft and gentle, like a tentative caress across his mind.

"What are you saying?" Jack was caught between needing Audra to leave now to get the pain over with and wanting to delay the inevitable.

"Make it easier on yourself, dude. Just rip off the bandage," Wendell had advised.

"I'm saying I don't have a pressing reason to return to Los Angeles Saturday night. I could stay an extra week or so." Her champagne eyes sparkled with hope.

Jack heard Wendell's taunt in his ears: *"Your ex-wife even left Trinity Falls, and she's from here. Audra's from L.A. What chance do you have of her staying?"*

He hardened his heart. "What's the point? You'll leave sooner or later."

The light drained from Audra's eyes. "Why are you saying these things?"

"It's the truth." His muscles screamed with tension. When would this conversation end?

"You're acting as though you don't want me here."

In fact, he couldn't think of anywhere else he'd want her besides Trinity Falls, Harmony Cabins, and his arms. "And you're acting as though you really think you can stay."

Audra frowned. "Why wouldn't I be able to?"

Jack took a deep breath to ease the pain in his chest. "You don't belong here. You belong in L.A.—with all the other Grammy winners."

Audra's caramel skin darkened with a blush. "Did Wendell tell you about the Grammy? Is that why you're so upset, because I didn't tell you myself?"

"I already knew about your Grammy. I read the papers."

Audra gaped. "Why didn't you say anything?"

"Why didn't you?"

Audra expelled a breath. Her shoulders rose and fell with it. "What was I supposed to do? Introduce myself as a Grammy-winning songwriter? That would have been a little pretentious, don't you think? And what about you?"

Jack arched an eyebrow. "What about me?"

"You didn't introduce yourself in any detail, either. You let me think you were the desk clerk. Your friends were the ones who told me you were the rental cabins' owner and a descendent of the town's founder."

She had a point. Jack inclined his head. "We were both at fault. The bottom line is, it's time for you to leave."

Audra's expression was a study in mutiny. "Why?"

Because if you don't leave soon, I'm afraid I'll beg you to stay forever.

He returned to repairing his porch railing. "You always knew this thing between us wouldn't last."

After a beat, Jack heard Audra move away. It sounded like she was running. He squeezed his fists to keep the pain at bay. He had to stay where he was. He couldn't—wouldn't—run after her. Whether she left next Saturday night or stayed a week or two longer, sooner or later she would leave. For once, Jack didn't want to be the one left behind. The problem was, it hurt the same, whether he was the one who did the leaving or the one who was left.

* * *

Her door was closed this time. Darius stopped in front of Peyton Harris's office Saturday morning. He glanced at the peace offering he'd brought—a dozen long-stemmed yellow roses wrapped in green tissue paper—then knocked twice on her door. *There was no need to be nervous. So why are my palms sweating?*

Darius leaned closer to the door, listening for movement on the other side. Muffled footsteps sounded. Darius straightened, stepping back. He was transported to the night he'd picked up his high-school prom date. The door opened cautiously.

"How did you know I'd be here?" Peyton stood framed in the threshold as though using her small body to bar his entrance. She'd dressed in a white T-shirt and navy blue walking shorts.

"One of your neighbors at your apartment complex told me." Darius cradled the bouquet in his arms. Had she even noticed it? "May I come in?"

Peyton frowned. "Who? I didn't tell anyone where I was going."

Darius shrugged. "She said she saw you loading boxes into your car. She thought that meant you were going to work."

Peyton's smoky gray eyes darkened with what looked like fear. "Why would she tell you where to find me?"

"Because I asked her." Darius frowned. Why was she so concerned? She still hadn't noticed the roses he held. Nor had she invited him in. "Perhaps we could have this conversation in your office."

Peyton stepped aside, then closed the door behind him. "Are people in Trinity Falls in the habit of telling perfect strangers where to find their neighbors?"

Darius cocked his head. What was causing the tension in her voice? "First, calm down—"

"Don't tell me to calm down."

"Second, I'm not a stranger. I grew up in Trinity Falls. I went to school with some of your neighbors."

Peyton leaned against her office door. "Suppose I didn't want you to know where I was. Would they tell you, anyway, just because they know you?"

"Obviously, they don't see me as a threat." He hesitated. "Do you?"

Peyton pinched the bridge of her small nose. "That's not the point."

"Then what is the point?" When Peyton didn't answer, Darius continued. "It's a small town, Professor. But take heart, nosy neighbors are the best crime deterrent on the market."

"I hope you're right." Her eyes challenged him. "I'm not giving you an interview."

"I'm not here for that." Darius desperately wanted to ask the professor what it was she feared, but he'd promised himself he wouldn't pry into her life. It was only fair, since he'd recently realized he didn't want anyone digging into his.

Peyton crossed her arms and angled her chin. "Then why are you here?"

Darius stepped forward to offer her the bouquet. "These are for you."

Peyton finally looked at the long-stemmed roses. She accepted them with caution. "Why?"

"Consider it a peace offering." Darius wondered

at her reticence to his gift. "We got off on the wrong foot."

Peyton's smoky eyes were suspicious. "Are you trying to bribe me? Sheriff Lopez said he'd spoken with you."

"The roses aren't a bribe. I promise not to write any articles about you without your permission."

Peyton studied him in silence as though she could read his thoughts. Could she? "How do I know I can trust you?"

That hurt. "If I'd wanted to write an article about you without your permission, it would've appeared in the paper already."

"That's good to know." Peyton opened her office door, an obvious but silent invitation for him to leave. "Thank you for the roses."

Darius crossed to her. "I'm sorry I made you uncomfortable. That wasn't my intent."

Peyton returned his gaze. "Just keep your promise not to write any articles about me."

Darius extended his right hand. "Fair enough."

Peyton shook his hand. "Thank you."

Darius smiled. "I'm not likely to cross you. After all, the last time I was here, you marched me out of your office."

Peyton's cheeks pinkened. "I'm sorry about that." She pulled her hand free.

"I deserved it." Darius closed his hand to hold on to her warmth. He turned to leave. "Enjoy the rest of your weekend."

"You do the same." Peyton's soft response followed him out the door.

Darius smiled as he strode down the empty, quiet

hallway. At least this time, he left without assistance. He'd consider that progress in their relationship.

Kerry crossed the lobby of the main cabin, belly first Saturday afternoon. His ex-wife looked ready to give birth today. Jack rose from his seat behind the registration desk.

"I'll get to the point, Jack." Kerry stopped in front of the counter.

"That would be refreshing." He crossed his arms and waited for her to continue.

Kerry squared her shoulders. "The only reason Isaac's returned to this dim little town is because you all invited him to help celebrate your sesqui-centennial. So I'd appreciate it if you didn't bring up our unfortunate past to the press."

He fought to find his voice. "'Our unfortunate past'?"

Kerry expelled a breath. "You know what I mean."

"You're talking about our daughter's death."

"She wasn't our biological daughter. She was adopted."

"Does telling yourself that make you feel better about what you did?"

"It's the truth."

"She was my best friend's daughter and you were my wife. After he and his wife died, we raised Zoey practically from birth."

"I didn't realize she was sick." Kerry's words were sharp and strained.

"So you just left her, left us?" Jack's muscles

were frozen with remembered anger. "She wasn't the perfect daughter you wanted, so you abandoned her?"

His ex-wife's makeup was expertly applied. Her hair was professionally styled. Her maternity dress was fashionably fitted. She was perfect. It had taken him a long time to realize that perfection was what she craved in every facet of her life.

Kerry shook her head, looking away. "I didn't abandon her."

"What would you call it?" Jack struggled to keep his voice level.

"I was scared."

"So were we."

"I didn't know what to do."

"Neither did we."

Kerry threw up her hands. "What do you want me to say? It's in the past."

"It's not the past to me. To me, it feels like this morning." Blood rushed through his veins. A pulse pounded in his ears.

"What do you want me to do about it?"

Jack lowered his arms. How could he make her understand the hurt she'd caused? How could he make her see the selfishness of her behavior?

In a moment of clarity, he remembered Audra's insistence that he get in touch with his feelings: *"The only way you'll heal from Zoey's death is to stop running from your emotions. You have to deal with them."*

He took an unsteady breath. "We were scared, too, Kerry. But we would've been stronger as a family, facing the uncertainty together. Being scared together. Praying together. Instead, I had to help our daughter understand why she was in so much pain. I had to do that by myself. I also had to explain why her mother wasn't with us."

Kerry's throat muscles flexed as she swallowed. "What did you say to her?"

Jack narrowed his eyes. "Is that the only thing that matters to you?"

"I want to know what you told her." Kerry pushed her chin forward.

Jack saw defiance in her eyes, but there were other emotions as well: fear, uncertainty. Shame? "Do you want to know what she told me?"

Kerry hesitated, then nodded.

"She said she must have done something really bad for her mother to leave. Zoey thought she got sick because her mother didn't love her anymore." Jack swallowed the lump in his throat. "She wanted to know what she'd done that was so wrong."

Tears welled in Kerry's eyes. So she was capable of crying.

Kerry blinked rapidly, wiping the corners of her eyes. "What did you tell her?"

"What should I have told her? That while she was lying in unbearable pain in a hospital, the woman she thought was her mother was screwing another man? That while she was dying, her mother could only think of herself?"

"*What did you tell her?*" Kerry screeched the question.

Jack held his ex-wife's angry gaze. "I told her the truth. That the day she was born was the happiest day of her mother's life. That even though her mother couldn't be with her now, she would never stop loving her. But I wasn't talking about you, Kerry. I was talking about Zoey's birth mother."

Kerry's chin trembled. "I did love her."

"Not enough." Jack's eyes dipped to her stomach and back up to hold her gaze. "I hope you don't treat your next child the same way."

Kerry gasped and stumbled backward. Tears raced down her cheeks. Without a word, she turned and rushed from the cabin. Jack sank onto his chair and let his own tears flow. He felt better, freer than he'd felt in years. Finally he'd been able to tell Kerry how he felt about her abandoning him and Zoey, most of all Zoey. That was because of Audra. The songwriter had taught him how to speak with his heart. She'd given him back his memories of his daughter. She'd brought him back into the community that was his family.

Once she was gone, how would he manage without her?

Audra marched into the Trinity Falls University auditorium. She fumed as she replayed for the umpteenth time her argument with Jack, mentally adding dialogue she wished she'd said to the grumpy rental cabins' owner.

"I hope you don't mind my being here." Doreen stepped into the aisle in front of Audra.

Audra rocked to a halt to prevent a collision with the other woman. "What?"

"I wanted to attend your rehearsal. I'm too excited to wait until next week to hear you and the band." Doreen searched Audra's eyes. The excitement on her features dimmed to concern. "What's wrong?"

Audra tugged her right earlobe. Her gaze circled the room: the three rows of roughly six hundred mahogany chairs bolted to the red cement floor, the large Gothic windows carved into the walls just below the ceiling, the choir balcony behind them, the stage before them.

Seated on folding chairs in front of the stage was the Trinity Falls University concert band. Forty of the university's best musicians—sophomores, juniors, and seniors—played wind and percussion instruments. They were talented, enthusiastic, and adaptable.

Audra fidgeted with the strap of her tote bag as she answered Doreen. "Jack and I broke up."

Doreen's eyes widened. "Let's sit."

She wrapped an arm around Audra's waist to guide her into a nearby row. She took the aisle seat beside her.

"It sounds ridiculous, doesn't it?" Audra dumped her bag on the floor beside her feet, then rubbed her eyes. Her fingertips came back wet. "We've been together only three weeks. Can you really break up after only three weeks?"

"What happened?" Doreen's voice was gentle.

Audra blinked away tears. "Jack told me he didn't see the point in waiting another week. He wanted to end our relationship now."

"I'm so sorry, Audra."

"So am I." She squeezed her eyes shut and pinched the bridge of her nose. *I will not cry. I will not cry.* "What really hurt is that he told me I didn't belong in Trinity Falls."

"He's wrong. It feels as though you've been here for years." Doreen rubbed Audra's shoulder. "I'm really going to miss you when you leave next week. And I know I'm not the only one."

Audra dashed away renegade tears. "I'll miss you, too. I'll miss the whole town."

"You can always come back for a visit."

Audra's blood chilled at the idea of coming back to Trinity Falls after Jack had tossed her unceremoniously from his life. She met Doreen's eyes. "Or you can come to Los Angeles."

"Do you know Morgan Freeman?" Doreen's grin was infectious. She had an obvious crush on the popular actor.

"I wish I did." Audra's heart felt lighter with her friend's teasing.

"Excuse me, ladies." Vaughn Brooks, the band director, seemed reluctant to interrupt them. "Is everything OK?"

Doreen stood, leading the way out of the row of auditorium seats. "I'm so sorry. I'm monopolizing Audra's time."

Audra pulled her sheet music from her tote bag. She hoisted the bag onto her shoulder before following Doreen.

Vaughn's brown eyes were dark with concern. "Do you want to cancel today's rehearsal?"

This was the final week before the Founders Day Celebration. The band was performing four pieces: "The Star-Spangled Banner," "America the Beautiful," "Happy Birthday," and the Electra Day song "Lifting Me Up." They knew the music and were playing together well, but Audra didn't want to cancel today's practice.

She offered the sheet music to Vaughn. "No, I'd like the students to learn this song for the concert."

Audra turned to Doreen. "Is it OK to add another song?"

Doreen's eyebrows lifted toward her hairline. "Absolutely."

"Thanks." Audra nodded toward the papers Vaughn was studying. "It's an original piece. I wrote it for myself. Can your students learn it in a week?"

"Of course." He returned to his musicians.

"Tell me about the song." Doreen's voice bounced with excitement. "Is it a ballad or a dance song?"

"It's a dance song." Audra shifted her gaze from Vaughn and his students to Doreen.

"What's it called?"

"'Prince Charming.'" Audra tugged her right earlobe. "I titled it before this morning."

Concern returned to Doreen's eyes. "Did you write it for Jack?"

Audra looked away. "Jack was the inspiration—before our breakup."

Doreen squeezed Audra's shoulder. "We'll see what next week brings."

"I suppose we will." But Audra didn't imagine next week would be any different from this morning.

⟨ CHAPTER 24 ⟩

A week later, Jack stood at the podium on the makeshift stage at the entrance to Freedom Park. It was August ninth, Trinity Falls's one hundred and fiftieth birthday. The noon sun was warm. The breeze was gentle and the air was still with expectation. A sea of faces—residents and guests—separated him from the Trinity Falls Town Center.

Jack gripped the edges of the podium and glanced down at his prepared notes. "Thank you for coming."

He hesitated. Ramona, Doreen, and Isaac Green had said the same thing when they'd addressed the expectant crowd. His speech was sucking before he'd even begun. Jack looked up. Ean, Megan, Quincy, Darius, and Ms. Helen sat together toward the front of the audience. Benita Hawkins, Ms. Helen's cousin and Audra's business manager, had joined them. Members of the Trinity Falls Town Center Business Owners Association—Belinda, Tilda, Grady, and Vernon—were scattered throughout the crowd. Simon and Ethel were in opposite ends of the area. They'd all been a part of his life for years, some since his birth. They'd helped him celebrate his joys and grieved his sorrows. And they'd waited patiently for his return when he'd shut them out after Zoey's death. They deserved better than his prepared speech. They deserved his heart.

Jack released the podium. He folded his notes and slipped the paper into the front right pocket of his black Dockers. "One hundred and fifty years ago, my great-great-grandfather, Ezekiel Sansbury, founded Trinity Falls. But this place is more than a town. It's one big extended family." He smiled at Ms. Helen. "Complete with overprotective parents." He glanced at Darius. "And annoying siblings."

Laughter interrupted him. Jack let his eyes roam the crowd, tensing at the sight of Opal Gutierrez, the *Monitor*'s junior reporter, taking notes on his presentation. "We have our family feuds and sibling rivalries, but running through it all is a lot of love. The type of encouragement that makes our successes even more special, and the support that carries us through our disappointments."

The people in front of him nodded and smiled in agreement. Jack continued. "My great-great-grandfather would be proud of the fact that he'd founded a family. I know this, because that's why I'm most proud of Trinity Falls."

The applause was enthusiastic. Jack turned back to his seat.

Ramona touched his arm. "Great job."

He nodded, acknowledging her words and the applause of the other people on stage with him.

Ramona took the podium. "That was a beautiful speech. Thank you, Jack." She led the crowd in one more round of applause before advancing the event's agenda. "I now have the great pleasure of introducing our next entertainment." She gestured toward the musicians on stage right. "Our own Trinity Falls University concert band will perform its final two songs. This time, they're accompanied by our new best friend, Grammy-winning songwriter, Audra Lane."

Jack joined the applause. He felt a slice of jealousy as Vaughn escorted Audra and her guitar onto the stage. Audra glanced briefly at him as she acknowledged Doreen and State Representative Isaac Green. She continued to the front of the stage, her hand outstretched to shake Ramona's.

Audra adjusted the microphone. "Happy birthday, Trinity Falls."

Her voice trembled a bit, probably from nerves. Jack was nervous for her. But the cheers and applause that followed her greeting let him know she'd already won over her audience.

With a nod from Audra, the band started the first song. She accompanied it with her guitar, as easy with the instrument as though it were a fifth limb.

There was dancing in and on the seats. Several members of the audience—young and old—left their chairs, giving themselves over to the music. All too soon, the song ended. People jumped up and down, roaring their approval. Jack was filled with pride at their reaction to Audra's performance.

She laughed into the microphone. "Thank you! Thank you so much, Trinity Falls. You're a great audience. This next song is an original piece, inspired by your lovely town. I hope you enjoy it."

Another opening chord played. It was reminiscent of the rushing waters of the Trinity Falls. The music was even more compelling than the previous song. After half a minute, Audra's smoky voice joined the band. She weaved the story of a sheltered woman, determined to convince a thick-skulled man that she loved him. This time, even more people left their seats to dance.

"'It's not a fairy tale. It's my love.'" Audra's voice gained strength as she sang, seeming to feed off her audience's enthusiasm. "'This pain is as real as it gets. It can't be healed by a magic rose, glass slipper, or tale.'"

Jack closed his eyes as her lyrics drew him back to their time together. "'It's like a fairy tale. Happily ever after.'" She'd said that to him on more than one occasion. Was she singing to him? His heart pounded faster and harder. Her words were tearing him apart. He prayed for her to stop.

Audra kept up her song of seduction. "'Prince Charming, you put a spell on me. Wake me up! Wake me up! We don't need three wishes, honey. I know the words to say for our happily ever after. It's not so far, far away.'"

Jack couldn't catch his breath. His body heated as her words called him back to their most intimate moments. His pulse raced with the memory of her limbs entwined with his. He tasted need.

Mercifully, Audra's song came to an end. The audience thanked her with more deafening applause. Jack breathed a slow sigh of relief, but his muscles were still strained.

Ramona returned to the podium. "Wasn't that a great concert? The band really outdid them-selves. And, Audra Lane, Trinity Falls can't thank you enough for your great performance. We hope you consider this your second home."

Audra blew a kiss toward Ramona, then waved at the cheering crowd.

Ramona continued. "Thank you all again for coming. We hope you enjoyed the celebration. Please join us in Freedom Park for a sesquicentennial barbe-cue with all our local favorites, including Doreen Fever's Trinity Falls Fudge Walnut Brownies."

Audra left the area with Vaughn and the concert band. Jack tracked her every move. The pleated skirt of her red minidress swung with each step that carried her away from him. His throat burned as he bade her a silent good-bye.

Two weeks later, Jack returned from his morning run to find Darius on his porch. What had brought his friend here so early on a Saturday morning? He slowed to a walk and stretched his shoulders to ease the tension stirring at the base of his neck.

The newspaper reporter stood from his perch on the porch railing. "I've been meaning to ask you. Were you referring to me when you mentioned 'annoying siblings' during your Founders Day speech?"

"Yes." Jack used the back of his wrist to wipe the sweat from his forehead. He mounted the stairs and entered his cabin.

Darius followed him. "It's been two weeks. I

thought for sure you'd have made at least one trip to L.A. by now."

Jack's stride faltered on his way to the kitchen. Darius bounced off his back.

Jack glanced at him over his shoulder. "Why?"

He crossed into the kitchen and poured himself a glass of water from the faucet.

"Come on, Jack. You've been regressing ever since Audra left."

Jack drained his first glass. He gestured toward Darius. "Water?"

"You see? You're back to your cryptic conversations. You've literally said three words to me since I've been here."

Jack refilled his glass. "Considering the reason you're here, that's three words more than you deserve."

Darius took a seat at the kitchen table. "I'll have that glass of water, please."

Jack took another glass from the cupboard and filled it with ice and water. He gave the glass to Darius before settling onto the seat opposite his friend. "Are you staying long?"

"Thanks." Darius accepted the glass. "That depends. How long will it take you to explain why you haven't visited Audra?"

"Why should I?"

"Because you're in love with her."

Jack almost choked on a mouthful of water. "I've only known her four weeks."

"Yet she's had a strong, positive impact on you in such a short period of time."

Jack couldn't deny that. The way he'd felt with Audra compared to the way he felt now without her was as different as day and night. Audra had led him out of the shadows and back into the light.

Jack moved restlessly on his chair. "I enjoyed those four weeks with her. But they were an aberration."

"What makes you think that?"

"She lives in L.A."

"So?"

Jack sighed with irritation—and regret. "Those weeks weren't real. Audra was on vacation, remember?"

Darius sipped his water. "It was a working vacation. She came here to complete her contract for three songs."

"A working vacation is still a vacation." Jack pushed away from the kitchen table and carried his empty glass to the dishwasher. "We live in different worlds. She's a Grammy-winning songwriter who lives and works in L.A. I repair rental cabins in northeastern Ohio."

Darius snorted. "Rentals that you own, in addition to the *Monitor,* Trinity Falls Cuisine, and the bank."

"Owning all those things won't make the twenty-four hundred miles between us disappear."

"You need to speak with Quincy and Alonzo. Ask them about the years they spent apart from the women they loved. I have a feeling they'll tell you you're being a fool for not trying to make this relationship with Audra work."

"How?" Jack spun to face Darius. He threw his arms up. "She has lunches with music executives and club-hops with other artists. How can I compete with that?"

"Why would you have to? Audra likes it here."

Why was Darius so stuck on this idea? Why couldn't he understand not every couple could have a "happily ever after"?

Jack leaned back against his kitchen counter. "She was fine here for a couple of weeks. After a couple of months, she'd start climbing the walls. Trinity Falls can't compete with L.A."

Darius rested his right ankle on his left knee. "What makes you so certain?"

"Kerry grew up in Trinity Falls. I thought she was happy here, until she divorced me. Ramona was born in Trinity Falls. She's spent her entire life trying to leave." Having examples that validated his theory didn't make Jack feel any better.

"Ean left Trinity Falls. He came to his senses and moved back." Darius's voice carried the satisfaction Jack didn't feel. "But there's an alternative solution."

"What?"

"You could move to L.A."

Jack stiffened. He'd never thought of living anywhere other than Trinity Falls. This town had been home to generations of Sansburys. Could he leave?

Yes, if leaving meant spending the rest of his life with Audra. "That's an option."

"What are you doing here?" Audra stood in the front doorway of her Redondo Beach townhome, scowling at Jack.

Her welcome was a frigid blast of air in the late August heat. Jack should have expected it, though. His good-bye to her had been cool, curt, and cruel.

Jack nodded at the cab driver idling at the curb,

letting him know it was OK to leave. As the vehicle merged back into traffic, he collected his courage to face Audra again. He took in her brown capris and gray Los Angeles Lakers T-shirt. Those were the darkest colors he'd ever seen her wear.

"I'd like to speak with you. May I come in?"

She stood, silently barring the entrance for so long. Was she going to turn him away, send him back to his hotel? Jack's palms began to sweat. Audra finally stepped aside and he entered.

"How did you find me?" She fastened the three locks on her front door—the doorknob lock, dead bolt, and security chain.

"Benita gave me your address." And assured him Audra would be home in the afternoon, probably working. It was a very different image from the one Wendell painted. *Why had I believed that guy?*

"In exchange for what?" She led him into her living room.

"She was impressed by your Founders Day performance." Jack's face heated with embarrassment. "I promised to try to talk you into making your own album."

"That won't happen." Audra settled onto a soft-looking, burnt orange armchair on the far side of the living room.

"At least I can tell her I tried." Jack sank onto the matching sofa.

The room was bright and happy. The walls were painted a sky blue. Potted spider plants hung in her bay windows. The hardwood flooring was the same oak wood as her bookcase and entertainment center.

"So talk." Audra was being as stingy with her words as she'd once accused him of being.

In her eyes, he'd previously found laughter, wonder, and desire. Now her champagne gaze was hard with temper.

Regret was sour in his throat. "I'm sorry."

Silence.

Audra arched an eyebrow. "That's it?"

"I . . ."

She rose from her seat. "You could have just called."

Panicked, Jack popped off the sofa and blocked Audra's path to her door. "I was wrong to push you away. I'm sorry I did that."

"That apology took three weeks?" Audra crossed her arms. "You could have phoned that in. Why did you fly all the way to Los Angeles?"

"I wanted to apologize in person."

Audra shook her head with a sigh. "Well, you've done that. Thanks for coming. Good-bye."

Jack stepped to his left, blocking Audra's escape again. She looked at him in surprise. He dragged his right hand over his hair. "That's all you have to say? 'Good-bye'?"

"What do you want me to say?"

"Anything but good-bye."

"I enjoyed your Founders Day speech."

That isn't any better. "Thanks."

He scrubbed his hands over his face. Why couldn't he communicate with her? He'd spoken from his heart to Kerry, to an entire town, but never to Audra. Why couldn't he let his heart speak to the woman he loved?

Because he was afraid she wouldn't love him back.

Jack pushed past his fear and pried open his heart. "The past three weeks have been hell without you. All the light you brought into my life has just gone away. I miss you."

"Now that's worth flying across the country to say." Audra's lips curved into a soft smile.

"It's just a start." Jack reached for her hand, relieved when she let him hold it. "Could you give us a chance?"

Audra cocked her head. The light returned to her eyes. "Are you suggesting a long-distance relationship?"

"I'm suggesting I move to L.A."

Audra stepped back, trying but failing to free her hand from Jack's. "You'd leave Trinity Falls?"

"For you."

Audra caught her breath. Did the stubborn, dense man even realize what he was saying? What he'd been saying since he'd showed up on her doorstep? "Your family founded Trinity Falls. You can't throw away your heritage."

"I'm not throwing away anything. I can always visit Trinity Falls, but I want the chance to build a life with you." Jack pressed her hand to his heart. "You make me a better person."

"Then why can't we live in Trinity Falls and visit Los Angeles?"

Jack frowned. "Don't you need to be in L.A. for your career?"

"I can write songs anywhere." Audra cupped his face, looking deep into his onyx eyes. "Trinity Falls feels more like home to me than Los Angeles ever has. I fell in love with your town—the place and the people."

"What about me?" Jack's voice was rough. "How do you feel about its rental cabins owner?"

Audra lifted up on her toes. She placed a soft, brief kiss on his yielding lips. "I fell in love with him, too. He's my Prince Charming. And I know he loves me back."

Jack smiled into her eyes. "How do you know that?"

She shook her head. "Oh, you silly, silly man. I knew you loved me when I saw you standing on my steps. When I first met you, you wouldn't leave Harmony Cabins. Now you're flying twenty-four hundred miles to say you're sorry? That could only be love."

Jack's laughter rumbled in his chest, making her knees weak. "I'd take a rocket to the moon, if that's where you were. You're my 'happily ever after.'"

Don't miss Regina Hart's

Trinity Falls

On sale now at your local bookstore!

CHAPTER 1

"I can't do this." Ean Fever closed the client folder. He leaned forward and laid it on Hugh Bolden's imposing teakwood desk. Hugh was his boss and one of the principal partners with the New York law firm of Craven, Bolden & Arnez.

"Why not?" From the other side of the desk, Hugh's laser blue eyes took aim at Ean's face. His frown deepened the fine wrinkles between his thick gray brows. "It's like all the other corporate litigation cases you've worked."

"I can't represent this client." Ean steeled himself for his boss's reaction.

"'Can't' or 'won't'?" Hugh seemed more curious than confrontational.

"Won't."

The walls were closing in on him. Ean freed his gaze from the older man's steely regard to take in the spacious office. It smelled like power and prestige. Thick silver carpeting complemented the teakwood furnishings—conversation table with four white-cushioned chairs, executive desk, cabinetries and bookcases. The entertainment center, including the high-definition television, was black lacquer. The picture window behind Hugh framed several Manhattan skyscrapers as they pierced the hot August sky.

Commendations and civic awards decorated the walls and shelves. But the partner's office didn't give any insight into the man: his loved ones, his hobbies, his beverages of choice. And after almost seven years with the firm, Ean knew the older man little better than on the day he'd interviewed with him.

Hugh shifted in his chair. He crossed his right leg over his left and adjusted the crease in the pants of his navy Armani power suit. "What's on your mind, Ean? You haven't been yourself for months."

Six months. Since his father's death in February, after a long illness Ean had been unaware of. Why hadn't anyone told him? "I need a change, Hugh."

"To what? Employment law? Contracts? Torts?"

Ean shook his head as Hugh rattled off the divisions within the firm. "I have to go home."

Hugh's gaze flickered. His frown deepened. "Is your mother sick?"

Ean appreciated his boss's concern. "No." At least, not as far as he knew.

"Then why do you have to go home?"

"I'm doing this for myself."

Silence stretched. Hugh took his measure, much as the seasoned litigator did during meetings with opposing counsel.

Tension ebbed from Ean's neck and shoulders as

he gained confidence in his decision. He hadn't made this choice lightly. He'd spent the past five months weighing the pros and cons, what he felt against what he knew. In the end, the two were the same. He felt the need to return to Trinity Falls, Ohio, and knew he had to make the move now.

Would someone like Hugh Bolden understand that? The firm appeared to be everything the partner wanted. Ean couldn't allow that to happen to him.

Hugh sat back in the tall executive seat made of brown leather. His expression cleared. "Do you want a leave of absence?"

"No." Ean rose, gathering his writing tablet and silver Cross pen from the table. "You'll have my resignation before the end of the day."

He checked his bronze Omega wristwatch. It was almost ten o'clock on the last Friday morning in August. He'd already put in more than four hours.

Hugh stood. Concern was evident in his expression. "You're resigning? Isn't this sudden?"

"I don't think so." Ean slid his hands into the front pockets of his dark gray Hugo Boss pants. "I appreciate the opportunities you've given me, Hugh, including the partnership two years ago."

Hugh shook his head. "You earned the partnership. You're a brilliant lawyer, Ean. I've enjoyed working with you. Are you *sure* you want to resign? Maybe you just need some time."

His family or his career, those were Ean's choices. He already knew how it felt to lose a family member. "Craven, Bolden and Arnez is one of the best firms in the country. But my life needs to go in a different direction."

"Are you sure this is what your father would have

wanted for you?" The question was surprisingly gentle coming from such a gruff man.

Ean tightened his grip on his writing tablet. No, he wasn't. Was that the reason everyone had kept him in the dark regarding his father's terminal cancer? Because his father was afraid Ean would risk his career to help care for him?

"I don't know."

Another long, silent scrutiny from Hugh's sharp eyes. "I understand. I'm sure this decision wasn't easy for you. But everything will work out. You'll make sure of it."

"Thank you." Every muscle in Ean's body relaxed with the other man's words. "It'll take me a few weeks to wrap up my open cases. I'll get Wendy up to speed on my new matters."

The second-year associate eyed his cases—and his office—with something close to lust. Would she be able to mask her pleasure at the announcement of Ean's resignation?

"What will you do back in Trinity Falls, Ohio?"

Ean offered a weak smile. "I don't know that, either."

"Stay in touch." Hugh extended his right hand. "If you need anything—a recommendation, your job back, anything at all—call me."

Ean clasped the other man's hand. His face eased into a smile. "I appreciate that."

As he turned to leave, his black Bruno Magli shoes sank into the plush carpet. He had a lot to do, but his thoughts kept turning to his late father, widowed mother, childhood friends and the woman who'd broken his heart six years before.

* * *

"You're full of energy." Megan McCloud huffed a breath. She picked up her pace as she jogged with Doreen Fever through Trinity Falls's Freedom Park Saturday morning. She'd thought they'd have an easy jog on the last day of August, enjoying the turning foliage and waning summer. Her friend must have had other ideas.

Doreen pulled back her pace. "Ean called last night."

Megan's heart hopped once at the name of her teenage crush. "How is he?"

"He's quit his job. He's coming home. Permanently."

Megan tripped over nothing on the winding dirt path. She caught her balance and her breath. "When?"

"That was my reaction." Doreen's warm brown eyes twinkled with humor.

In her lemon yellow jersey and black running pants, Ean's mother looked at least a decade younger than her sixty years.

Megan forced her numb limbs to keep up with Doreen as they continued jogging. "He's coming back to Trinity Falls?" *Seriously?* "Why?"

"Didn't say." There was maternal concern in the older woman's breathy voice. "He thinks it'll take eight weeks—give or take—to finish his cases and move."

Megan's heart reacted like that fourteen-year-old girl she'd been as she called to mind the eighteen-year-old Ean. He'd been larger than life to her

adoring eyes: long, fluid muscles, broad shoulders
and a sexy smile. But his almond-shaped olive eyes
had never noticed her. All he'd seen was her older
cousin, Ramona.

The path veered left around a group of bushes
lit by one of the park's many security lamps. They
followed the trail deeper, past morning walkers
and a few other joggers.

Megan drew in the scent of warm air and packed
dirt. "Is he all right?"

"He said he is." Doreen didn't seem convinced.
"He sounded fine. Better than he has in a long
time."

The last time Megan had seen Ean was during
his father's funeral, more than six months ago. Did
he even remember their exchange? She'd shaken
his hand and expressed her condolences. But Ean's
eyes had looked so lost—not even Ramona's touch
reached him. Megan knew well the pain of losing a
beloved family member. She'd lost two—four, if you
included the parents she barely remembered.

Megan's thoughts returned to the present. "Did
you have any idea he'd been thinking of coming
back?" Had Ramona?

"None."

Megan couldn't wrap her mind around the news.
"Ever since high school, all Ean's wanted to do was
leave Trinity Falls. Why is he moving back?"

Doreen chuckled. "Paul used to say Ean had
been born with a road map out of town."

Megan smiled at the mention of her friend's late
husband. "Ean always had a plan, which is another
reason this decision is so out of character."

"I know. My son has never been spontaneous."
Doreen paused as they jogged past two women
speed walking on the trail. "He chose his college
when he was in elementary school. And he selected
his law school before he graduated from high
school."

Megan had been devastated when he'd picked
New York University's law school. It had seemed so
far away. "It was always his dream to become a
partner with a prestigious New York City firm. Now
that he's achieved that dream, he's going to throw
it away to return to Trinity Falls, Ohio, population
less than fifteen hundred?"

In the seven years since Ean had been working
for that law firm, Megan could count on her hands
the number of times he'd come home.

"I don't understand his decision, either. But I'm
glad that he's coming home."

Megan's face warmed with guilt. Doreen's re-
sponse put this situation in its proper perspective.
She reined in her panic and focused on her friend.
"I know you've missed him."

Doreen was silent for several paces. "A lot has
changed since he's spent any real time here." She
wasn't talking about the new buildings and wider
roads.

Megan reacted to the tension in the other
woman's voice. She reached out, giving her friend's
shoulder a bracing squeeze. "As long as you're
happy, Ean will be, too."

Doreen's expression was hopeful. "Do you really
believe that?"

Megan let her hand drop. "How you choose to

live your life is your decision, Doreen. Ean can either get on board with it or not."

Doreen mustered a halfhearted smile. "I hope he gets on board. It'll be nice to have him home again."

It would be nice for Doreen. And for Megan? That would depend on whether Ean and her cousin picked up where they'd left off.